One Heart

One Heart

A NOVEL

JANE McCAFFERTY

HarperCollins*Publishers*

The first chapter of *One Heart* was previously published in the *Kenyon Review*, Summer/Fall 1998, Vol. 20 3–4.

HarperCollins books may be purchased for educational, business, or sales promotional use. For information please write: Special Markets Department, HarperCollins Publishers, Inc., 10 East 53rd Street, New York, NY 10022.

FIRST EDITION

Designed by Kyoko Watanabe

Library of Congress Cataloging-in-Publication Data

McCafferty, Jane.
One heart : a novel / Jane McCafferty. — 1st ed.
    p.   cm.
  ISBN 0-06-019263-1
  I. Title.
PS3563.C33377O53   1999
813' .54—DC21   98-49469

00 01 02 03 ❖/HC 10 9 8 7 6 5 4 3

In memory of Casey Hyde

and for my mother and father

Acknowledgments

Thank you to the following people, who in various ways helped this to become a book:

Nicole Aragi, Marjorie Braman, Jeffery McGraw, Shelley Perron, John Edgar Wideman, Sharon Dilworth, Diane Goodman, Sherry Wellman, Kristin Kovacic, Jane Bernstein, Kathy George, Evelyn Pierce, Jill Weaver, Bruce Burris, Jim Daniels, and Jackie Litt.

Thank you also to my family: my parents, my brothers, Aunt Shirley and Uncle Butch and all Ackermans, Bjorks, and Lowes, Joshua, Jordan, Rosemary, and Annajane.

Most especially, and always, thanks to Dan.

Ivy

When Your Mind Drifts

I BEEN COOK AT CAMP TIMBER OUTSIDE OF LAKE CATAMAN here in New York State for almost twenty years, and the rest of the year I cook for the Timber winter school. I live on the premises in a small blue house on top of a hill that's covered with a carpet of dark maple leaves every autumn.

The winter school's a red brick building set down in the valley with spruce and ash circling all around it, and the camp's up on the other hill, all spread out on the flat land. They got cabins and what you call lean-tos for sleeping, and in the middle an outhouse someone painted purple. The children are sent up here just as soon as they spell *cat*. They're wealthy children, but brokenhearted. You can see that initially.

My sister, Gladys, cooked with me the last ten years

or so. She's forty-eight now. Let's face it; she's a rather heavy woman, like me, so the children get their laughs. For children "fat" is the joke they hear over and over and still it's funny. Gladys thinks the children are mean-spirited (a few are) and can't understand it's like we're the fat ladies in the circus, no harm intended. But then again I been fat since birth. Gladys only blew up after she had troubles.

And neither me or Gladys are huge and unsightly. We're just big, full-figured, nice-looking quality women. We have always attracted the men. We couldn't really work in the circus. No possible way would the circus hire us.

In the summertime the children are more scared to death of Gladys than the winter boarder kids are. Winter kids get used to her ways. In the summer when they file into the eating hall behind their counselors, Gladys stands near the wall in her white uniform, watching them with her big green eyes and her wire-rim reading glasses low on her nose and her hair sweaty and dark from the kitchen. Stands stone still like a fat lady statue. If a bold one ever waves to her, maybe she nods her head, maybe she don't.

But this past spring everything changed up here. It happened there was a counselor come up here, a young girl of seventeen called Raelene. Raelene was a pretty little thing even with her crooked teeth, but she was all alone in that camp, since the counselors are mostly kids who used to be campers here, rich cliquey kids from the Ivy Leagues. There's a lot of ideas some of these people learn to carry, the main one being they're better than others. You can see the nicer ones trying not to think this way; it's not even their fault really. It's been ground in, and they're limited by what they've seen.

Now Raelene, take a quick look at that girl and you'd know she was from elsewhere, other circumstances, like you could imagine her in a wintry town where the industry died and the windows of the stores are boarded up. You could see Raelene with her long hair and pale face walking through the closed-up town on a bitter evening in her Salvation Army black coat with a fur collar smelling like a dead woman's perfume. And no gloves. Her hands bare and chapped with bit-down polished nails. She would be the sort to just stand in the circle of streetlight and tap her foot. Or maybe that's just in my head she does that.

Not that I'd even let her in my head much if Gladys hadn't known her. I make my little friends up here at camp and school, but I'm drawn to the cheerful. Life is short and I'm not here for the gloom. I been a good sister to Gladys, and that's enough gloom for any one soul, and I don't say that to blame her, and it's not like we haven't had some laughs even in the darkest of dark years. But Gladys had a hard life. I say *had* not because she's dead. I say *had* because I think it's changed now.

The reason Raelene even ended up at camp in the

first place has to do with about seven or so years ago, back when the war was going on in Vietnam, and Gladys's boy, Wendell, bless his soul, was over there captured. Raelene, who back then lived in Philadelphia, ended up wearing one of them bracelets they gave out to the young people. A prisoner of war bracelet, which Gladys didn't like the idea of. A few winter school kids wore those bracelets, and Gladys could see the names didn't mean much. The kids couldn't know what any of it meant, no matter how many times they sung "Where Have All the Flowers Gone." She didn't like thinking her son's name, Wendell J. Pittman, would be on some ignorant child's wrist, some child who wore the name like a piece of jewelry from a gum machine.

And sure enough there was a child out there in the world wearing Wendell J. Pittman on her wrist, and this child was Raelene Francis. One day in November, I believe 1969, Gladys got a letter in the mail.

It was a child writing to her saying she was praying for Wendell to come home every day and every night, and lighting candles in two churches every morning. The bracelet company had sent his picture, the one where he's almost smiling in his army uniform that Gladys kept by her bed, and the child said she thought Wendell looked cute. Then the child goes on to tell Gladys that she had no parents, that she was a real live orphan down there in Philadelphia, and if Gladys wanted she would come and be her little girl.

Gladys read that letter out loud to me at the supper table late that night. I can see it clearly. We're having wedding soup. Gladys has her Jack Daniel's in a short glass. She's wearing her old cat-eyed drugstore glasses with the thick lenses so her eyes are magnified. Outside it was snowing. It was snowing for days, and our little blue house on the white frozen hill looked lonelier to me when I walked back toward it after cooking down at the winter school all day. In this weather Gladys tended to be worse off than when the sun was out, with Wendell being over there. I believe the snow on the mountains made her feel farther from him and farther from the good times she had known before certain parts of her life just broke down. She would get busier than usual cleaning the house or the kitchen at work, humming to herself all the while when normally she weren't a hummer.

I remember before Wendell and his friend Tim McGreen went over there we had to buy a map and spread it on the kitchen table to show the boys where they were headed. And show ourselves too, truthfully. We'd forgotten all kinds of geography.

So in the snow Vietnam was even farther and Gladys was always reading the papers to try to bring it closer and it made her meaner. If some child didn't take their tray over to the rack after eating, she would find that child and yell and call the kid spoiled or worse. She would redden their faces, she could make them cry if she wanted. She knew how. And once they started crying she would walk away, regretting it all. I could see that regret. Her face would scrunch up in painful regret when she thought no one was looking. Even when she was mean there was part of Gladys that didn't want to be mean. Maybe she just couldn't stand how those rich kids seemed to believe invisible servants followed them everywhere they went with silver platters, but I don't think so. I think her meanness surely had other tangled-up roots.

"So," I said that snowy night. "A little orphan wants you for her mother. Maybe this is God's plan, maybe you should write back and say for her to come on out here."

Gladys just stared across the table at me, no expression whatsoever on her face, maybe it was boredom; I believe I bored Gladys much of her life. I don't really know.

"It sure sounds like a nice little orphan," I said. "Maybe she'd like it out here. She could go to the boarding school free of charge and then camp in summertime."

Gladys was still looking at me. She had a way of studying my face. Finally she said, "Ivy, are you forty?"

"Yes," I said. "You know that." And I felt my face grow warm for no reason.

And then Gladys shook her head a few times. She didn't say another word that night. She cleared her plate and sat in the red chair, drinking and watching the snow in the darkness. I sat there like a damn fool eating one kernel of corn at a time trying to figure why she said *Ivy, are you forty*.

That's how Gladys was then, she'd just say a few words, and leave you in the dark, like she wanted to put you there because that's where she was.

But I see now any talk of God's plan was ridiculous and offensive to the mind of Gladys. She was forty-one then. If she believed in God, which she didn't, that God wouldn't exactly have *plans*. That God would be sort've *planless*.

So a week later, another letter from little Raelene Francis came. It came along with a painting of a brown horse wearing a blue saddle. It was a good painting. I believe the girl traced it from a book, and I could see Gladys, who loved horses when she was a child, liked it. And the girl said in the letter she was praying novenas for Wendell's safety and she was also offering up her bed. She was still lighting candles and sleeping on the bare Philadelphia floor by the window as a way of asking God to help.

I understand your Catholics because I dated an Italian one, a pope-loving doozy in my late thirties who had me on the road to conversion, a man who had a conniption fit when I put his rosary beads on like a necklace one night, but Gladys had no contact before Raelene, and after she read the letter she said, "Now why would sleeping on the floor convince God to help Wendell?"

I said, "The Catholics believe sacrifice tugs on the heartstrings of Jesus."

Gladys said, "Do they now. That's cute."

But she didn't throw that letter away like she did letter number one. And the horse she taped up on the back door of our house under the curtained window. I was surprised at that. I think it was the first thing Gladys hung up in ten years or so. She never was your interior decorator type. Maybe it was just the idea of some Philadelphia orphan girl sleeping on the floor for Wendell that got to her.

Only the next letter Raelene had a confession to make. The confession was that she was no orphan after all, she was only a "half orphan" and "a daughter of bad circumstance." She wrote like a girl who loves the dictionary, with fancy words like *perplexing*. Her mother, a perplexing woman who must've thought she was a cowboy, had "gone west" when Raelene was nine. This was surprising, since she'd been "sedentary," Raelene said, I'll never forget that. And her father, she said, and I'll never forget this, had glued the nipple of a baby bottle to the bottom of his cane so he wouldn't make the tapping noise that drove her mother crazy. That was all she said about him. I'd call that disturbed. Another painted horse with a blue saddle came with this letter. This time Gladys finally wrote back to the girl. She gave the letter to me for mailing uptown, since I used to drive the truck in every other day for produce, and I'm ashamed to say I tore open the envelope and read the whole thing, which weren't special or long, so I doubly regretted doing it. It was just the kind of thing my sister would've hated. Behind her back I believe I was always doing unforgivable things, maybe hoping she'd catch me so I could test her out. How far could I go with that sister of mine before she'd cut me out of her hard life like she cut out the rest of the world during the past fifteen years?

I sat in the truck outside of The Duke of Bubbles Car Wash (a man who believed he was a duke owned it) on a stone cold gray winter day and read what Gladys wrote to Raelene. She wrote,

> *Dear Little Girl, I appreciate you praying for my boy. Don't worry about your lie, we're all of us orphans here. Please don't sleep on the floor, and thank you for the horse paintings which I've hung up. From, Gladys J. Pittman.*

I remember I sat in the truck wanting to cross out "Little Girl" and write in "Raelene." Why couldn't Gladys at least use the soulful child's name? Not many people ever reached out to Gladys anymore, and I didn't want her to miss this opportunity, whatever it was. Even then I guess I was sensing this little Philadelphia girl was important in some way.

It was around this time Gladys nearly got fired from the winter school because of some parents complaining she beat their kids. This wasn't true at all; what was true is Gladys and me were getting our windows soaped and egged in February, so don't think it was Halloween pranksters. Gladys stayed up late one night and spied in the dark at the window while the two boys, Sinclair Barnes and Cale McGovern, wrote with white soap on our windows HOUSE OF WHORES, EAT ME RAW, and other pleasant things of this nature.

Gladys has an old rifle (she found it in the woods once and never loaded it), so she went out there in her white robe and yelled, "Freeze or I'll shoot your ass to the moon!" I was in bed, listening with a rattled stomach. It wasn't what Gladys said, it was how she made the whole house feel, like the air was made of sharp bits of rage.

The boys saw the rifle and froze. She said, "Get your skinny asses in here." They must've walked into the kitchen like scared sheep; I heard the door slam shut.

Then I heard the sound of four slaps. She had slapped their faces hard, quick, twice for each boy.

"You can't do that!" one of them cried. "We'll sue you!"

She slapped them again.

"You fat bitch!" the same boy cried.

"You get the hell out of here, both of you; I don't want your kind stinkin' up my house!" Gladys's voice was almost always strong and steady, but that night it was shaking and higher pitched.

They ran out. I watched at my window as they tore through the snowy fields, two scared, skinny animals under the moon. I know Gladys was standing at the door with the rifle, watching them, and somehow I knew her eyes were wet, and it made me think of when she was a girl, when she could still cry, when she wasn't all dammed up. And I missed that girl terribly.

Gladys came into the bedroom that night and sat on the edge of her bed and watched what she thought was my sleeping face. She sat there breathing. She watched me for ten minutes or so, and then she looked at Wendell's picture, picked it up, and sat it in her lap so his handsome face was staring up into hers.

I missed Wendell too. I thought of how he ran as a small child, with so much coordination and grace his father said he'd play ball. Why, when children are gone from you, do you so often call up not the recent memory but the memory of when they were smaller, needier? Gladys brushed her fingers over the features of his face. Then she laid down on top of the covers and slept.

The next morning she said, in a voice that wasn't like her own somehow, a softer voice with an almost smile, "I dreamed of that child from Philadelphia. I could see her. She wore red shoes walking by a river and a bird was flying above her, following her. A captain on a white boat was sailing by, but he didn't see the child and she didn't see him. It was in a different country. Maybe Portugal. It weren't clear."

I knew right away there was more to that dream than red shoes and a captain on a Portuguese river.

More letters came, more horses, not all with blue saddles, fact they got more colorful, imaginary colors for the horses like purple with green dots, and one with sunglasses and platform shoes; Gladys got a kick out of that one and put it on her mirror. And every letter told of how hard she was praying, how much she was sacrificing, she had given up Almond Joys and wearing socks, for instance—and how she thought Wendell was like a big brother to her. She never had a big or little brother, she said, she just had a cousin and the cousin was unsuccessful as a Philadelphia puppeteer so had to live elsewhere. I believe Miami. And the father with the nipple on his cane, turns out he was a drug user, with a new drug-user girlfriend who he wanted Raelene to call "Mom," so mostly the poor thing tried staying out of that house late as possible, and leaving in the morning soon as she woke.

But there came a time when Gladys didn't read me the letters anymore. I don't remember when that was, but she didn't leave them around for the likes of my deceitful eyes either. And Wendell didn't come home, and didn't come home. Tim McGreen had been back for months. Another boy we knew, Lad Kane, he was back without a leg. I worried about Gladys then more than I could tell her. She'd already lost one child, and that's a whole other story. I watched her closely, I couldn't help it, I'm protective of others. Maybe she hated that. I kept wondering when she was going to cry. I know I felt like crying all the time; I loved Wendell too. But I was waiting for Gladys.

Then we found out he was never coming home.

When she got the news it was a windy spring day, the kind that bangs the shutters, and after she closed the door on the officers Gladys just bent in half. She had her hands on her stomach and she bent completely in half. *Oh*, she said, *Oh*.

She stayed bent in half with her hands on her stomach for less than a minute. Her face was dark red. I was afraid to speak. She finally straightened up and walked back to the bedroom and closed the door quietly behind her. She came back out in five seconds, left the house with a stone face, and walked down the hill.

Gladys came back an hour later. I remember I had made macaroni and cheese. I could tell by Gladys's face she hadn't cried yet. Gladys was conversational that night, drinking her whiskey. She said things like, "I'm bored with the Sunday stew we make. I'm bored to tears with the same damn thing. We should get some new cookbooks, Ivy. I need some variety in life. We need to change the menu. No wonder those children are half insane. Jesus, Mary and Josephine, Ivy, what have we been thinking?" I remember her eyes were wet, but it was like the tears that wouldn't fall were clear, solid shields, and she kept smiling, and then her eyes weren't even wet anymore. Before she went to bed that night she sat on the couch and read one of her books (she usually read the classics, and never the excellent mysteries that I recommended). She looked up from that book and said, "I wonder if James will ever know."

James was Wendell's father. We hadn't heard from him in almost a year, and hadn't seen him in five. He must've felt something. He called just six days after we'd heard Wendell died, and I answered the phone, and he said, "Ivy, hello, this is James. Just calling to check on Wendell."

"Hold on," I said. "Hold on."

Then I held the receiver in my hand with my heart pounding. "Gladys?" I said. She was asleep in the bedroom; it was six in the morning. "James is on the phone, Gladys." And so she gets out of bed smoothly like she'd rehearsed all this a million times and she comes and takes the phone from me and says, "James?" And then she puts her hand on her throat and her chin lifts itself up in the air and she hands the phone back to me, and goes to stand over by the window.

"Bad news, James, Wendell died over there."

He didn't gasp or make a single sound.

"James? You there?"

I talked to him about the service we were having for Wendell in the Unitarian chapel, and he said he'd be there, but he never made it.

"Let me talk to Gladys," he said before hanging up.

So I gave the phone to Gladys and the only thing she said was, "I'm okay, yes. Are you?"

And that was that.

Raelene's letters didn't stop coming. Gladys put them in the night table drawer. I didn't read them, or ask Gladys whether she ever wrote back. When I think back to those days, it's like Gladys and me are all alone in that house, two women in our early forties already feeling old, and the house is underground, like Wendell took us right down with him somehow.

When you looked out the window all you saw is the earth, and it was filled up with boys.

You can be a sister to Gladys and feel your own luck as evil, or not quite evil, but unfair. Like I said, Wendell's not the only one she's lost. No sir. And the fact is, I haven't had a single tragedy. My son Louis grew up flat-footed with asthma, and missed the war. His father and I parted early, both of us happy to do so; it was back in the days where you married up after knowing someone only a few weeks, and that's what we done, when I was just a girl, and him a boy, and soon we said to each other, "We're opposites, but we don't attract." It weren't too painful and Harry and Louis kept in touch, and after Louis was six he had the counselors at camp to spoil him. He was always riding on someone's shoulders wearing his plastic fireman's hat and laughing his quiet laugh. I was blessed with a soft-spoken child with just the right mixture of mischief and pity in his heart. He cared for hurt animals; the asthma must've gave him sympathy. I remember he liked to serve me breakfast in bed when I was on the melba toast diet. He'd smear peanut butter on melba toast and top it off with Christmas cookie sprinkles, but I ate it anyway. His eyes were a shade bluer than my own, shining under the fireman's hat he never took off, not even in the bathtub. He was husky voiced with a funny way of winking at you like he was an old man, don't know where he got that. One of those little boys who wouldn't look too abnormal with a cigar in his mouth. Now he's on a ship. A fisherman by trade. Calls me from various ports, and visits when I least expect it, always with a present. Last time he called he mentioned he was getting serious with a woman and I'd meet her soon, maybe.

So you might think to yourself that I've been a lucky woman, and you're right, though it hasn't all been a dream. I'm not deaf to the world. I'm not blind to the veterans of one war after another. And there's part of me that knows the bomb is bound to be dropped soon enough. I'm not like Louise Daley down the road who feels safe just because we don't live in D.C. or New York City. I'm not someone ignorant about the powers of destruction.

On a personal level, the Italian Catholic broke my heart years ago; I thought I loved him and cried for a month, and sometimes in my mind I still see the way he looked when he drove, like he was always expecting to happen upon something great, but who needs to think back on that? It's not my habit. And Gladys said he was a fool. Finally I came to agree.

See, Gladys had an opposite sort of life, a life of one thing happening after another. It started happening after she was seventeen, when she met James.

His full name was James Gehrig Pittman. Gehrig for Lou, the great ballplayer. We called him James or Jimmy, or sometimes Gladys called him *Louie the hula boy*, some private joke of theirs. They were always that way—Mrs. and Mr. Private Jokes. Jimmy was originally from Kentucky, but Gladys met him back when we lived in southern Delaware, near Rehoboth Beach. One May evening Gladys met James Gehrig Pittman on the boardwalk. A warm night with a dark pink sky, the beach and the ocean empty. Gladys had always loved the off-season.

That night James was sitting on a bench with his legs out and his arms crossed. One of his feet was moving like he was nervous; the rest of him was still. Gladys had gone to the boardwalk to talk to her friend Jean Ann Reilly, who worked in a french fry and vinegar joint looking right out at the ocean back then. I'm talking years ago, when Gladys was seventeen, and the war was over but still a feeling in the air (fading fast), so remember, she's not a fat lady in this story. She's not a thin girl, she's a girl with meat on her bones, but Jimmy must've liked it that way. Back then it weren't like a girl had to starve to be cute.

Gladys with her dyed red hair was walking in her skirt and sweater in the early June night, maybe the sun not all the way down yet, but nice and sparkly on the water. Maybe she was walking like she used to walk with her arms crossed, thinking to herself about the world across the sea, where the Nazis had been. She wasn't the sort who could walk near the sea in 1946 and not think about what had happened on the other side a few years back. I knew because she would talk to me at night when we laid awake in the dark with the cows looking in.

So on that old boardwalk, Gladys and James looked at each other and knew, both of them knew, something was happening. He was not quite your movie star, but he was exactly Gladys's type.

That's hard to put into words what her type is. Her type is a man who is not good but whose goal is to be good, who works to be good because he believes in it. She liked that in Jimmy, I think, that struggle. You could see in Jimmy's face that he was struggling. Yes, struggling men is what attracted Gladys. The hidden motion they had in their faces was the motion of their troubled thoughts. Jimmy wasn't really her first struggling man, that was Ben, a farm boy, a two-night stand when Gladys was fifteen, something else entirely. I had my share of a boy like Ben too, don't think a heavy girl gets no experience. We were looking for love, like any girls, and it interfered with our morals early on, but I can't say I ever cried too hard over that spilled milk.

So this James, or Jimmy as only I mostly called him then, he had a child already, the child was Wendell, soon to be Gladys's adopted son. Wendell was three years old then. That night on the boardwalk Wendell was on the carousel in the pavilion with his grandfather, Jimmy's father, who was exactly Jimmy twenty years down the road (still struggling). Jimmy said to Gladys after their eyes met, "Will you sit down?" He patted the bench beside him. I think she probably looked out at the ocean for a second, narrowing her eyes, then sat down, and crossed her arms.

They sat and talked a bit, staring straight ahead, and though their bodies weren't touching they could feel each other. And then Jimmy's father in a black suit and baseball cap (which apparently was a kind of uniform he never took off) and Wendell in red overalls come walking out of the pavilion, and Jimmy says to Gladys, "That's my boy and father walking this way." And Gladys almost got up and ran, thinking the boy's mother would soon be stepping out of another pavilion. But Jimmy touched her on the arm, first time ever, and said, "The boy's without a mother."

She swallowed. She was only seventeen, and on a beautiful May evening with a struggler who's watching his child and father walk toward him, a girl feels romantic. She thought Jimmy's wife must've died of a terrible disease, but the truth was Jimmy never had a wife, just a girl he got pregnant, a girl who ran away seven months after the baby was born because she was a young and wild tobacco-chewing colt from the Blue Ridge Mountains and Jimmy was off at war. The girl had left the baby with her mother, then Jimmy came home from the war and grew attached to little Wendell. You could feel how he loved that boy. If the two of them were standing behind you and you didn't know it, you'd turn around anyhow because you could feel it. The love, I mean.

Really Jimmy was only twenty-two years old, but when I met him I was sixteen and thought, Now who is this older man Gladys drug home? because in Jimmy's expression there was age and a kind of wise look. He wasn't usual. He was a college man thanks to the GI Bill. He was tall with these blue eyes welled up with kindness, a kind of weight that kept him separate, cut off, like you didn't really know him. He was looking at you kindly but from a distance.

I believe he was lonely and Gladys always noticed loneliness in people, and felt for it.

The two of them were so in love it made me nearly sick to be around. Jimmy came out to the farm with

Wendell and some Ballantine beer stashed in his old Ford every evening, and half the time they'd leave the child with me, and I'd sit and swing him on the porch swing, and tell him little stories, but my mind was on them, knowing how they'd be drinking and talking deep and using their hands out in the dark field. The swing would squeak and whine, squeak and whine. The one-night stands I'd known did not seem sweet next to the love my sister had with Jimmy. I felt inside like I was empty then, so empty I had to be as fat as I was just to store the emptiness. I would sit and sit and swing Wendell and hum "Ain't Misbehavin'" like I was cheerful. That has always been my way. Wen smelled like a milk mustache and cut grass. We'd look at the summer moon bright in the sky, we'd hear crickets, and the squeak of the swing chains, we'd smell the dark roses growing up the side of the house, and every three minutes he would say, "Where's Daddy?" till it drove me crazy and I began saying, "Daddy went up to the moon. See him there?" or "Daddy's in Paris selling Bibles" or "Daddy's joined the Chinese Circus." That just amused old Wendell, he was so smart. He'd joke right back. "He joined the circus?" he'd say, "Is he the man on the flying trapeze?" And you could tell that even though he was only three, he was being sort've sarcastic.

"That's right, he's the man on the flying trapeze, Wendell, hope he don't fall."

"Oh, me too!" smart Wendell would say. He loved me

for telling him these little tales, he really did, but I wanted love from someone more my size.

Gladys weren't the same after Jimmy. Before Jimmy at night we stayed awake talking in the twin beds, two sisters on nine acres with six cows and two parents. Gladys was not always serious. Not at all. She could talk down-to-earth too, and we would compare the boys we knew (some only in our imaginations), who was the good lover, who was the lover that hurt, who was the lover who couldn't hurt if he tried. We would tell each other what the boys said in passion and how their voices changed after passion, how they didn't want a thing to do with us then, their fine bodies all rigid and twiny and their eyes off to the new horizon, and how we were glad because they were all a bunch of wood-tick hicks from Dover. (Take the *D* out of *Dover* and it's *over*.) They were so dumb when they went to the movie theater and saw the sign saying SEVENTEEN AND OVER PERMITTED they went home and rounded up seventeen friends. That kind of thing is what we'd say in the dark when we were two foolish girls before Jimmy came on the scene.

"Tell me about Jimmy," I'd say on those summer nights after Jim and Wen drove off in their Ford.

"He's a good soul," she'd say. Like she was an old, tender woman.

"You told me about his soul already. I mean tell me about him. Tell me how he is."

"He's a good father, and a good man."

"What's he say after he's through with you?" I asked her one night. I wanted her to say just one funny thing, like old times.

"Not a word," she said. "No need for those kind of words between myself and James Gehrig Pittman." Sometimes she'd just come right on out with his full name like that. I'd be rolling my eyes so far up in my head they might've got lost.

"Oh," I'd say.

"Someday you'll find it," she told me. She was eighteen now. She was going to marry him. She sat up on her bed by the window in a pale green negligee she got from our blind neighbor down the road for weeding. Her voice had a new sort of gentleness, like everything in the world was something she loved because the love she had for Jimmy just spilled right over. Her hair was long, and still dyed red, and when I think back to her face, which was filled with the prettiest, what was it, *sureness*, *certainty*, the kind that belongs to *innocence*, it can startle me to think we were ever that young. She was so changed. She'd say things like, Isn't it amazing we're alive, Ivy? Look at that willow! Isn't a goat the most incredible thing? I mean when you really consider it, really see it? Not to mention the stars! The Milky Way!

I was lonely then, and sure I liked the goats and the Milky Way, but I knew I was missing something, and Gladys for the first time felt almost like a stranger. I'd still lie awake at night and so would she, but between our beds it was like a dark river, her on one side with love, me on the other without.

Gladys never would look at old pictures. I suppose she couldn't bear it. And she thinks they've been trashed. She's unaware I rescued them all the day she threw them out so many years ago. I don't look either. Because I'm not one for looking, at least usually. It's a waste of time is what I always said. But sometimes now at night, now that Gladys is gone off with Raelene, which is a whole other story I got to tell you, I lay awake thinking I'm going to get up and get the pictures out and sit at the table with a glass of milk and look at us all back then. But I never do get up. I let myself drift off to sleep. I got work to do early in the morning, and Gladys isn't here helping me anymore, so there aren't many laughs in the kitchen. Not to say that Gladys was a laugh factory, but we had our times.

If I brought the pictures out I would look for the one of Gladys, James, Wendell, and myself, sitting on the steps of our house that summer they got married, a black and white my mother took. I can see the way my mother looked taking it just as good as I can see the four of us in the picture. I can see her cheap blue sneakers in the wet grass and her flowered, old, ugly dress with the hem line too long and her skin on her thin legs so white they just glowed like marble in the dusk. Wendell's already calling Gladys "Mama." Jimmy's black Ford is not in the picture, but I would feel it on the border just the same. That picture was taken the night Gladys left the house for good. I cried for days. Maybe I'd take that one out and hang it up. Maybe because that was the first time Gladys left, and this is the second, only this time I think it's really for good.

Raelene kept writing to Gladys for four or five years, and I don't know for sure how many times Gladys wrote back. Raelene was a little girl who needed a mother substitute, I guess, and she thought she had one in Gladys, a kind of pen pal–mother. But she finally stopped writing. I forgot all about her, to tell you the truth.

Then last spring, late April, when some of the early-bird counselors were up here for special training, this knock comes to the screen door one afternoon. One of the new counselors is standing out there on the shady step.

"Does Gladys Pittman live here?" she says.

"Certainly does," I say.

"I'm a girl who used to write her letters."

"Oh. You are?"

I was so surprised. And then in the very next instant I weren't surprised at all. That happens sometimes, one moment is so strange you feel you're dreaming, then something *shifts* and you feel "of course. It makes sense." Like you were expecting it.

"I'm her sister," I told the girl, and she says, "Ivy, right?"

So Gladys must've mentioned me at least once.

"That's right," I say. "I'm Ivy, now come on in for a soda pop."

She was a pretty little thing, but not real healthy looking, with dark circles under big eyes, pale skin, long curly brown hair, and nervous to the point you want to send her up to Doctor Wichert for a Valium. She had on a big T-shirt with some rock stars on it, the sleeves cut off near her shoulder and near the one shoulder a blue angel tattoo I hoped was a rub-on. Even though it was chilly, she wore a pair of blue jean fringy shorts like they all wear in summer, with her long legs scratched up from the woods and then these little pink Chinese slippers on her feet when most of the girls wore sturdy sneakers or hiking boots. Also she wore baby pink socks to match. On her big-eyed face was some eyeliner and a little blue shadow, and it just made her look younger and paler.

I gave her a soda pop and sat at the table with her thinking Gladys was going to walk in any second. She was only out back on the stoop drinking ice water. We were on break between lunch and dinner. Gladys liked to sit out there alone in the shade on the cool cement steps. She'd pull on an old sweater. Usually she read a book, and maybe had an afternoon highball. I'd see her look up from her book and into the spring light for a second. In the distance we still had snow on the mountains. She'd squint at that bright white. Then it was back to the book.

Raelene was not easy to talk to that day. She was polite, but not easy, not cheerful, and it was like she was afraid to say, "Where's Gladys?" Like she was worried I was going to tell her, "Gladys is dead."

So I hear the door opening and we both look toward it and Gladys is stepping inside still in her uniform and she's put her head under the garden hose, so her hair is plastered down. She had her wire-frame glasses on, but she still squinted at Raelene. She weren't at all used to having visitors.

"Who's this?" she said, and walked to the sink. She filled her glass with water, her back to us, and Raelene looked right down at her own long folded fingers.

"It's Raelene," I said. "The girl who wrote you all those years. The little girl who prayed for Wendell." I remember saying Wendell because I think it was the first time his name got said in that house in seven years. At the sound of it I could feel Gladys stiffen over there at the sink.

Raelene's dark eyes were even bigger now and she looked at Gladys and said, "I'm just starting to work at the camp now, so thought I'd say hello. It's been a while."

The poor girl's face was red now, and she was smiling right through her embarrassment. And she had her chin lifted, she was a proud girl, she weren't about to sit there and let the embarrassment win, not Raelene.

Gladys slowly turned around, then said, "Well hello." I think Gladys almost smiled. It seemed like I could hear Raelene's heart pounding behind the rock stars on the little cage of her chest.

A silence falls, and I'm coughing to fill it. I'm the one always taking care of awkwardness.

Raelene said, "The lakes are real pretty around here."

Gladys said, "Sure are, if you like lakes."

Finally Gladys sat down at the table, but she didn't talk to Raelene. She talked to me. About what? About rhubarb. "Aren't the winter schoolers slackers?" she said. "We were supposed to have rhubarb pie tonight. The little slobs pick too damn slow."

After some more of this talk Raelene stood up and said, "I'll be going," and Gladys said, "Good-bye," and I said, "Stop back."

Raelene walked out the door and only I got up and watched her walk back down the hill toward the camp. She was just a proud, sorry little colt in pink Chinese slippers. Gladys stayed put and said not a word, but you could feel her thinking.

"How sweet," I said. "How sweet that she'd come here to visit you after all these years."

"Looks like she needs a good bath," Gladys said, and fixed herself a drink.

*　　*　　*

After a couple of weeks, when some of the campers began to show up, part of Raelene's job at that camp was to wake up Monday, Wednesday, and Friday mornings and play the guitar at 5:30 A.M. with the younger girl campers gathered around her out on the porch of the main building where Gladys and I cooked. Raelene had a beat-up red guitar and no case. She could play decent, but her real talent was her voice. She sung pure as a night bird in a marsh. The children always made her sing the old songs like "Leaving on a Jet Plane" and "A Hundred Miles," not the real little kids but the elevens and twelves; those girls liked to sing and feel their eyes well up with tears. "Lord, I'm five hundred miles away from home," they'd sing and then they'd cry, partly homesick and partly happy that in the world was a song exactly about them. Raelene would stop and try to play a different tune like "The Cat Came Back," but the girls didn't like it much. The porch is right outside the kitchen. I've heard "Leaving on a Jet Plane" for ten years of early mornings. Case you're wondering, it don't hold up.

So the first time I noticed Gladys taking a shine to Raelene was one morning when Gladys was standing by the kitchen window with a mug of coffee watching Raelene sing. Gladys almost never smiled, but she did that morning. It was like Raelene's bird voice got into

Gladys's body. She was singing that song called "The Dutchman." On Gladys's lips was just a small smile, a gentle smile, but somehow it seemed like her whole body was smiling. Gladys didn't know I was watching her, and I wish I didn't do what I did; I said, "Isn't that a pretty voice?" and wrecked the spell Gladys was under. The smile fell off her face, her body went back to itself, and she looked over at me without saying a word. I had trespassed. I had caught her beginning to love.

It's strange that she's no longer cooking here. Gladys always cooked.

My first memory of Gladys is when she's only five years old, standing in the old sunny kitchen and she's stirring something in a bowl. Since I'm barely four, she looks big to me, and so wonderful. I wanted to be her. Who wouldn't? She was five years old and she could make a cake!

My father said when she was a little older, maybe nine, "Gladys, you cook better than your mother. Now how is that? What side of the family are you taking after? Not mine. Not your mother's. Where do you come from, girl?"

He was always asking Gladys that, about once a week. It was his little joke to pretend Gladys came from somewhere else, that she was so fine you couldn't explain her origins. Me, he could explain too easy. He would peer at me and say, "You're just like my mother. You look like her, you talk like her, you screw up like her." He'd say it smiling. I'd always laugh like he was just joking with me, but I knew all the same it was not really joking; even when he rubbed my head it was too forceful. But I had my mother there to love me; I did all right. She would make excuses for the man. "Your father's had a long day, honey." "Your father's gruff on the outside, but inside he's tender." "Your father loves you, he just don't know how to show it." Some women are born to make excuses this way.

I'd pretend to believe her. She was a fragile sort.

For years Gladys would cook the family dinner because my father said she was such a fine cook, that she had the knack, that it was inborn, that my mother never spiced anything up and burned half of everything. *Burned the shit out of it.*

"Really, Frank, you're exaggerating. I can cook. I can put more spices in. Just ask! Gladys shouldn't take over, she's a child."

"It's practical," he'd say. "If you got a natural cook in the house, you make her the cook."

He was not a man who needed to yell to get people to follow his orders. In fact, he was usually soft-spoken, and used big words he learned at night school. But somehow he made you feel if you stepped out of line, if you said the wrong thing, if you asked too many questions, he'd kill you. You knew he'd never really kill you, but that was what you felt anyways.

He bought Gladys four aprons, all pretty, some with hand-sewn flowers from the Farmers Market, one from a department store. I remember he tied an apron on her and had her spin around the kitchen like it was a ballerina dress. "Beautiful," he said that day, and whistled, still in his work clothes, his hands and nails dirty. He was learning to build houses. He ran with the Italian stone mason crowd up north in the city of Wilmington. They were good craftsmen like you don't see anymore. He was also slowly going to college at night. He was a book-smart man, I'll give him that. He could pass a test when he was drunk. He was often drunk, but also in control. He wasn't a sloppy kind of drunk, usually. He wouldn't have stood himself being out of control.

So maybe Gladys was ten then. But she was cooking every day after school, and she liked it, because my father made her feel like a special queen, and she made casseroles and stews and simple chicken or beef with green beans. And she made pies—pumpkin, apple, peach, cherry, key lime. And when she was older she made bread. And my father would rave every night; he couldn't get over it. He would tell the neighbors and all our relatives about Gladys, and she would smile and feel proud. He said she was not just a cook, she was an artist.

Maybe you'd think my mother felt bad, like she wished she was still cooking, but it weren't that way. My mother thought my father was right, she always thought that; it was ground into her early on that the man knew better. They got married in 1927. I guess most of your 1927 brides weren't asking a lot of questions. My mother weren't exactly a suffragette in comfortable trousers.

So instead of getting upset that she was ex-head cook she used the free time to make a great big garden, and to grow her rosebushes. She liked being out of the house in her old sleeveless dresses and her scarves on her head. The scarf never did match the dress. It was a sin the way she looked sometimes. Kneesocks rolled down like sausage links around the ankles. Who was looking? Who cared? Well, I cared. She would get red shoulders from the sun and her skin would peel and she liked that too. She would sit there on the back stoop and peel off her skin like she wanted to peel her whole self away. It was hard for me to look at that thin little day-dreaming woman sometimes. She had bright green eyes, same color as Gladys's only softer, and they'd look up at me as if to say, Don't worry, honey, life is long, you won't always be watching your sunburned mother like this.

But if Gladys went out in the sun my father made her wear a hat to protect her skin, which was snow white. He wouldn't let her go out in the garden without sleeves.

Maybe Gladys didn't get fat when she lived there because she was always cooking and a cook never eats as much as others. They get bored with their own creations. I should know.

I ate too much of what Gladys cooked and went from being a plump child to a plumper teenager, and my father never told me to sign up for reducing classes or sent me off to fat girls' camp. But if Gladys started looking too plump, which sometimes she did, he'd have her walk ten miles into town and back, or swim laps in this bay down in Lewes, or maybe run back and forth on Slaughter Beach. He'd drive her down there, sit in the car, and watch her swim and run. Meanwhile he was no slim-jim himself, but it never occurred to us then that a man should reduce. You look back and things seem obvious, but at the time you're being hypnotized every step of the way.

Gladys didn't mind. He was her hero absolutely, and nobody could say a bad word about her father, including me. She was a little like him, you didn't want to push any wrong buttons. So I just swallowed up everything I thought about the man and when we talked at night and she said something about how fine Daddy was I'd say, "Uh-huh."

So when James came on the scene, when Gladys was only seventeen, my father at first told her no, she could *not* see a man who was twenty-two, he was too old for her, and he had a child.

"You'll regret it, dammit, you don't want to be mother to some other woman's child!"

"How do you know what I want?" Gladys said that night. The two of them were on the front porch, on the swing. I was on the steps. My mother was in her own little world out there in the garden, suffering, I think now. I remember Gladys saying, "How do you know what I want?" because it wasn't her habit to snap at him like that, and the way she said it was a real snap crackle pop.

For a long time he was quiet. You could hear the sound of my mother's shears snipping in the garden.

"I suppose I don't know what you want. Suppose I never did," my father finally said, and then he gets up off the swing and walks inside. I turn and watch him walk through the light of the doorway, a big man in his work boots, and secretly I'm thrilled his feelings got hurt.

The squeak of the chains is all I hear now. Gladys is swinging on the swing with her arms crossed. It's quiet, and I wanted to say something but I just could never figure out what to say. Then the swinging stops and there's a stillness, and all the sudden Gladys is crying, crying hard, like I never heard her cry before.

I stood up and walked over to her. "Gladys?"

She said through her crying, "Get away from me!"

So I did.

And by the time of her wedding day, which my father did attend, Gladys and him weren't talking. He walked her up the aisle of the small white Baptist church none of us had ever set our heathen feet in; he wore a suit and had his hair slicked down and walked tall, but they hadn't talked to each other in over two months.

I cried my eyes out at that wedding. People cry at weddings, especially young girls, so nobody thought a thing. They thought, Sweet Ivy. Sweet Ivy is so happy for her sister. But I was crying with a dark heart. Watching my father hand her over like a present to James, I knew the future of our house. I knew my father would disappear. He wouldn't know how to live in the house with Gladys gone. I wouldn't miss him, exactly, I'd miss who he'd never been, some father who never was. I wouldn't see him for a long time. He wouldn't even show up at my wedding.

Gladys and Jimmy would just ride away with Wendell. My mother and I would be left behind. She wouldn't know what hit her. She'd just milk the cows and work the garden and maybe try to figure it all out. She wouldn't try too hard to. She'd tell herself, That's life. I wouldn't really have any words to explain anything either. I watched my sister, the beautiful bride in the lace wedding dress, her cheeks rouged up and her lips painted too red and clashing with her dyed red hair, but the gown fitting her curvy body perfectly, Jimmy tall and painful looking and handsome, and Wendell the ring boy in pants that were too short and patent leather shoes that looked like girl shoes if you asked me.

I now pronounce you man and wife!

It started raining just as he said it. I kid you not. The rain slithered down the colored glass windows. So the reception couldn't be outside under the elms. We had it in the fire hall. My father danced to the sound of thunder and Nat King Cole with Gladys, kissed the top of her head, and then he was gone, and nobody knew where to.

The fire hall was decked out in pink and white streamers. Flowers on every table. The small high windows framing hard rain and lightning. I danced one with Wendell. I can see him looking up at me with his smiling boy face and his dark hair slicked back like a man's. I also danced with Herman Lock, a prematurely gray boy from Gladys's grade in school. Mostly I watched Gladys and James, how they were always looking at each other even when they were talking to other people. And James kept checking his watch. They weren't holy people who had to wait to get married before they knew each other in the biblical sense. As I told before, they had been lovers in the fields. But still they didn't want much part of the big reception, you could see that. They wanted to drive off and be married. They had their own private little world going. My mother sat at one of the tables in a blue dress smiling and being sweet when people came up to say congratulations. If she noticed my father gone, she weren't letting on.

And when I stood out on the gravel road and

watched the bride and groom and child drive away that evening, I could feel they weren't headed for easy street, even though the rain had cleared and the sky was soft and blue. Under that pretty setting sun I thought to myself, That little world of love they have between them, it's just too nice. Something's going to bust it right open. How I knew this I can't say, it was a feeling in my stomach, and as it turns out, I was right.

Wendell turned around and waved. I knew that wave was for me. I realized then how much I loved that child, but I couldn't bring myself to wave back. Maybe, I thought to myself, if I don't wave, they won't go. I just froze up there for a moment, maybe saying to myself, if I don't feel this departure, it's not happening.

Now I'm hoping for some luck when I finally visit Edgel Greely. Almost forty-seven years old, and I'm on a diet for a man named Edgel Greely. You might think it's a strange time for me to decide to reduce. Why didn't I try sooner? What's the point?

The point is, I have a plan. In Edgel I have a man I could love, and I believe he will love me, in about twenty pounds. This sounds foolish, but I have a feeling about it. I am not and never was unsightly, fact I'm far from it. I am not the kind of fat you worry will get stuck in the doorway. But I am heavy, and I'm a woman, and the two don't go together in this world lately, do they now.

But it didn't matter for years. For years it was me and Gladys, and sometimes I had a man, and most times I didn't, but I was so busy, so tired, and so occupied with Gladys somehow, I never gave much thought to my body. I always knew I could lose fifty pounds and be a beauty, but the beauties I knew didn't seem much happier than anyone else so what was the point.

But now, especially in the early mornings cooking thousands of blueberry pancakes with my new coworker Mike Stanley, a whistling man twenty years my junior who talks about politics like he's Jimmy Carter's best friend, and who objects when I pour salt on the bacon grease we spill on the floor when we don't have time to stop and clean it up, and who won't wear frozen towels around his neck, which anyone who works in a 120-degree kitchen knows is part of the uniform, the fact that Gladys isn't with me is still a surprise. On one level. On another level I'm used to the absence. And I like checking the mail each day because it turns out Gladys is a letter writer. She doesn't write so often, but the letters she does write, it's worth the wait, if you can read the penmanship.

No campers this year have taken to talking with me. Usually a few of the little ones like to come by and get an extra cookie. This year they don't. I guess I'm not the same woman; I don't invite them with my smile as much. I'm still cheerful, but work isn't the same. I make the hotcakes and eggs and bacon, the stews and sandwiches, the huge bowls of fruit, and the whole time I've got my mind on a certain man I plan to drift toward. And if my mind isn't on that, it flies to Gladys.

I used to be a woman who thought of the eggs when she made the eggs—I liked that scrambled yellow color, and the bacon when she made the bacon—the smell and sizzle. When I was brushing my teeth at night, my mind was on that, how good it felt to give your teeth a clean slate, how good it was to *have* teeth. When I was talking to a person, my mind was on the person's words.

Not anymore. I'm just not the same. I can hardly recognize myself some days.

It's not as pleasant when your mind drifts. It's really not the right way to live. I'm against it. But I can't seem to make it stop.

Gladys
Out of the Cave

WHY WAS I MEAN?

Raelene wanted to know that. Wanted to know a lot more than that. A long time ago, this was. Over fifteen years since she came to camp. That's a long time ago, I suppose. It doesn't feel that way. But I was a different woman then. God knows.

I learned to appreciate Raelene. When she was seventeen she came up with her big eyes and pink Chinese slippers and her accent from Philadelphia. She wanted to save me. You know the sort. The child who couldn't save her own parents. She's just ripe to save a stranger she thinks needs fixing. Just ripe to wrap herself around a shipwreck like me. Oh yes, Raelene rescued me, at least for a while.

She took me away on a Greyhound bus. She was an

odd piece of work. She said, come on, Gladys, let's just go! And something in me knew I'd scram then, or never scram again. I was forty-eight. Not exactly your traveling gypsy age.

When Raelene first came up to camp I was what you might call dying on the vine. I was living with my sister, Ivy. Ivy's a good woman. Sometimes too good. But she got on my nerves back then. She was always watching me, and she knew too much about me. She'd been there when it all came tumbling down. Looking at her face was somehow looking in the mirror of my past. It was all right there.

I didn't even know this then. I didn't think much about the past, but it was always there just the same. Like bad background music. I couldn't get away from the glorious past even for a second. Not as long as Ivy was there. My whole life story was caught in her eyes because she'd watched it unfold, and the problem was, neither Ivy or me said a word about it. Words get stuck in your eyes if you don't let them out of your mouth.

Ivy always meant well. I know that. Didn't I always? And I'm not blaming her. Even if I wanted to, I'm too old to blame anyone now.

Ivy was there when I was a girl, drunk on hope, falling hard for my husband, James. She was at our wedding, of course. She knew James well, knew my son Wendell well, knew A., my daughter well. And her heart broke each time there was big trouble for me. When Ivy's heart broke her eyes broke right along with it. Painful eyes, at least when she looked my way. Sometimes I couldn't face her. I'd look elsewhere. She pitied me. She thought I was the big shattered, pitiful mystery woman. Maybe I was. A mystery to myself too.

When Raelene first showed up at our house, I said to myself, no thank you. I was unprepared, and I'm not fond of surprises. I was rude, I know that. Partly because she'd stopped writing to me and never told me why. After years she just stopped. I didn't particularly need another child disappearing like that. And she sure didn't look much like the little girl I met once before in Washington, D.C. (That's a long story.) Her long brown hair was curly wild. And I thought she needed a good bath, and she had the blue tattooed angel on her arm. I had a problem with that. Don't ask me why. Tattoos always disgusted me. After a while, I told Raelene that.

"I don't like 'em much either," she said. "This guy I was goin' with convinced me to get it. But I figure a tattoo on your body's not too important compared to the things that end up tattooed on your soul."

This was Raelene. A real life philosopher from Philadelphia. I got a charge out of it. I liked that girl's way of talking. And there she was, working in the late spring at the camp where I cooked. Campers weren't there yet as I recall. She was being trained, fixing up the lean-tos. She'd come up from Philly, where she'd been her whole life.

I'd been cooking at the camp over ten years by that time. Ivy had been up there cooking forever. She followed some man up there when she was too young to know better. Can't even remember the man's name right now. Arnie? He was a handsome plumber from Lake Placid. Had money because the rich summer people hired him for every little leak. He invited Ivy for a vacation. She was only twenty-some years old. Well, she vacationed all right. The highlight of that vacation was Mr. Lake Placid disappearing on her. She had no money, and she was in a strange, cold place. And too proud to call our father. So she ended up getting a job as a cook down at Camp Timber. Didn't expect it would be her whole life. Who would? Didn't expect I'd come join her, either. But she called me a few years after being up there. "Why don't you and James come settle?" she said. "Then Wendell would be near his Aunt Ivy." That was late 1960. In early '61, she called and said, "I'm lonely, please come." So we all went up to see her. I didn't think we'd end up calling it home.

Now little Raelene Francis didn't fit in, believe me. She and her tattoo and her wild hair. She wore eyeliner like a cat woman, not exactly your camp girl look. She chewed big wads of gum too often. She had that accent from Philadelphia. If she wanted to tell you "have yourself a very Merry Christmas," she'd say "Have ya self a vurry murry Christmas." It was an awful way to have to talk, but you can't help where you're born. Her big dark serious eyes just sat back in their sockets staring at you like they had serious answers if only you could ask the right questions. And her eyebrows were always raised up like she was ready for trouble. Ivy thought she always looked like she was about to cry. But that was Ivy. Raelene never cried. Not Raelene. Not back then. She was beyond tears. So was I. Beyond Tears is like a place, a meeting ground, and it's where we met. Right out there by the old campfire, a nice place that could've had a sign: WELCOME TO BEYOND TEARS. POPULATION: 2.

See, Raelene was on late-late shift one night. All the counselors had to take a turn at it, every other week. This was maybe three weeks after she'd shown up, and some of the early session campers had started trickling in. I suppose I had a case of guilt. I wasn't sleeping. Here was this child who had written to me for years. I'd written to her too. The least I could do was be her friend.

Now, that was going to be hard. I hadn't been anyone's friend in a long time. Not my own friend, either. I read books and mostly kept to myself. I worked. I slept. I said hello to folks. Sometimes I even enjoyed them. Part of me did, anyhow. But I'd been frozen, I see now, all my insides just frozen up. It's easy to freeze. I understand why I froze. Now I understand.

So Raelene was out there by the fire that night, the late-late counselor, sitting on a rock, poking embers with a stick. Chewing gum. I can't imagine what she thought when she looked up. I had turned off my Sonny Boy Williamson and stepped outside. I had walked in the dark, down the hill from our house, through the valley past the school, and up the other hill to the camp. This was not a hop skip and a jump.

I'd never been over late at night before. Now there I was on the other side of the flames. Big old Gladys in blue pants and jacket. Just standing there in the night, firelit. I tried smiling. I imagine she saw the fire reflected in the lenses of my glasses.

"Gladys?" Raelene said.

I went and hoisted myself onto a rock across from her. The flames were hot and dancing on my skin. Above us were the usual stars.

"Thought I'd come on out and keep you company," I told her.

"That's great."

"Even though it's two in the morning," I added, "And I'm crazy not to be in bed."

"It's crazy just living, as the old song goes," Raelene said. Her voice was sweet and high. She was smiling.

"What old song's that?" I said. I sat and poked some embers around.

Raelene shrugged. "I don't know. I can't believe I'm even here. You must think I'm really pathetic, and I can't say I blame you."

A small wind bent the flames. I peered over at Raelene's firelit face, which looked young, dangerously young. Needy. I rowed back inside myself all the way for a clear moment. I could row myself back inside like I was a cave. A cave with ice on the walls, nice and dark. I could see the world and anyone in it standing at the cave's mouth, framed and manageable. I had to do this right away with Raelene. Because I see now she scared me. The little girl believed she knew me. Thought she knew old Gladys.

Oh, she knew some things. But she didn't know me. Not then. You can't really know a person just from letters. I had told her some things I hadn't told any others. True enough. She was my secret pen pal. I had told her how broken I was inside a while after Wendell was killed, for instance. Broken up. A smashed heart. Hatred in my veins for the whole country was the only thing whole inside me, and I expressed that page after page. To a child I expressed it! This I'd call desperate. I wrote that letter at night out on a picnic table off the interstate. I sat in the dark and wrote my hatred out. I almost ripped the letter up. I remember it seemed to demand too much tenderness from me to fold a letter and put it in the envelope. I remember I had to force myself to go through those motions that seemed beyond me. Because I was pure hatred and rage. Shaking with it.

Now Raelene hated the whole country too. She was no dummy. But she had a child's hatred for the men in power. A baby's notion that if only the right men got in power, there wouldn't be war. She didn't understand a damn thing, but she did have her anger. She couldn't stand any of it. She was just a baby watching the whole thing on television.

Ivy never knew it, but once I went to meet Raelene in Washington, D.C., for a protest the hippies were throwing. It was 1970. I went, Raelene went. It was her idea to go there on a bus with a church group, and meet me at the monument. She was just a lost child with crooked teeth and red bell-bottoms. Pretty little thing with those big eyes. Flashing the peace sign at strangers when I first saw her there at the foot of the monument. "Is that you?" I said, but I knew. Her face had Raelene written all over it. We were both lost souls in that mob. All those festive hippies, Raelene and me eating hot dogs. The sky blue. It got dark slowly that day. I remember a nun in her blue habit came up to me, tapped me on the shoulder and said, "You have a fine relationship with your girl. It's obvious." I remember her white nun face in the dark like I remember some of my dreams. It was late and Raelene and I sat on cool grass behind the White House. I knew I'd remember her sleepy face on that night, and I do. She was so young I felt I should carry her back to the bus. But I didn't. I was relieved when the day ended.

Raelene loved Wendell in a way, though she never knew him either. His name was on her little bracelet. And she had his picture. She was lonely, a lonely kid from Philly with no mother. A boy named Hambone West lived across the street from her, and he was a kind of friend. She also had some school friends, but they didn't cure the loneliness. They didn't cure the mother who ran off with a man to the West, leaving Raelene with a pile of presents. They didn't cure the father who liked his needles. So she latched onto Wendell, the idea of him. I believe she talked to his picture. And certainly loved him and prayed for him and that cured her loneliness for a while. She had a Catholic imagination back then. It was one thing the drug addict father and the runaway mother handed down. They'd been the sort to have a party on the saints' feast days. Raelene went to some grammar school called Immaculate Conception, if you can believe that.

So I had told her an important bit of the past, but just a bit. So out there at the fire she looked at me like she knew me. Only it was someone else she knew. Have to admit I enjoyed that. I think now I enjoyed being someone else in her eyes. It was like a vacation, a vacation from my self, from who I knew I was, from who Ivy knew I was. To Raelene I was a big strong woman who'd seen hard times but who was somehow just great. Lonely but wonderful! A real interesting woman. I just needed some encouragement. I just needed a friend.

People can free you up. They see you a certain way and you suddenly buy that vision. You eat it up directly. You get to be someone else for a while. Moments come along where you can stand yourself a little.

So out there at the fire Raelene is looking at me with a load of admiration that first night.

Now, I'm complicated. So to be truthful I'll have to say this. That admiration in her eyes was not real welcome by one part of me. While one part liked it, another part wanted to slap her face.

Why? Why the meanness? Well, you tell me. When someone admires you and you don't admire yourself, don't you feel like slapping them? Like you have the responsibility to wake them up?

I couldn't stand it when someone turned their naive eyes on me. Of course I liked it too. Like I said, I'm complicated. Bear with me. I've beared with me for all these years. Jesus Christ I'd like a medal.

I told Raelene I didn't think it was pathetic that she'd come up to camp. (This was a lie, I thought it was one of the most pathetic things I'd ever heard of.) I told her, "I'm glad to meet you again, I really am. But I warn you, I'm nothing special. Not like you thought I was when you were small. I'm better in letters. I really am."

"Your letters were like the best thing in my life for years, Gladys," Raelene said.

"Is that right? I'm sorry to hear that."

She laughed. She was an easy laugh. Surprising.

"Gladys, whenever you wrote me, you had this way of saying everything. I'd read those letters like fifty times. I kept them under my pillow and I read them by flashlight when I couldn't sleep. It was like I could feel you out there, same as I used to feel my guardian angel when I was six. I bet I could recite lines from those letters all these years later."

As she talked, she looked straight into the fire without squinting. When she stopped talking, she looked at me.

"Your letters meant a lot to me too," I told her. And saying that, I was surprised to realize how true it was. I hadn't thought about it in a long time. "And those horses you always drew. It was real nice. I always did love horses."

"You still have them?"

"Oh, probably. I imagine they might be stuck in a box in the basement."

She said sometime it would be fun to see them, and I said yes, it would, and then I hoisted myself up off the rock and said good night. I started walking away. I could feel her puzzled eyes on me. I was headed with my flashlight into the dark field. I was headed right toward the hill so I could get back to the house. I really was. But I stopped. Or something stopped me. I turned and walked right back to the fire. "Changed my mind," I told her. "I'll stay a bit longer." Don't ask why. It wasn't like me to head back to a place I'd decided to leave.

I stayed for a while, and then walked with her to wake up all the bed wetters at 3:30 A.M. I remember this like it was last week. She would go into the cabin and nudge the kid awake saying, "You have to go to the outhouse now, honey." Most of the little bed wetters woke up quick. A few cried. We'd walk them down to the purple outhouse. I was interested, seeing the kids this way. They were mostly asleep. They were baby sleepwalkers in pajamas. All moonlit. Like orphans. Angels. Not the loudmouths they were in the daytime. I had pity on them, seeing them half asleep and walking barefoot on cold grass in the dark. They were so young. And it hurt me having pity like that. It warmed me up. Was this the beginning of my unfreezing? Maybe. I do remember it hurt terribly! Like hot liquid pushing through a hole in my frozen heart. I grit my teeth. Crossed my arms. We just kept waking up the little kids. Or Raelene did, and I watched. Tried not to watch, but watched all the same. It was more like a dream. The goddamn camp was packed with kids who peed their beds. A bunch of nervous bladders. Some were only seven years old, like Becky Kalmus, I'll never forget her. Slept in a cowboy suit. Guns in her holster. Seven years old, a bed wetter, a cowboy in her dreams.

She slept this way every night according to Raelene.
Made her feel safe. She was a little bird. Most kids just
walked barefoot on the grass to get to the outhouse.
Old Becky had to put her cowboy boots on. White
boots with fringe and too small for her. She wasn't a
sleepwalker. She was wide awake, or at least looked
that way. And she sang to herself quietly the whole way
to the outhouse: "Hello operator, give me number nine,
the boys are in the bathroom, pulling down their flies
are in the kitchen, eating bread and jam, my mom
doesn't give a darn and I don't give a damn . . ." Raelene said that's what the kid sang every night as she
walked to the outhouse under the stars. Anyhow, I
watched her closely. Couldn't help it. And something
about her face was getting to me.

"I think I'll go now," I told Raelene, after we walked
Cowboy Kalmus back to her cabin.

I felt angry. I remember I walked back to our house
full of anger. Why in hell had I just walked around with
the late-late counselor waking up the bed wetters? Goddamnit, I had to work in the morning.

But before I fell asleep, I kept seeing that little
girl, that little seven-year-old Becky. Her face under
her cowboy hat. The eyes looking up at me. Brown
eyes, not big or small, just brown regular eyes. It
came to me that night that she'd reminded me of A.
My daughter.

I'd stay away from her for good, I thought. I fell

asleep mad. Raelene dragged me out of my cave. Mad at her for even showing up. I wished she'd go back to where she came from.

Of course, once you're out of the cave, you're out. You're rearranged. Bigger. So if you try going back in the cave, the fit's no longer quite right. The next day I woke up and knew it. Because I'd had a nice night. I really had. Old Raelene knew how to show a person a good time. Just walk them around in the dark and wake up some bed wetters.

So I believe I had this sense of expectation. Nothing familiar about it. The anger from the night before was mostly gone. Ivy said to me at breakfast, "What's up?" I said, "Nothing." She said, "You're different." I said, "For Christ sakes, Ivy, stop watching me!" Poor Ivy. I hurt her a lot. Why didn't I just say, "Well, Ivy, I stayed up late with Raelene. She's a nice girl. She likes me. She depends on me. She might just turn out to be a real friend of mine."

I didn't say that because poor Ivy was just too hungry to hear it. Now that's another mean streak in me. If someone was too hungry to hear something about me, they got nothing. Jesus said feed the hungry, so I'll go to hell, but I couldn't control it. Not with Ivy. Ivy thought I needed her kind of love, but I needed privacy. Don't we all? And I see now I needed Ivy to get her own concerns. She didn't have a life outside me back then. Or maybe she did and I couldn't see it. I'm smart enough now to know I don't finally know too much.

So that morning I'm in the kitchen. I've got a new sense about things. It was unclear what it was, but I could feel it. I stood washing my hands at the big sink. I noticed the sky. Purple. The sun coming up orange. The mountains in the distance. A lot of young green leaves on the edge of the woods windblown upward. Everything hushed.

I stood with the water rushing over my hands noticing sky. How long had it been since I'd seen the sky? Ten years? When I was young I'd noticed it every day. Now, here it was again. The sky. Mountains. Pressing in on me. It was like seeing it all for the first time.

And then Raelene, who was the music counselor, was out on the porch. The wandering minstrel with fifty kids following her. She was not in her element. Not naturally playful. That you could tell by looking at her. She liked kids, but she was a worrier. She cared too much. It was a little bit pathetic. She tried too hard to listen to every single kid. Then she just gave up. She stood there with her hands over her ears, smiling. They all asked questions at once. Finally they'd get quiet. I watched at the window. She unplugged her ears, and sat down to do her job. Her job was to get the kids singing before breakfast. Five-thirty in the morning, and Raelene hadn't slept on account of late-late shift. She looked like a bewildered raccoon. She was a pretty little thing sometimes, but that morning she looked terrible. But then she started singing.

The chorus of the song was:

Let us go to the banks of the ocean.

That's all I remember of the chorus. The song was "The Dutchman," about an old couple. The old man's falling apart. Thinks he's still in Rotterdam. The old woman walks him around. She sings old songs while she makes the bed in their little house by the canal. They sit in a dark kitchen. You can see them. They sit there with a candle burning, eighty years old. They don't speak. They've said it all.

Well, it was a nice enough song. I would've especially loved it when I was a girl. But it was the voice that impressed me. It was Raelene's voice. A real beautiful voice. You couldn't think otherwise.

Now I was born a music lover. You either are or you're not. You know it early in life if you're a music lover. Because songs will make you cry. They teach you something deeper than words when you're small. They teach you about time. Even the early lullabies do this. *All aboard for blanket bay, won't be back till the break of day*. And they teach you that someday you're going to die, you're not always going to be a small girl spinning in a nightgown on a dirt patch in the back-yard looking at the cows with your mother singing quiet in the window above you. The song's going to end.

So there I was at the sink listening to Raelene. All the kids were singing along, but I listened to Raelene. I felt a tightness in my throat and thought her voice was *terribly lovely.* Those were the exact words I used inside my head. They alarmed me. It was not like me to think like that, ever. That's how good she sounded when she sang. I stopped listening after the second verse. To save myself from feeling it.

It wasn't easy getting to know Raelene because they keep the counselors busy. And I was busy too. But Raelene would come by for coffee on the days when she wasn't a minstrel. Before anyone else had to be out of their tents and cabins, Raelene would wake up and head down to the kitchen. Ivy and I would be in there, sometimes a radio on so we could hear the international bad news. We'd have to start cooking soon, but not yet.

"Hi," Raelene would say in the doorway, her long curls flattened down with water. She always woke and took the GI's bath. And what a fashion plate! I don't know where she found those clothes. I guess it was the style in Philadelphia. She wore tight shorts like they all wore, but Raelene went in for the halter tops. They'd have to be a godforsaken color, like electric blue. Bright green with silver glitters. And then she had a dress.

White with apples and oranges all over it. It zipped all the way down in the back. Like the dressmaker didn't know a zipper stops halfway. And then she would go ahead and wear those damn pink Chinese slippers under the dress. They were the only damn shoes she brought with her.

We'd sit together at the table by the door and have coffee. We talked a little, but not much. The kitchen was big, clean, and quiet. The convection oven, the regular oven, the three-bin sink, the six-burner gas stove, the flat grill, the walk-in, the tile floor, all of it was clean because we left it that way the day before. Ivy and I took pride in our work. The kitchen almost had the feel of a peaceful garden on those mornings. Sparkled. Raelene was soothed there.

Sometimes Ivy would come over to the table and join us. I never appreciated that. I would turn to stone when Ivy joined us. Raelene told me about Hambone on one of these mornings. "He lives out west in Oregon now and told me to come on out if I want. I wish you could meet him. He's been my friend since I was six. He's like the one guy I can trust."

"I'd like that. I'd like to meet old *Hambone West*." Somehow I pictured an old black man with a blues guitar singing Ivory Joe Hunter's "I Almost Lost My Mind." Of course Hambone didn't eventually live up to that.

Then, another morning, Raelene came to visit with tears in her eyes. Her voice shaking with sadness.

She sat at the table. I poured her coffee. I said, "Easy now, easy." I was not prepared. I didn't know her that well yet.

Not well enough for the tears I could feel were coming. I didn't want anyone's tears falling around me. Maybe because I kept my own dammed up inside and expected others to have the common courtesy to do the same.

"What's wrong?"

She shook her head, bit her lip, wouldn't speak.

"Ivy, heat the girl a sticky bun, will ya?"

Ivy did, and brought it over. "Is she okay?" Ivy asked me. Raelene was looking down at the table, biting her lip. She was wearing another godforsaken halter top that day. She looked about as much like a camp counselor as I did.

I let her get her bearings. I went and got the pot of coffee and put it between us on the table. Then I gave her the newspaper's crossword puzzle.

"This will help," I said. "Do this puzzle."

And then I went over and started cooking breakfast. That's just how I was. My shoulder just wasn't ready for anyone's tears. But as I was cooking breakfast, I had Raelene in the corner of my eye. It was like I was holding her there. I half wanted to tell her to get out of the kitchen. The other half of me was confusion and feeling for her. Empathy. Not pity. Lord she knew how to make inroads.

Maybe I was glad because finally, after all those years, here was a counselor who liked me, and not Ivy. That sounds childish, I know. But you don't know how it was. You don't know how the other counselors regarded me all those years. Fat, mean, and dumb. They size you up in a flash. You can read the faces too easy. You're the cook, you're a bit overweight, so you must be dumb. And their asses are headed to Harvard in the fall, so what the hell do they care?

Now Ivy, she was different as far as they were concerned.

(But not as different as she thought.) She was happy-go-lucky. Blue eyed with golden hair. That won her some points. The jolly fat woman. Santa's wife. They all said, "Hi, Ivy!" with big smiles on their faces. And there were a few groups of girls through the years who invited her canoeing or to a little cookout. She was "a good sport." She played along with who they thought she was.

I never got invited anywhere. (This didn't astound me.) And I never thought it bothered me, but maybe it did. One child, ten years ago, a boy named Neal, he liked me. Made me lacy valentines in July, and gave me a goldfish in a Baggie. But when I walked up to his table to thank him one night he put his hands over his face and shouted, "I'm ascending into heaven!" He wouldn't take his hands away from his face, and he wouldn't stop saying "I'm ascending into heaven." In other words, he was out of his mind.

So really Raelene was my first real friend at camp.

I let her sit there and stare at the crossword puzzle. The sun rose in the window. She was all lit up now in sunlight. It seemed to bother her. She put her hand over her eyes. Then she got up and left, not saying a word.

"She's upset, Gladys. You don't just give someone a crossword puzzle," Ivy said.

"Always helped me," I said.

But I knew damn well she was right. And I thought about Raelene that day. And that night I left my house and walked down the hill and up the other hill. Got to her cabin at ten o'clock. She was one of the few counselors who had their own cabin. She'd started out with a college girl in a golf shirt from Boston, but Golf Shirt wanted to live with someone else. Surprise surprise.

I walked down the path in the woods. There was hardly any moonlight. I saw her cabin didn't have any lights on. She was probably sound asleep. I wouldn't wake her.

"Who is it?"

Her voice rang out into the dark woods.

"Gladys," I whispered loudly. "Be quiet."

There she was, standing in the doorway of the cabin with a long white T-shirt on and those long bare legs.

"What's up?" she said. She didn't sound friendly as usual.

"I came to check on you. Are you all right?"

"Sure, I'm fine. I'm feeling better. No big deal."

She didn't move out of the doorway.

"Well okay then," I said, and turned to walk away.

I headed down the path, and then she called out my name, and told me to come back.

I suppose that's the night we became real friends. Raelene's cabin was a nice place. She had little impatiens on the sills and a stuffed bear sitting next to them, real cute. Screens on the windows with flittery moths all over them. She had two cots, with white sheets and scratchy blankets. And I sat down on the one that was made, and she sat down on hers. She lit a lantern and set it on the floor. On the wall she had taped up some snapshots. Her mother. A lady on a couch with tall, dark hair. She didn't look like the sort to run away, don't ask me what I mean by that. Her father in a baseball cap holding a small white dog on the front stoop of a brick row house. Just how I pictured Philadelphia. Another snapshot was Raelene with some long-haired boy with an open shirt. Hambone.

Soon we had both stretched out. We were there stretched out talking with our eyes on the ceiling.

Raelene said she felt like she didn't belong at the camp, that the other counselors didn't like her, and that she wasn't good enough with the kids.

"You could get yourself some preppy clothes from a catalog and do something cute with your hairdo," I told her. "And new shoes. But why would you want to? What the hell do you care?"

"Feeling alone gets old," she said. "I never felt like I was the weird duck back in Philly." She laughed. "Up here's like a different country. I never thought I'd get homesick for Philly, man." Laughed again. Then she told me a bit about her father. "When I left he was high as a kite. I tested him by saying I was going off to Texas to get married. He was so high, and so was Peggy, that's his girlfriend, they just got teary eyed and said, 'Aw, you're gettin' married! You found true love! Aw, Raelene, that's so sweet.'"

I didn't know what to say to that. It was quiet, then Raelene said, "You know, Gladys, I been up here worrying he's dead."

"He's fine," I told her, "I can feel it."

"You can feel it?"

"Sure. I can feel things."

"Psychic?"

"Hell no, I just feel things."

I remember she laughed too hard and too long at things like that, then she'd catch her nervous breath.

"So you think my dad's fine, huh?"

"Yes he is, and he'll be fine in the future too. He'll find his way. So don't fret it."

Was it true that I could feel this? I thought I could. Or did I just assume that everyone would be fine, in one painful way or another? I thought I could see her father sitting in a dark kitchen at night with a radio ball game. A man in a dark cap wondering why he ruined his life. The radio ball game reminding him he was once half normal. He was once a boy who collected baseball cards. It's true I could feel things like that. I could sometimes look at a person and see their mother and father or maybe their true love, even before they showed their snapshots. Just some trick my mind played?

I could feel certain things about James too, my lost husband. I knew he was alive, and living far away. I even had a sense he was in a warmer climate.

Slowly but surely, I worked James right into our talk without even knowing I was doing it. Once I started, I felt a kind of pressure inside. Like the words had been waiting to come out. Waiting for years. I'd started, and there was no shutting my big trap now. The words were coming out.

Of course Raelene was curious. She was interested in me. In every little chirp that came out of me. Interest is *bait*. I mean someone interested in you like this can make you talk, if you feel the interest is pure, and not just some kind of idle curiosity. Most people you meet in life, let's face it. They're not interested, they just got a case of idle curiosity.

But then someone comes along with their interest. Their pure interest, and it gets you interested again.

*　　*　　*

It was that way with Raelene there in the cabin. I told her all about James, how after he got back from a year in Korea he and Wendell and I once lived in a house not much bigger than the cabin, a place Ivy found for us about a half hour away from the camp, a view of the Adirondacks out the back window. How we just let Wendell paint and crayon all over the walls, and how that looked just fine. I told her of the claw foot bathtub in the backyard with the makeshift wall around it that I decorated with pictures cut from *Look* and *Life* magazines and how Wendell loved it. Never wanted to get out of the nice warm water we'd heat on the woodstove. And how he would sing to himself "Silent Night, Holy Night," no matter what the season. His voice was sturdy and made my eyes water on certain nights back then. I was a sentimental girl at least when it came to that child. I also told Raelene how James worked in a lumberyard and came home smelling like fresh wood and fresh air. And always had a story to tell me, though he was not a real talker. Could I believe I was saying all this to Raelene, a camp counselor in a cabin? No. She kept asking questions anytime I'd pause. Questions mainly about Wendell, which was natural.

James and I, we'd eat supper with Wendell, then put him in to play with his trains and cars and stuffed whatnots. We had a whole room for his pleasure. We never made him pick up his toys in that room. He could do what the hell he wanted in there. His father and I believed in letting him be natural. It was our own idea. We'd tell him, "Go use your imagination." And sometimes we'd play with him. And other times, maybe two or three times a week, we'd get out the Jack Daniel's and listen to music, and talk. Sometimes Ivy would come over and join us.

We never thought much about it, James and I. His father and my father, and sometimes my mother, they drank like sailors. And their friends did too. So we never thought even for a minute, Maybe there's a problem here. Maybe it's not good for Wendell to see us drinking. We just thought, The wars are over for a while, so here's to what we call life.

Raelene said, "People back then didn't know any better."

She was trying to make me feel better.

We drank. We played our music. Everything from Bill Monroe to B.B. King. Some nights we were perfectly sober. We were never really out of control. We loved Wendell to death. And sometimes the three of us would sleep right out under the stars, Wendell in the middle in a blue hooded jacket.

Meanwhile all my old friends from Delaware were moving to houses with natural gas furnaces and H-bomb shelters. I'd get a letter from someone and they'd have to tell me about watching *The Aldrich Family* or

Milton Berle on the television, and what did I think of
Betty Furness, the Westinghouse lady. I visited once or
twice and saw how they thought they had the good life
under their belts because their houses were brand-new
and clean. You could eat a meal in their toilet bowls.
Sparkling clean and new! Out with the old. New everything. And they'd send me *Reader's Digest* articles that
said the Communists were taking over our children's
minds in the schools. They believed the articles were
true. They were smack in the middle of things.

We were out of it. Our house looked like Hogan's
alley. We read the paper, sometimes we went to David
Walton's bar to watch Ed Sullivan. And we had a radio.
But other than that, we entertained ourselves. The more
McCarthy stirred up the fear of reds, the crazier people
got. We had neighbors two miles away who were crazy
like that. They avoided us entirely.

But things were booming out there. It was boom
time. The country was rich. Clean! Happy! A new car
born every second, and two or three lucky babies. America the beautiful. But we could feel the lie of that. James
and me could feel the evil in the air. After Fat Boy and
the other bomb, what the hell did they call it, I forget,
but we could feel how the air was different, the world
was different. No matter how new the houses were, no
matter how many sprung up, no matter how clean.

So, we could feel some things, but we were out of it.
Wanted to be.

*   *   *

Then one day when Wendell was twelve I thought I might be pregnant, and I went to the doctor, Doctor Elwin Fry. He looked exactly like a walrus, I'll never forget that. Doctor Elwin Fry said to me, "You don't want to gain weight now, Gladys. You want to keep your figure." I did have a nice Betty Grable–type figure, if you can believe that. I had every eye on my legs when I walked down a street in those days.

So the walrus says, "When you get the urge to snack, have a cigarette and a highball." Raelene didn't believe this. I had to explain. Things were just different back then. The doctors didn't want the ladies losing their figures. This was the biggest concern. The ladies cannot lose their figures! No figure loss by the ladies allowed! You could hear the doctors saying this throughout the land of plenty.

I was used to that. My father, to save me from turning to fat, made me run and swim until I wanted to die. But that's a whole other tale.

So I was pregnant and happy. It weren't planned. We'd wanted to wait for a while. But we were so happy. About three months into that pregnancy, James's father died. We all went to Kentucky for the funeral, and James and I cried together with his mother. This was the mid-fifties. Later that year we moved from New York back to the state of Delaware for a few years. Only we lived in the north, in Wilmington, an hour from where I'd grown up. My father ended up landing James a job down on the docks as a loader. We were happy and Wendell was happy too. He was thirteen now, and he was looking forward to a brother or sister. I missed our old house up in New York State, our old way of living. Ivy missed us and kept saying, "When you coming back?" But James was making decent money at his job. And whenever we got the chance we got out of the city and camped.

We missed the land. Both James and me loved land. There weren't so many real land lovers back then like there are now. Or if there were they didn't talk about it as much and hang so many posters. I'd grown up on a farm, and land was in my blood. I weren't so big on loving animals, but I loved the *land*. James had grown up in a town, where he said he felt "shackled." Part of why he fell for me I think is because I had the land in my blood. The old farm in my heart.

One night by a river he and I made a pact to avoid boredom. We drank to that promise. We were so young we believed boredom would be the worst possible thing to face in this life.

Now how do I describe A.?

Well, not yet. Not yet. It's not that time yet. I'll just tell you she was nice. She was a good baby that didn't keep us up all night too much. I can't hardly stand thinking of her so I won't. I'll talk but I won't think. Not about this. Yet.

Now one day A. was three years old, Wendell was a teenager, and James and myself took them on a little trip to a pond. This lake was back in New York State. (We were there for good this time, in another decent little house in the woods.) We had never been to the pond before. Bennet Thane, a man James worked with, recommended it. He had a cabin nearby. He said we could use the cabin and swim in the pond, have us a getaway.

So there we were, a family by a pond. Sunshine, a little bench of old stones by the edge of the water. Woods all around.

Wendell was a quick-eyed, handsome boy, with his short black hair and his hawk nose. He looked older than sixteen. He had the usual recklessness of that age. Well, that day at the pond he met a girl. Her name was Jan. She was fifteen in a green and yellow flowered two-piece. They ended up running around together in the woods. I don't know what happened in those woods. We didn't worry much then. I remember we watched Jan and Wendell swimming off together in the green water, laughing.

"He's a young man now, isn't he?" James said with mixed emotion.

"He is. And he's turned out fine," I told James.

"Everything happens too fast," James said. He was pouring us some white wine into small glasses. I ended up throwing those glasses out. Along with everything else we had with us on that trip.

The glasses had Scotty dogs on the side, white and black. I think they were from James's father. I can see the golden liquid shot with sun and pouring into the glass. A. was sound asleep on the blue blanket she loved. I had her face covered up with a sheet. She was pale skinned and burned easy. On her feet were blue socks. They made her legs look whiter. She still had some baby fat then. This is a picture frozen too clearly in my mind. I thought of covering her legs and then thought, no, I should let her get a little color. I can't for the rest of her life protect her from all the sun in the world.

When really, as it turns out, I could have.

I began to feel the strange sensation that I was a girl again when I talked with Raelene in the cabin that night. Because I spent my whole young life talking in the dark to Ivy. Twin beds, windows, summer night, quiet voices . . . it was familiar at the very core, even though it was Raelene over there and not Ivy. Even though the things I was saying, that girl I was had never dreamed possible. I weren't comfortable. But I kept talking. Not able to control it, really.

I told her how James and me kept drinking that day.

We weren't completely out of control. It was never like that with us. We could hold it. And it was only wine. We had tolerance like nobody's business. The sun was brilliant. Way high up there in a great blue summer sky. We were on the pink blanket lying down now and turned toward each other. That's how we were, we just liked to lay there and stare at each other, and laugh and try to feel young. Sounds stupid but it was a good feeling. To feel comfortable like that. There's no denying I felt at home with that man for a while.

But we got too comfortable. And we fell asleep. It was Wendell who woke us. He was dripping wet, so was the girl standing beside him, Jan. I remember looking up at them and thinking, Why are they so wet and cold?

"Where's A.?" Wendell was saying. "Where's A.?"

My hand reached over to the blue blanket, but it was an empty space. I sprung up. And as I sprung up, the whole world got dark for a second. And in the dark there was something evil, a force, or a face. It was there for a split second. I began to shake.

James squeezed the back of my shoulder. He was trying to calm me. I pulled myself away from him. I screamed her name. I screamed it and ran along the edge of the water. But I knew even as I was screaming. I knew that she was on the pond's floor. So I was screaming her name with no hope whatsoever. I could feel that she was gone like I could feel the water was wet when I dived in. James and Wendell and the girl dove in too. It was a fairly big pond, but not all that deep. We were diving for her, all of us.

We dove and dove and finally James said, "She's not in here. Jesus Christ, Gladys, why the hell did we assume the worst? She wandered off into the woods is all." He called her name. "Where'd you get to, love?"

James's voice was packed with hope. I tried to believe it. But I knew. And I was mad at James for not knowing, hated him for being able to enjoy that bit of hope. I watched James head into the woods. He turned for a split second and looked at me. From that moment on nothing was ever the same between James and me.

"I'll stay with you," Wendell said.

"No, no, go on with your father."

I wanted to be perfectly alone. I was so calm.

"Calm?" I remember Raelene saying. "But weren't you screaming on the inside?"

"No, I had the kind of calm that's on the other side of screaming." It's not possible to say what that's like. But I was where I'd never been before. And never been again. Though part of where I was I suspect is still inside me.

I knew if I kept diving I would find my child. And when I found her, I knew I would find a hole in the world that I would fall through. It would be the deepest, blackest, hungriest hole in the world, and I would fall through, and nobody would follow me down, and I wouldn't want them to. But first I had to find her.

Her body was not on the edge of the pond, but out

near the middle. At the time this made sense. Only later did I try to figure out how a child who couldn't swim made it out to the middle of the pond.

And to Raelene I didn't say a thing about how it was to swim with her body toward the land, and I won't ever say a thing about that to anyone, though I did tell James.

I didn't tell him until many years later after this happened, though. Because I hated him so much, hated him immediately, hated him more than I loved him, and hated myself even more than that, which was powerful hatred.

I hated myself too much to weep. Weeping in grief is a kind of pleasure. The only pleasure when it comes to grief. I felt I didn't deserve it. No release. Not for a minute. No pleasure, ever again. *No consolation.* So back at home, with Wendell locked in his room throwing a ball against the wall for hours, and James in our room weeping for two days straight, I was sleepless and out on the back stoop chain-smoking. And hating James more and more the more I heard his crying. The grand indulgence of his crying.

So you can see by nature I'm partly cold hearted. And even then I knew that. I thought to myself, *A good woman would go comfort her man, a good wife would hold her husband as he weeps. A good woman wouldn't sit here frozen up with rage, a good woman would run to Wendell and tell him time will heal.*

*   *   *

Does time heal, or is that just something we like to say to people? I don't believe it *heals*. Not really. Time goes by, and the buried pain gets duller, true enough. But is that healing? Was I healing as I froze? No. Healing is something else entirely. It happens within time, but it's not just time doing the trick.

Half a year after we lost A., I got the news that my father dropped dead of a heart attack. It happened in public, on a street in New York City, where nobody knew him. I went to his funeral, but I didn't digest a thing. Not possible. And years later, when my mother died, which was four years after Wendell was killed, I went to that funeral too. All I know is I sat in the front pew with my eyes closed. I tried to hold a picture of my mother in my mind, but couldn't. I'd see her, then she'd start to shatter into pieces. It didn't hurt a bit. And the faces of my children would blend into her shattered face. Then the face would explode like confetti and fall. I watched the explosion, didn't feel a thing but dizzy. I looked at the coffin and thought, She's in there, and didn't feel a thing. But the person I suddenly missed was my father. Missed him like I was a child, like he could come and gather me up. I remember my heart like a car starting to plow into a field of quicksand. I remember I slammed on the brakes and coughed too loud until I felt safe again. Everyone has a time in life where they think, *Cry now and you'll never stop*. Maybe it's these times where you have to say, "Okay, ladies and gentlemen, I'll cry for the rest of my life." But of course nobody in their right mind makes such a choice. Not usually. You slam on the brakes, thinking you'll save yourself. You won't make a show. You'll be strong. Ivy sat beside me, her head down. I felt her look at me several times with her side vision. Her hands trembled. What she digested, I never knew.

After that night in her cabin, Raelene would sneak out of her cabin sometimes and sit with me, out on the back stoop of the house. The end of May. A number of the summer campers hadn't even come up yet, just the ones from certain private schools that let out early.

Raelene didn't make too many inroads with the other counselors. They'd asked her, "Where do you go?" Meaning what college. She just looked at them, not understanding the question. They said, "What college?" and she said, "Not sure, maybe next year I'll go somewhere." Well, that would've marked her an Ada the Fringer in their book. If they hadn't already decided that.

She was glad for my company out there on that stoop. My reading stoop, as I called it. Ivy would poke her head out the window and say, "Do you think this is right?" or sometimes, "Keep it down, ladies." Because we would be laughing and talking and drinking beer. "Come join us, Ivy," we'd say sometimes, but Ivy felt left out anyway and always said, "I got too much to do, maybe some other time."

One night out on the stoop on the first of June after it had rained all day and the kids were all wild banshees doing indoor arts and crafts and Raelene was feeling restless, Raelene said, "You ever want to leave here and go someplace else? I mean someplace that's not a *camp*?"

I really hadn't given much thought to that. But I said to her, "Hell yes."

"Maybe you and me can get some bus tickets. Remember Hambone? The friend I mentioned? He's like a guy I can trust. We could visit him."

"He's like a guy you can trust," I said. I liked to tease her about the way she talked. She never minded.

"Yeah," she said, "He's like that."

"I don't know Hambone from Adam," I said.

But I was already seeing myself flying through the country.

You might not want to put yourself on a Greyhound when you're almost forty-eight. Unless the trip's short. The destination particular. Don't just get on the bus with a young girl like Raelene. Buy a train ticket if you need to get away. Don't let a girl tell you, "We can just waitress our way across the United States!"

"You waitress, I'll sit on my hind quarters and watch, honey," I told Raelene. She gave me one of her smiles.

And I was already on the bus. I have to say at first it thrilled me, just looking out the window. I didn't expect it to feel so good. I put my head against the windowpane and felt the vibration of the bus. I watched the land open up, the sky get bigger. I got off and on the bus with Raelene, the tour guide. Greasy spoons were palaces to Raelene. "Look, Gladys! Real genuine midwest coffee cups!" Whatever that meant. We got off and spent one night in a motel called The Wayfarer in Indiana. That was also a palace for Raelene. "Look at these great little soaps! They're so cute!"

Of course on the bus I was putting up with the usual Greyhounders. Half had just escaped from the nuthouse. A man named Albert across the aisle never shut his mouth. I had to hear his couthless stories. He would look across the aisle and say, "Your arsehole gettin' sore?" He didn't understand when I ignored him. "I *said* your arsehole gettin' sore yet?" he'd say. And when I still didn't answer he'd say, "Blessed are the bus riders, for they shall inherit sore arseholes!"

"If he's still here tomorrow we'll need to kill him," I told Raelene, who threw her head back and laughed her way through the whole ride. Laughed and laughed.

That's what you do when you're young on a Greyhound. It's all a big adventure. It's all a laugh riot. You think every lunatic in your path makes the world a little more special.

Finally Albert got off the bus. A girl took his place. She was Amy, she was a talker too. We had to hear all about her rock and roll band, the Helen Kellers. But she was a relief after Albert. She had some couth. We got off the bus with her in Lincoln, Nebraska. She promised us showers.

I'm forty-eight years old traipsing down the street in Lincoln, Nebraska, to visit the house of one of the Helen Kellers. It's getting dark and I'm thinking, Okay, Gladys, you can wake up now, the dream is over. The little dream is over.

Our tickets let us get off and on whenever we wanted. I wanted off, but not in Lincoln. At that particular point, I wanted off the earth, not the bus. But I walked down the street to Amy's house. Raelene and I sat and drank water on her lumpy couch. "So here's to Nebraska," Raelene said. Amy changed into a purple robe and what looked like white go-go boots, then took us out to her backyard. I thought I'd leave then, I thought I'd go find the bus and just go home. Rather than stay and feel ridiculous.

Instead I sat down in the room Amy had set up in the back of her house. It was a ridiculous room in the middle of a wheat field. A blue couch covered with plastic. A rickety blue table, a hat stand. I thought, Now I'm dreaming someone else's dream. Amy smoked marijuana from a small pipe. "Do you mind?" she said. "I'm not your mother," I said. "If I was, you wouldn't be wearin' those go-go boots." She smiled. "That's cool. That's cool." Then she inhaled too much, had herself a minor coughing fit. She passed the pipe to Raelene, who said, "I hate drugs, I hate all dope, I don't get near it, I'm straight." She folded her arms. She'd seen enough of drugs in her life.

"Really? You look like you know how to party," Amy said.

"Well I don't," Raelene said.

Amy told a long story about her friend who was going to be famous soon, if his record "Come to the Salmon" caught on. I could try hard and never forget the name of that song. She sang it for us. She stood looking down at the ground.

> Come to the salmon
> with me and me
> Come, come to the salmon.

"Can I use your phone?" I said when she was done. I went inside and called Ivy.

It was quite a phone call. Ivy said, "Heard from James, Gladys."

"Did you really?"

"He called to see how you were."

"Is that right? And how am I?"

"Sound like the same old Gladys to me, only now you're far away."

"I'm in Nebraska, Ivy."

I wanted Ivy to say, "Why? Why on earth are you in Nebraska? You should be here, helping me. The kitchen's falling apart."

But she said, "Nebraska. Bet that's pretty."

I wanted to say, "Ivy, I miss you." I did miss her. How could I sit in an outside room and watch a young girl smoke marijuana and sing a song called "Come to the Salmon" and not miss my sister?

Instead I said, "It's flat," meaning Nebraska.

I never could say things like "I miss you."

I said, "Bye, and tell James if he calls again I said hello."

I didn't sleep that night. I sat in Amy's outside living room on the blue couch. All night long. A big moon lit the room. I might have dozed, but mainly I just sat there. I sat there wondering what I was doing. I couldn't begin to tell myself.

Amy drove us to the bus station the next day. She drove shaking her head and saying, "Pretty pe-culiar, pretty-pe-culiar."

"What's peculiar?" Raelene said.

"You two. Not even mother and daughter. Traveling together. Peculiar, that's all, peculiar."

Amy liked that word.

Back on the bus, I slept. Raelene met a boy. This boy would change her life. Funny thing to say, I know, but it can happen like that. Unexpected. He was a scrawny kid with a goatee in a white undershirt. A hyper kid with what they call a boom box for his rock and roll music. Next time we stopped, it was Fargo, North Dakota. The Frank Powers Hotel. The boy and Raelene holding hands, Raelene with her eyes on me, afraid I'd feel left out. "Relax," I told her. I was happy to get off the bus. Happy to see that hotel. I wanted a shower. That's all. I wanted to get the grime of the bus out of my hair. Off my skin.

Now poor Frank Powers was ninety or a hundred years old, and he took us up on a manual elevator, and charged us each a dollar for a shower. Terrible showers. A trickle. No pressure whatsoever.

"Might as well hire a dog to piss on your head," I told Raelene and her boyfriend. His name was Anthony. The two of them practically threw themselves down on the floor laughing. Like I was the funniest woman alive. I stood and watched them. I closed my eyes. I was homesick. But not for any home I'd ever had. Not for any home I could even dream up.

And that night back on the bus, Raelene and Anthony kissed in the seat behind me. His hands all over her. I could see them in the reflection of my own window. I rode and watched them. Finally I turned around. I said, "If you need to do that, go sit somewhere else." And Raelene pushed the boy away. Looked up at me with big eyes.

Then they went and sat somewhere else.

I watched the road in the dark.

Ivy
Ghosts

A PERSON MIGHT WONDER HOW I ENDED UP WALKING OUT of my kitchen job and into my garden job and that's the easy part to explain so I'll start there. I just had to get away from the townie fellow who temporarily replaced the man who replaced Gladys after she'd left on a bus with Raelene. I had to get away from the second replacement not because he looked like a young Merv Griffin, which he did to the point where I had to ask him if Merv was his long-lost brother, but because he was boring me to tears with talk of gubernatorial races in a nasal voice and at the time I couldn't see any good qualities in him. I'm a person who can usually see a good quality or two in most anyone without even trying, but somehow Gladys leaving for so long made me less of a friendly soul. I was lonely without her and angry that her travels were lasting so long and surprised that she could get on so well without me. Standing on my feet for a total of seven to nine hours each day in a kitchen so hot I ate salt tablets like candy began to hurt in a different way without Gladys there to share the burden. And Merv Griffin had the habit of leaving sharp knives in sinks filled with soapy water, which anyone who ever worked a minute in a kitchen knows is the most inconsiderate mistake you could make. I almost cut my finger off one day. Life didn't feel quite normal.

Not that I wasn't still counting my blessings. My son, Louis, visited and brought me sixteen dolls from Thailand, for one thing. "Dang, you look great!" he said when he saw me. "Like a twenty-five-year-old! What's your secret?" You'd think it was flattery, but he weren't that type, he actually thought I looked great and it is true a little extra weight on a woman my age can smooth out the face and make her young looking, plus I had Shine for Life on my hair. I lined the dolls from Thailand on the kitchen shelf and they looked real pretty until he left and they started seeming too alive, like they were watching me, and the quiet in that house started sounding like a loud noise in my head.

So I abandoned poor Merv (I privately called him this in my mind) in the kitchen one morning and walked all the way up the mountain to the cabin where Brent Quinn lives; Brent's the boss of the whole camp—fact, his father was "old money" and he owned it way back when, and started up the winter school, too, where Brent used to teach. And now Brent's sixty-some years old, and calls himself "your basic old lefty escaping the madness," and he liked me enough not to ask too many questions about why I had to quit the kitchen work. He gave me a cup of coffee and I sat and talked to him in his old striped pajamas and he told me I belonged in the garden and feeding the animals. "I can see you in the garden," Brent Quinn said. "Fresh air, the company of children, shorter hours, it'll do you good. You can be there until the fall really hits us. And by the way, stop by and visit me if you want sometime. Must be lonely without Gladys."

"I will." I liked him, and once a few times a year I'd drop by to drink some beer with him, and I never minded when he went on his art history tangents, fact I liked it, he was educational.

So I started that garden job the first week of July, which meant I had to wake up at five in the morning and walk down to the dewy garden in the dark and wait for the children to poke their sleepy faces out of tents like little hatchlings. They were nice enough children, most of them eight or nine or ten, and I felt for them, since they'd been shipped out by parents for a whole summer. The parents wanted to travel in foreign lands without any nuisances. About 5 percent of the kids were scholarship campers from the inner cities, mainly black kids, and they didn't generally mix in too well with the others. In the old days I'd sneak the city kids donuts. Then I got yelled at, certain counselors saying donuts are bad for their teeth and doing them special favors would make them feel more like outcasts, so that was it for my donut sneaking days.

As we all picked the peas, the green beans, the first peppers, and the last of the strawberries, I can't say I felt too good about the new job initially. It hurt my back to bend so much and my hands ached too. I was using different muscles than my cooking muscles. It wasn't so hot as the kitchen was, though. And each day it got better and finally I came to stop dwelling on Gladys and when she might return. I had my own life and my health and this garden job, which was more than a lot of people had. I never was one who felt too smart complaining.

We would work until nine in the morning, then go down and feed the chickens, goats, and baby calves, who most of the girls were mad for with their spindly legs and big sad eyes. "Aw! Look! Aw, isn't he cute!" They were getting early practice for the sad-eyed spindly legged boys they'd learn to love in a few years.

Then the day was mine, all mine, and what was I to do with myself? All my life I'd mainly worked hard, come home, relaxed, and slept. Any worrying I did was wrapped around Gladys. Now there was this space. This whole person named Ivy who was *there* now in a strange way I don't have words for.

I became a walker, walking each day into town

dressed in a shift and sneakers and a nice hat and sun-glasses, and I'd just happen to swing by Edgel Greely's garage, where he'd be working in his big blue shirts under cars or talking to his partner. Once or twice I brought Edgel Greely some iced tea and once or twice I convinced my heart it was falling in love but it weren't and I knew it. "Call me Edge," he told me, but I couldn't. I did like Edgel but not like I liked him when he was in the far-off distance. He was like a house you pass on the road and think its pretty for years, then it goes on sale and you walk inside and think, This isn't the house I imagined, it doesn't have enough light and the ceiling's too low. Turned out Edgel was the sort who laughs too hard and too long at his own jokes, so you end up feel-ing all that laughter is privately tied up with things you'll never know about because he barely does himself. So there I'd be on one of them vinyl genuine barbershop chairs that Edgel Greely had two of in the corner of his garage, and I'd be feeling kind've sad for Edgel that he had to laugh like that because I don't imagine it won him many friends.

I gave up on dropping by the garage, which didn't feel real good because I'd been counting on Edgel as a kind of new interest for months and now there was nobody. This didn't stop me from being a walker. As I walked I felt light as a girl.

I lost some weight, enough so a few workers at camp called out, "Lookin' good, Ivy."

One particular day as I was headed into town just breathing in all that blue air and watching the very beginning of August's red and yellow leaves in the sun, I heard a car slowing down behind me. It didn't scare me because I was in a fine mood and figured it was someone I knew stopping to ask if I needed a ride, or maybe some parent trying to find the camp, because the kids were going home now. The winter school kids would stay, and some new ones would come up. I was all set to decline the ride or give directions. I weren't at all set for the man who turned out to be at the wheel.

He slid his car up beside me. His window was rolled down and he was framed there in that rolled-down window and I just stared at him with the cat on my tongue.

"Touch the car and make sure I'm not a vision," he said.

"Jimmy? James?"

He smiled at me and reached out the window to grasp my hand. His was clammy, not the strong dry hand I remembered. His dark blue eyes were heavier or maybe older looking, and his face more weathered and streaks of silver filled his hair. But he was still James, a man too tall for his own car.

"James G. Pittman. I'm not dreaming, am I?"

"Can I give you a lift?" he said.

"A lift?" I said. "A lift?"

"Into town."

I got into James Gehrig Pittman's old Valiant, the

same car he'd had when he left, with the same faint gasoline and old leather smell basically, and the same mixture of chaos and cleanliness.

"James, why the corduroy coat? It's summertime," I said. I don't know why, but I wasn't calling him Jimmy like the old days.

"It was cold early this morning. I'm not used to the north anymore," he said.

I had the oddest feeling in that car, like the tires underneath us were enormous, like we were up high in the air because the tires were so big. I don't know what that was all about.

James talked in the same old way with his jaw tucked down near his neck, head bent and blue eyes straight ahead. Every five seconds he'd glance over at me, half-smiling as we rode into town like two people in a stranger's dream on those big fat tires.

We were quiet for a while and then James tells me that two nights before he'd been visiting some friends in Clairton, Pennsylvania, and they watched a nice documentary about people and their pets. And he goes on to tell me all about this nice documentary of pets and the folks who loved them like they were children, just like he'd seen me the day before. I was glad this was how James was.

"So it was mostly dogs and cats these people were grieving?" I said.

"That's right. And there's animal graveyards all over

this country. People go visit the graves and leave things like Milk-Bones and toys that squeak. Or sometimes painted portraits of themselves and the pet. Or one fella left a violin."

"Is that right?" I said.

"These people were noble," he said.

"Noble."

"They were noble because of how much they loved. All that love was simple and ennobling."

"Well I'll have to watch it sometime myself."

"You should. The line I liked was *Animals are put on this earth to love and be loved.* I like the simplicity of that. I keep running it around in my head."

So there we were after eight years of not seeing each other just riding along talking about this pet-lovers' documentary in his old Valiant filled with faded maps and hardback books he must've forgot to take back to the library. Or maybe he bought them at used stores, I don't know.

We headed past the big lake and James looked out across it, then back at the road. "Nice to see this land again. Nice to see mountains," he said. "So how's Gladys?" he added, and I felt him tense up as he waited for an answer.

"She's still traveling," I said. "She left with Raelene, this girl she knows. Did I mention her on the phone? The girl—well, it's a long story."

"I'd like to have a drink somewhere," James said. "Is the Little Moon still open?"

"Sure is," I said. "Haven't been there since I last saw you. But I know it's still open."

The Little Moon was your basic bar in the woods with a little door so you had to duck to get through if you were over five feet. Once you got inside you were fine. The two of us were struck by how much the same it was, with Seany, the old bartender, still doing crossword puzzles, and Mrs. "Sloe Gin" Kingston, a white-haired six-footer in her thick glasses, still writing letters at the center table to a man named Professor Danicki, who most people thought was dead. And on the old Wurlitzer were the songs we used to play. When James and I walked over to the booth under the high window with the dark red curtains I think we both felt the ghosts of him and Gladys. We just sat right down on the laps of those ghosts and had some draft beers.

James wasn't looking up much, and when he did he wasn't smiling exactly, and his eyes were friendly and worried.

"I have some things to tell you," James said. "But you know me, it'll take a while. I'm adjusting to this now."

"This?" I said.

"Everything," James said.

"Where were you before you came here? Maybe you can start at the end of your tale and go backward. If you feel like talking, that is."

"Louisiana," James said. "It's a long story."

"I got time." I smiled at him. It was so good to see him.

"But I'll give you the short version. The long story is something I couldn't tell you. I can't even tell it to myself."

"Long or short, it's up to you."

He took a deep breath and looked sideways.

"A child grew close to me. Her name was Cecile, but they called her Pie Pie. I was with her mother for three years."

James spoke in his quiet voice without much expression. You had to listen hard to him to figure out what his words meant, which ones were the most important. This wasn't how he used to talk, and I got the feeling he'd rehearsed this speech in his car as he drove.

"Pie Pie's mother," I said. "What was her name?"

"Nicoletta Graves."

"Nicoletta Graves," I said. "With a girl named Pie Pie. Pie Pie Graves." I was smiling.

James didn't smile.

"She grew real close to me, Ivy. Too close. She didn't look a thing like Ann, but all the sudden all I'm thinking of is Ann. It snuck up on me. Because Pie Pie was three years old going on four."

Ann.

We never said "Ann." Gladys never said it, so I never said it. I took a deep breath. All the sudden I wanted to say "Ann."

"Three going on four," I said. "Like Little Ann was."

James looked down, wouldn't meet my eye.

"Like Ann," I said again. I wanted to say it a hundred times.

"Pie would sit out on the dirt under the laundry line with her metal cars. She had three metal cars, and one metal ambulance, and one dune buggy, and one Barbie doll. That was her whole toy collection. She'd make that doll walk and leave footprints in the dirt. She'd sit out there by herself for hours in the evening and play in the dirt."

"And you'd play with her, right?"

"No, no. I'd sometimes sit on the front stoop and watch her. And sometimes she'd tell me things."

"So you left the little girl, James. Is she heartbroken?"

"She's got a father. I'll never be her father. Her father came over once a week and took her out on the town. He was a comedian. I mean he made his money that way, locally. Pie Pie loved him. He told her he was going to take her around the world when she was ten. She'll miss me a few weeks, but then she'll forget me. I'm no father to her."

"I don't think you're real forgettable, James," I said. "I don't think Gladys forgot you for a second."

"I don't know why I even want to see her," he said. "I might just want to say hello and good-bye. But I have to see her to know."

"That's understandable."

"Anything really *new* with her? Anything I should know? She ever go to night school like she always said?"

"Night school?"

"She always said she would."

"Oh, that's right. No, no night school that I know of."

"Would you say she was happy?" he wanted to know.

"No, James. I would never say that."

"She talk about Ann?"

"Oh no. Never."

"She talk about Wendell?"

"Maybe once or twice."

Before we left the bar James played "Ring of Fire" on the jukebox, a song we all loved in the old days. Him, me, Gladys, maybe a man I was seeing, we'd all sit in that same booth singing.

We left that day before the song was even halfway through. James said he wanted some fresh air, and I knew that whatever he thought the song would do for him, it did something like the opposite of that.

He drove us down into the valley, asking me questions about my own life now. Was I happy? "Sure," I told him. "Happy enough."

"What's that mean?" he said.

"Can't complain," I said.

"Go ahead and complain. You could do it if you tried."

So I complained that maybe I was a little lonely now that Gladys was gone. A little out of sorts.

"I venture that's an understatement," James said.

Maybe that was the sort of conversation that made me like James so much. You don't often find men who ask you to complain.

Men who know you well and know when you're making an understatement. Men who know you well enough to say, "So, Ivy, can I stay with you a while?"

"Sure you can."

"Won't put you out?"

"Hell no, James."

We were in the kitchen and James was looking taller than usual because of the low ceiling, and I was suddenly remembering him as a young man with bare arms and Wendell sleeping on his shoulder at Rehoboth Beach on a lazy gray day. We all left the beach that day just as it started to rain. Most of the other people ran off the beach headed for shelter, but we all walked slow as usual, and for a second I saw James had his face lifted to the rain and his mouth open. And Wendell opened his sleepy eyes, then went right back to sleep with his head on James's rainy shoulder, and a smile came to James's lips for just a moment, then was gone.

For a second I could see James the fifty-two-year-old and James the twenty-four-year-old at the same time, like both men were in my kitchen. The older man might have looked over at the younger man like he was a complete stranger, but I could see that James was still James and his best quality was still a kind of gentleness.

I fixed him some supper and gave him three glasses of ice water, and he ate and drank in silence while I sat and looked out the window, over at him, out the window, over at him.

He stood up after he was through and thanked me in a formal way and asked if he could go to sleep on the couch, so I went and got some clean sheets and a pillow and made it comfortable, and he took off his boots and lay down and fell asleep in about two minutes with his legs bent because he was too tall, and for a while I just stood in the doorway looking at him because I never saw a grown man sleeping in the dusk light, only children.

That whole first week James stayed was nice because he inspired me to fix the faucets and helped me repair the roof, which I'd been putting off for years. And one morning he even came down to the garden with me, not to work but to see what we were growing, which weren't much because the fall was coming, and the children all looked up at James and studied him. He smiled at them and said hello. "You people good gardeners?" he asked them.

"Yes," they all said.

"Not afraid to get your hands dirty?"

"No," they all said.

"I admire that," James said. "From the looks of this patch of ground you all do a fine job."

The little anorexic girl, Cassie Dean, stayed by James's side the whole morning, the two of them weeding partners, James just praising her ability and telling her about what a lousy weeder he was when he was her age, how he always ended up leaving in some roots. She finally took off her red plastic sunglasses, which I'd never seen her without. Her eyes were small blue jewels. She had a smile on her face and that was for James.

I like to remember James walking beside me toward the garden before the sun even came up, everything cool and dark and dewy, James in a T-shirt and jeans and his boots, stopping once in a while to pick up a stone and turn it around in his hand.

During this time Gladys called, and I told her James was here. I expected a big reaction and I thought she might start coming home. But she said otherwise, and I never mentioned it to James. I guess I didn't want to talk about her with him for a while.

In the evenings we'd go for drives together in the valley, which James loved and said he missed. I can't explain it, but the tires underneath us felt bigger than ever. We were way up high, almost floating down the road.

At the end of that week on one of our valley drives with the windows half open and the smell of red leaves in the car, James reached over toward my hand, and I wasn't too sure what he was doing so I didn't give my hand over to him. I just looked at his hand and did nothing so he took his hand back and put it on the wheel.

But after that my heart started pounding and it just got louder when I told myself to calm down, because there was a new feeling in the car and it dawned on me that James wanted to hold my hand so I reached out and touched his hand on the wheel and my throat swelled up. Without looking at me his hand slid off the wheel down to the seat between us and our fingers just linked up like they were old friends having a reunion.

I mean to say holding the hand of James didn't feel *new*, it felt *old*, like I'd held it a million times. I don't have an explanation.

So I'm riding along trying to breathe in the piney mountain air and trying to say to myself, this don't mean much, Ivy, you're just holdin' hands and bein' friends, honey, so why the racing heart, why's your throat swelled up, old girl, and why so warm? Warm in the face and the body?

That's all understatement, the truth is that just hold-ing his hand that day in the car felt better than most anything I could remember. A pleasure in my body like a steady flame that got stronger when James took his fin-ger and traced little patterns on my palm.

Maybe when he was tracing those patterns on my palm is when I said to myself, Ivy, this is more than friends.

Back at the house he helped me make the supper, which was fried chicken and a lot of nice vegetables. James cut all the vegetables up and sat at the table in his new-looking white T-shirt with a glass of beer beside him. I was at the stove and kept looking over at him, thinking he might look up and smile, but he didn't. And if he had, I would've looked away, since the air was thick and still with all our feelings.

I was frying that chicken saying to myself, Ivy, this is not your man. This is your sister's old husband. This is not your man. This is not your man. This is not your . . .

And another voice would come into my head that was more like the sound of the wind in the leaves, or someone saying, Shhhh.

And pretty soon I listened to that voice and got qui-eter than I'd ever been in all my life. The whole kitchen filled up with quiet that was coming from me and from James, so now you could hear every sound from the pots and pans like it was coming through a mega-phone.

So we ate the meal together and still we didn't say a word, and now it was like we both understood that we shouldn't talk and break the spell.

After that meal we go out for a ride and end up in the valley and we walk way down to the very bottom of it. The sky was all thick with clouds like a hard rain was coming. Some of the mountains are hiding behind the clouds, some aren't. And James is talking more about pets now, about a man he knew with a dog who learned to steer the wheel of the man's Chevy. The dog would sit between the man's legs with its paws on the wheel and the man would tell the dog "left," "right," and the dog, who wore a Yankees cap, would steer just fine.

"The man never got into a single car accident," James said as we went deeper into that valley. "I've been in three, myself. You think I should get a dog to do my steering, Ivy?"

"Maybe that would be just the thing," I said.

And then we were down on the grassy ground in the darkness, no blanket under us, no stars over us, no hesitation left inside us.

We were good together, that's an understatement. James was a man who could make you forget yourself when he kissed you. He was a man whose weight felt good on you, like his weight was made up of things you wouldn't mind knowing. Some men, their weight feels all wrong, and even as they're making you feel good, if someone said, "Would you like to see everything inside his heart?" you know you'd answer, "No I wouldn't, thank you."

With James I wanted to see everything.

The problem was the ghost of Gladys hovering over us or stretched out beside us so that any time I remembered myself I felt a burning in my heart and a need to sit up and say "Stop, I'm not Gladys." But see, I never did sit up and say this, in fact I never sat up at all unless he pulled me that way. Ivy the rag doll.

So what happened, or what seemed to happen, was that the spirit of Gladys somehow slipped into my body. Now don't think I don't know that sounds mystic of me, me who thought I didn't have a single mystic bone in my body.

All I know is that while James was making love to me my own face felt like my sister's face. And when I cried out it sounded like her voice.

And after that first time James said, "I feel a bit worse off now than I did before. I'm not sure this is the right thing to be doing. Considering everything."

I didn't know what to say to that because I didn't want to think. I just looked up at the dark sky above and tried to feel exactly like myself but I believe I wasn't sure what that was anymore. Though I did feel a bit like a patch of dry earth with a brand new stream running down through the middle.

* * *

One night in the middle of our love affair I made up some spaghetti sauce. All we were doing with our time was making love, and we weren't hungry at all, but we needed to eat to keep going. I stood at the stove on a warm fall afternoon making that sauce and feeling furious at James all the sudden.

Because he had this power over me no man ever had before. I had a hunger for him I never had for anything or anyone before. All I had to do was look at him and my whole body hurt from desire. He came into the kitchen and said, "Ivy, are you okay?" because he could feel my anger. Hell, Brent Quinn could probably feel it all the way up on his mountain. I kept stirring the sauce and said, "Fine," but I snapped it out. So he leaves the kitchen. And I start pouring hot pepper into the sauce. I pour about three or four times the usual amount. Then I taste it. Then I add a little more hot pepper.

I served him his spaghetti and served myself some too and we sat at the table together. "Wow," James said after his first taste. "Hot! Are you trying to kill me?"

"Maybe."

I sat there and ate and felt angrier and angrier because all he'd have to do was reach out for my hand and I'd be leaving the table and following him to the bed. He knew this was the case too.

"What did you do, pour a whole jar of peppers into this sauce?"

I shrugged my shoulders. He smiled at me. I think he understood.

"So when do you think she might be coming back?"

"Oh, I don't know. If she knew you were here I imagine she'd come back if she had to walk across America on bare feet."

"I don't know about that."

"Maybe not," I agreed.

Because who knew anything about all of this? Who knew what time had done to the heart of Gladys?

You might think I started feeling overwhelmed with guilt like any woman would have after sleeping with the long-lost husband of her own sister, but it didn't happen like that. The guilt was there, but it was like a little bad music in the background or an itch or sometimes at moments a knot in the chest, but it was not the main feeling at all. The main feeling was lovesickness as bad as a girl's, but not as innocent, and not with the same kind of promises for future lifelong happiness. In fact I felt the promise of doom. But it was love all the same. And there was this rudeness, this rude part of me that thought only of myself, and hurt. I never felt so bad or so good in my whole life. After we made love each night I'd lie there and talk to James and he'd listen for a while and then fall asleep and I'd lie there and look at his sleeping face for a while, then lie there some more staring up at the ceiling, then maybe walk outside, look at the sky, then come back in and toss and turn and finally sleep.

One day James slept most of the morning, and when he woke up he wouldn't look at me. He sat and ate breakfast at the table and neither of us said much, until he finally said, "I'm in bad shape."

"You've been through a lot," I said, real quickly like I could feel what was coming.

"I'm in worse shape than I can say," he said. "Shouldn't keep coming into your room."

"I don't mind."

"You should mind."

"Why's that?"

He didn't say anything.

"Why's that?"

He looked me in the face then and said, "I came to see Gladys. I'm not sure this is the right thing to be doing. I came to see Gladys."

"And Gladys is gone," I said.

"I was just lonely, Ivy. And now I'm even lonelier," James said.

"That's something," I said. "That's something. Because I'm *not* lonely, and I can see now I been lonely all my life and never even knew it."

James just looked at me while I cast my eyes down

and thought about my words and wondered if what I said was true or false.

When Gladys called again I told her he was still visiting, but nothing else because it didn't seem like something I could say over the telephone. I asked her if she was coming home and she said "Not sure," and I was glad of that. Because by the time she called, I knew I was in love with James.

Maybe he was lonelier after each time we were together but maybe that was his goal, to get lonelier and lonelier, all the way to the very last edge of lonely, so he could see his whole life clearly. Or why would he have kept coming back to my room, and why would we have taken those walks in the valley at sunset with neither of us speaking and sometimes holding hands and sometimes just lying right down on the dark green earth?

And I wasn't eating anything because love like that takes all your appetites away, it's like your appetites for sleep and food and other people just get sucked up into your appetite for your lover, and suddenly you're fifteen or twenty pounds lighter and you have these dark circles under your eyes but you still look good because your cheeks are pink and your body is filled with a secret hunger and a kind of sorrow that feels like happiness.

Meanwhile I was still working the garden with the

little winter-school children. Pretty soon it would be too cold for gardening, but it was perfect in late September, with a sharpness in the air you could take inside you. And hundreds and hundreds of ripe tomatoes we'd can. I learned something about children out there. They're a lot more interested in you if they can feel you're carrying around a secret world, a world you consider more important than the world of children. The campers always liked me well enough, but out there in the garden they liked me even more and asked me questions no child had ever asked me, not even my son. "Ivy, when you were small, did they have televisions? Did you have a nice mother? Did you hate school? Did you hate boys? Where did you live when you were eight?"

I'd answer all the questions and they'd ask others and the gardening went quickly like a smooth dance and afterward I'd always walk down the dirt road alone, carrying my shoes and feeling like some kind of queen because the children would sing, "Bye, Ivy! See ya tomorrow!"

And a fine-mannered Indian boy named Apoorva made me a nice lanyard. That was a first.

Sometimes at night after a warm fall day we'd take a sheet down into the valley, a white sheet that we'd spread out on the black grass. James would get undressed and I would kneel beside him and massage his back and his legs. I was good at this, and sometimes James returned the favor, and he was good too.

One night as he was returning the favor I kept having a vision of my father standing on the hill just looking down into the valley at me and James. It was a childish wish of mine and I understood it was childish right away. What I wanted was for that man, my father, to see me with James and see that James loved me, even though I knew deep inside me that James really didn't *love* me, but it *looked* like love and *felt* like love to me if I didn't think too hard, and I wanted my father to come back from the dead to see me as a woman who James was loving. The man who loved Gladys was now loving me.

This surprised me because I hadn't given much recent thought to the man. My father, I mean.

"Guess who I'm thinking of?" I said to James. He was sitting beside me, one hand on my spine.

"Who?"

"My father. I keep picturing him in his black hat standing over there on that hill."

"He had the heart of a bull, your father."

"What?"

"Your father was a bull."

I thought about that for a second, and started laughing, and laughed harder the more I tried to figure out what it meant, and I kept seeing a real bull, a live bull, walking around in my childhood house, snarling, and the bull had my father's face, and I couldn't stop laughing at the thought. But I laughed myself sick and started crying.

Basically I see now I was a whole different person by this point, crying like that.

James looked over at me and was quiet for a second.

"He showed favoritism, no denying that," James said. "He favored your sister. I always wondered how that felt for you."

He had started to refer to Gladys as "your sister" and never said her name during this time.

"Why do you think he favored her? Why was he so hell-bent on pretending I didn't exist?"

"I don't know," he said. "A mystery."

"Come on, James."

"Maybe he knew your sister would be harder to tame. Maybe he liked the challenge. He was a certain kind of man."

"Maybe," I said.

I was unsettled. It was all happening too quickly. I had always thought of myself as happy, my life as easy, but something about this love affair was cracking me open like a safe where I'd locked away pain. Because really, Gladys had it harder with my father. It was easier to be ignored and dismissed and every so often teased. Not always easy, but easier. Because I did love him. You don't come into the world as a child with a choice about who you'll love, you just love whoever's there. And it's deep inside you the rest of your life no matter how much you know your love's unreturned. But still, it was easier to be all that than to be beaten. Not only beaten, but made into a little wife in an apron. Made into a prize possession.

Gladys was beaten with a belt at least five times that I remember and I wasn't even once struck with his hand as far as I know. I put almost all of my energy into giving him no reason to hit me, I think. I remember the first time Gladys was beaten hard enough so that she had red welts on her legs she was only eleven or twelve years old. In those days the boys from school had the habit of visiting girls in their class in the evenings. They wouldn't knock on the door, they'd just roll around on the front yard like gymnasts. They'd be dressed in white T-shirts and dark gray baseball pants. They'd do headstands and backward somersaults and things like that while the girl would stand in her bedroom window or maybe on the front porch dressed nicely because she'd have been expecting them. Gladys was out there on the porch one autumn evening in a dress and her white patent leather shoes that she wore all year-round when everyone else only wore them in summer because she was an individual. She watched the boy gymnasts performing under red trees with a small smile on her lips, not giving them too much appreciation, but just enough. My father wasn't home when this was going on, just my mother, and she thought it was sweet. She'd stand behind a curtain and watch the boys herself.

That night Gladys whispered out to the boys, "Come around back in about five minutes." Which they did, and Gladys let them in the basement door and gave them each a shot of whiskey. My father kept all the spirits down there in the basement. So after they had their shot they all went running off except for Digger Kovaleski, who Gladys had a case on. Digger and Gladys stayed down in the basement kissing too long, because the next thing they knew my father was there beside them pulling their hair to separate them, throwing Digger Kovaleski out onto the ground, and ordering Gladys up to her room. The other boys were waiting for Digger, hiding on the side of the house. I looked out the window at them from the dining room. Next thing I know Gladys is being beaten with my father's belt up in our bedroom. All the windows were open up there. I could hear the belt get louder on her skin, and a few times she cried out but mostly she stayed quiet. And the boys on the side of the house could hear this beating, could hear the sound of that belt against Gladys and could hear her cries. They just stared at each other wide-eyed, some of them smiling, and all of them listening until it was over, and then they ran off.

Gladys had welts on her legs and her back and they lasted a long time. My father told her he wouldn't beat her so hard if she'd behave, and it hurt him more than it hurt her. My mother didn't know much better, since she'd been beaten too (maybe most people had, spare the rod spoil the child and all that), so she didn't say a whole lot. She had a heartbroken look and tried to be extra nice to Gladys, but that just infuriated Gladys.

I told James this story and afterward nothing was quite the same between us. I could feel I'd changed everything, but I kept on talking. James had a Quaker mother who raised him without any violence, so for him the story had more impact than it would a more regular person, I guess.

I told him a story from when I was a girl, a story that I never told anyone, and the problem was even as I was telling it I could hear how it couldn't mean much now, not to James and not to me. Still, I talked on. I told him how when I was just a little girl back in southern Delaware, twelve years old, I thought I loved a man named Willy who worked behind the counter in the local drugstore. I considered him to be the most romantic man in the world because his fiancée had run off on him. The fiancée was a pretty girl who wore a Stetson hat with a dress, and everyone thought it looked good because she gave you the impression she was a queen, even when she was slouching at the counter waiting for Willy to take a break and smoke a Lucky Strike with her out front.

Willy had thin black hair, too long for those days, so it made him stand out as a bit unusual, and he wore old shirts with his father's name stitched onto the pocket, *Warren*, and I could smell his body when he set my Coke down on the counter, and I'd want to touch his arms with their muscles, and whenever people came into the little creaky floored drugstore and Willy gave them a slow, sad dip of his head, I'd have to bite the edge of my fist I liked it so much.

I kept telling this story to James, maybe trying to erase the story of the child Gladys, and the more I told it the more I felt like the child Ivy was a figment of my imagination and only the child Gladys was real. I was telling the story fighting for the child Ivy to be real as I talked. I just laid on my back and looked up at the sky and kept going.

I told James how I wrote little love letters to Willy sometimes right there at the counter, all hunched over so he wouldn't see the words but wanting him to be curious, and then one day he was. It was four in the afternoon and I was at the counter on the red vinyl stool that twirled up and down, though I weren't much of a twirler considering my size, and that little store was half lit with orange afternoon light and half in the shade, and Willy was by the window biting his nails, which on most men wouldn't look good but on him it did. He was looking out at the street when suddenly he turned from the window and called down, "Hope you're not writin' some boy love letters down there."

James was trying to perk up a little, trying to forget my sister and remember me, and his hands were pulling up the grass and he said, "So did you give Prince

Charming of the drugstore your little letters?" and I could see on his face he was working hard to be interested, and maybe he was a little bit, so I told him how my face got red and my heart pounded and I yelled back to Willy, "No, I'm just doodling."

And Willy said, "Don't be duped."

"I won't be duped," I told him.

"Because you only got one heart, partner. One heart."

"I know."

Then he turned right back to the window.

Even then I sensed that Willy was planning to waste his life biting his nails behind the counter and warning others to protect their hearts, but at that age it seemed romantic to me. Then one evening I went to Willy's house and spied through his window while he ate his dinner from two cans, can of beans, can of corn, and he used his bed (unmade) for a chair and his dresser for a table and he wolfed down the dinner like a starving man, looking at his own reflection in the dresser mirror the whole time.

I just stopped going to Willy's after that I felt so bad to have seen all that, and I never could get it out of my mind, fact it'll just come to me about once a year when I least expect it, clear as a bell, like I'm seeing it all over again.

James pulled me to him all the sudden. It surprised me.

Something reached his heart in the memory I told him, or maybe he just felt it was pitiful how hard I was trying.

We both stayed quiet for a minute.

"Don't understand why she never mentioned something like that," James said. "She told me most things."

"Who knows," I said, and turned away my face because my eyes were stung by confusing tears.

We kept on with our love affair, and we kept on talking.

It just wasn't quite the same.

My son, Louis, called in mid-October to wish me a happy birthday. He said he'd be coming home to visit for Christmas. He asked me if anything was new and I stood by the kitchen window and said, "No. Not a thing." I saw right then I had turned into a woman with too many secrets.

Then, a week or so later, when James and I were about to take a drive into the valley, me in a new sweater and lipstick, both of us almost at the point of thinking she might be gone for good, Gladys was at the door, battered brown suitcase in hand, the evening sun behind her. She wore a white cotton blouse and a blue skirt, or rather a blue sarong. On her feet were black Cuban heels.

"Hi," she said, smiling.

I must've looked at her funny, and mumbled hello. Then I reached out to her, and gave her a hug, but it was stiff.

"What's wrong? Something wrong? Am I a stranger?"

She had made her way into the house. I followed her. Then the toilet flushed.

"James is here," I explained.

"He came back for another visit?"

"He stayed."

James walked out of the bathroom and saw Gladys standing there still holding her suitcase.

Those two looked at each other for a long moment, and I'm feeling a sort of crumbling take place inside me.

"Hi, James," Gladys said. It looked to me like she suddenly had tears in her eyes.

"Hi," he said. Then he looked over at me for a split second.

"It's all right," I said. I was talking to myself but James thought I was talking to him and he looked over at me like he was thanking me for saying it was all right.

A small part of me was glad to see Gladys. Most of me just kept on crumbling.

Gladys started walking back toward the bedroom with her suitcase and I stepped in front of her and said, "Let me take that for you, here, sit down on the couch, James get her some cranberry juice, she still loves it, I'm sure. . . "

Gladys let me steer her toward the couch. She was tired. She had been on a Trailways bus for three days.

I let James wait on her while I took the suitcase back in the bedroom, closed the door behind me, and hurried around that room to gather James's shoes and his books and his pants and shirts on the hook by the window. I stood there with all of it in my arms and thought I'd throw it all out the window then go out and deal with it later.

But I remembered I was not a child and not a fool or a liar. I wasn't sure what I was but I knew what I wasn't. And the smell and feel of James's belongings began to pierce my heart just as if he were wrapped around me saying, *Good-bye, Ivy, it's all over now.*

I finally set it all down on the bed. I could hear Gladys's voice out there in the living room and I heard what I thought was James's laugh once. I figured Gladys was thinking I was back in the bedroom to give them a little privacy.

So all his belongings were on the bed and I began to fold his shirts and pants neatly. The maroon flannel, the two worn plaids, the gold T-shirt, the two white T-shirts, a robe I bought him, his jeans, his underwear. I put his shoes on the floor.

Then I walked back into the living room and for a second saw it like I'd never seen it before, saw that oil painting of the ship on the rough sea at night, saw the way the couch sagged underneath it, saw the little statue of the girl in the yellow dress like it was brand-new.

I didn't really *see* Gladys and James now. They were

blurs, and I took my seat on the couch next to Gladys and across from James and for a few seconds it was silent.

"I think we oughta tell Gladys something," I said to James.

And the odd thing was I wasn't a bit nervous about it, mainly because I knew I'd lost everything that really mattered to me then, meaning James's love and companionship, and whenever a person loses like that a kind of bravery sets in, maybe a hopeless bravery but it's better than being afraid.

James looked at the floor and said, "Well, I guess so. Seems an odd way to say hello to her after so long, but I guess you're right, Ivy."

So I looked at Gladys and said, "James has been mine for a while."

"James has been yours for a while," she said. "Now what's that supposed to mean?" She was smiling. She knew what it meant.

"James and I are lovers," I said.

"Whoah!" she said. "Whoah Nilly!" She was still smiling.

"I'm sorry, Gladys, it just happened," I told her. I felt no emotion at this point other than a bit confused about that smile on her face.

Then she starts laughing. She throws her head back and laughs and says, "Ivy! Ivy and James!" And she keeps on laughing.

*   *   *

I went for a walk alone when that laughter died. Gladys wouldn't look at me. I wasn't sure what to make of it all, but I knew that I was the third wheel in that room, that James and Gladys had a long life together that maybe happened long ago, but it was there in the room just the same, and I felt like a girl again, a girl excluded, alone on a porch swing in the dark.

But I couldn't stay on that swing in that dark because I was a whole different person now, and my heart was in great pain, and all I wanted was to turn around and head back to that house and say to James, "James, tell Gladys you love me. I know you love me. I know you do, James."

But of course I kept walking into that autumn night because I knew James didn't love me.

When I was twenty-two a man named Stewart Rivers dated me half a year. Stewart was a nice man in most ways, and a handsome man too, often in a tie because he was an architecture student. My mother told me he was the best I'd ever get. He might have been, but I didn't love him, so I had to break his heart. Stewart didn't take that heartbreak well, in fact he called me on the phone crying, he showed up at my house with roses once a week for three months straight, and he wrote me about sixty letters signing them "Love, Stew" when all I'd ever called him was Stewart.

I walked that night straight out of the camp and down the dark road that led to town, and the whole time I thought of how Stewart Rivers became smaller and smaller and less like someone I could love the more he persisted that way.

I would not be Stewart Rivers with James. I'd be the opposite.

I'd go on with my life, and whatever he wanted to do, well that was plainly his business.

There was no moon that night, only stars. I couldn't see where I was going, but I didn't much care.

Next thing a car is shining headlights on my backside and Gladys is hanging out the window saying, "Ivy, get in!" And I turn around and walk back toward James's car and get into the backseat. Gladys is at the wheel, James is in the passenger seat, and a football game is on the radio for a second until Gladys changes the station and now we've got the singer Al Green.

Sha-la-la-la-la-la oh baby
Sha-la-la-la-la-la

I'll never forget it.

Gladys drove straight and James turned sideways in the passenger seat, reached back and squeezed my hand, and all the sudden I'm filled with the most painful hope I ever had. I squeezed his hand back.

"We going to the Little Moon?" I said.

"We just came out to rescue you, sister," Gladys said.

"So where *are* we going?"

"Back home," James said. "Gladys and me need some time to talk."

"So why can't I walk if you two need to talk?" I was angry all the sudden. Terribly angry.

"It's too dangerous out here, Ivy. You could get hit by a car."

He squeezed my hand again.

Al Green kept on singing.

I let them take me home.

Gladys
Do You Love?

GUS GUNADOS WAS A MAN I DRANK WITH AT THE VFW IN Eugene, Oregon. That's where we got off the bus for good. When I say we, I'm speaking of myself and Raelene and Anthony, boy of her dreams.

Gus was no veteran. And the VFW was not your typical old soldier bar. It was the misfit watering hole. Doors wide open for your down-and-outers. Bums spent the night in the booths. Some mornings, the odor was sickening. But you had to admire an operation like that. Course there were vets in there, but they weren't the sort to hold it against you if your feet never wore combat boots. They played old music in there. Glenn Miller and Fats Domino, mainly. Sometimes Johnny Cash. I liked to sit and talk to Gus and hear Johnny Cash in the background.

Gus was a flat-foot in thick glasses. He and I hit it off, mainly because we were both afternoon drinkers at the time. It was company for a while. Nothing to compare to James. In fact, just being with Gus got me thinking of James.

We stopped there in Eugene, Oregon, because that's where Hambone West lived in a big old house with a few other youngsters. One of those young people called himself an artist. He'd paint the Pillsbury dough boy, Mary the Virgin, and an automobile on a tin can, then sell the damn thing for fifty-five bucks at the Saturday market. I just kept my mouth shut about that.

The other young person was a college girl. Hardly saw her. She had an older man professor in her life. Tell you the truth, he was my age. Bumped into him one night in the hallway. He had a towel wrapped around his waist. We just looked at each other, then moved on.

It was a place to stay for a while.

I was all pains and aches after that bus ride. Raelene and Anthony and myself got off the bus and there was Hambone West. He had himself a car the size and color of a toad. "Get on in," he told us. I looked at the car and thought, How? Raelene squeezed into the back, and I sat beside our chauffeur.

Hambone was a curly red-haired boy who talked too fast and too much. The sort of young man who blasts off like a rocket when he's sixteen, then crashes down to earth by age twenty-five. He was still blasting when I met him. I looked at him and pictures came right into my mind. An exhausted mother and a General Motors father, hard-working folks with dark circles under their eyes, and all their dreams in Hambone. I liked him. He didn't seem to care that I was old enough to be his mother. When he talked, he talked to both Raelene and myself. He didn't pretend I wasn't there, and he didn't change himself because I was. Every other word out of Hambone's mouth was *shit*. And it brought out the cusser in Raelene and Anthony. "Are you shittin' me?" they'd all say.

"You people got cute mouths," I'd say. "But use your imaginations. You got a lot of curse words out there, why stick to one?"

The house was surrounded by roses. Two blocks away was the Willamette River. I would go for walks on a path there. Thundercloud plum trees lined our street, dazzling deep purple if your eyes never saw one. My room had a bed and a rusty mirror on the wall. And two windows. I wasn't complaining. Something in me was different. Maybe I just made myself enjoy the distractions of novelty. I knew it wouldn't last long.

But I see now it was good that I headed west on that bus. It was good getting away from my life. They say you can't run away from your problems, but I found that's not true. You need to sometimes, and you can. It's possible. It's not like you stay the same if you put your carcass on a Greyhound and take it to a house of youths across the country. You don't tend to haul that same old carcass with you. You change.

Not in a big way, but that's all right. You need little changes. You need a stranger on a bus to sit across the aisle and tell you the story of the time her uncle painted everything in his house bright red. I said to the baffled niece from Detroit, "Everything? Even the toilet paper?"

"Even the toilet paper," the woman says.

And that's when I knew I left myself behind. Laughing with an ease I hadn't felt since being a girl. My eyes tearing up with the laugh. I turned toward the window. I thought of the uncle with his paintbrush not being satisfied with a red house. He'd want to paint the sidewalk next. He was trying to make the world simple with his paint. For a while I sat and rode and thought about that man and laughed.

It weren't like me, and I liked it.

Old Raelene. She stirred it all up. I can see she's a mystery now. The fact that she came into my life. Mystery. Where would I be without it.

For employment in Eugene, I cleaned houses for three families—it was easy work, and the one family paid a fortune because the father was one of those men who hate exploitation of any kind. For decorations in that house they had posters from this protest, that protest. "Want to join us on an antigrape march?" the mother said one day when I was eating lunch. "I'm not a marcher," I said. And the mother got very interested, pulled up a chair, like I'm a scholar on not marching. She says, "Really? Why? How did you come to that decision?" No matter what I said, that family thought it was interesting, so I just said, "Bad feet."

Meanwhile Raelene picked strawberries. Walked around with stained hands. Still wearing Chinese slippers, only black ones now. She'd bring home baskets of the very ripe ones, and we ate.

Anthony worked with some carpenters. He got brown and muscled in the sun, started looking too much like Omar Sharif for his own good. Grew a thin mustache. Raelene told me she was going to marry him. "That's how much I love Anthony," she said one night on the front porch. They would have three kids (she had three god-awful names picked out, including Illuminata). They'd stay "out west where the air was vury clean." And maybe she'd eventually look up her mother, she said. Her mother was out west, had been for years.

"Out west is not an address," I said. I looked at her face. She was biting down on her lower lip.

She said, "Oh, I got the address. I got the address exactly."

I understood then that the girl had wanted to go out west not just to see Hambone. Not just for the adventure. And I figured she wouldn't be able to wait. Marriage and babies would come later. Tracking the mother, sooner. I could see it in her face.

Wasn't too long before Raelene says, "Will you go visit my mother with me?"

She needed my company. Omar Sharif had to work, and she couldn't face it alone. Part of me wanted to go so I could say to the mother, what ails you?

Turns out the mother lived in the city of Portland, Oregon. Raelene borrowed the tin can artist's car. Away we went with the twin Virgin Marys on every door. Raelene at the wheel.

Here's what that girl told me on the way to Portland: "Gladys, I'm going to have a baby." The way she says it, soft with a big smile, her eyes all lit up, I know I was supposed to say, "Congratulations." But I just stared at her. Then I said, "What?" And she says it again, with the same innocent happiness. She was like a film star playing a farm girl. Odd, because she weren't much of an actress usually.

"You tell Anthony yet?"

"Not yet. I want to take him somewhere nice, like down to the river, make it vury, vury special when I tell him."

"Uh-huh."

"You're the godmother, if that's all right with you."

"Raelene," I said. For a moment I clenched my eyes shut. I was overcome with an emotion. A kind of sorrow for Raelene, maybe. For all she was going to lose. And besides this sorrow, I felt something like jealousy. A grown woman jealous of a girl in trouble. It alarmed me.

"Don't worry," she said. She smiled over at me. Then she turned back to the road, still smiling.

"You're tough," I said.

"I am," she said.

"I can't stick around much longer," I told her.

She looked over at me.

"This little trip's not my life, Raelene," I said. "This is diversion."

She smiled. "You never know, Gladdy," she said. She had started calling me Gladdy. First and only person to ever give me a nickname. Gladdy.

Raelene's mother's apartment building looked like a motel. It was on the second floor. This was a gray day in July. I had stopped in a bar for a drink. I was eager to knock on the mother's door and get this over with.

But Raelene was a wreck. She stood on the balcony with a pocket mirror. Chomping her nails like a war bride on D day. Pushing her hair behind her ears which weren't flattering. She wore a long olive green dress. "I look terrible," she said.

"You look fine."

"I can't do this," she said.

"You got every right."

I said all sorts of things, but words didn't help. I

thought this whole idea was a bad one. I could feel it.

When we knocked the mother answered. Raelene lowered her eyes. Couldn't look up. So the woman says to me, "Yes?"

"I'm Gladys, this is Raelene," I said.

I didn't like the woman. Never had, ever since I heard of her. She was a pretty woman, I'll give her that. Even in an ugly brown pants suit with gold buttons. She was an hourglass redhead with blue eyes. Only thing she had like Raelene was crooked teeth.

"Can I help you?" she said.

Raelene still couldn't look up. So I said, "I'm Gladys, and this is RAELENE."

The hourglass stepped back.

"Come in," she said. Her face went whiter. We stepped in. She led us into a long, narrow kitchen. Three toddlers sat at a little table. One was a little Chinaman. Red bowls full of lima beans on the table. I can still see it. Raelene just stared at the children.

"Can you say hello to our visitors, kids?" the mother said. She said it singsong.

"Hello," they sang.

"You kids be golden while I sit and have a grown-up time," she said. She led us to the other end of the long, spare kitchen. Toward the horizontal window framing Portland sky. She walked real fast like she was racing. Then slowed down all the sudden. Slammed on her brakes, so I nearly fell on top of her. Raelene looked at the floor. Then we were all on a sagging couch set under the window.

"Surprise, surprise," Raelene mumbled to herself, smiling. She had a nervous laughter brewing in her, I could see that.

In the corner a small TV with tin foil antennas was tuned into a talk show.

"I didn't think I'd ever see you again," the mother said. "Is this your stepmother?" she said, big blue eyes looking at me.

"No, no, just my friend," she said. Then her nervous laughter spills out.

The mother's hands rose to cover her pretty face. She had long red nails.

"Go ahead, tell me you hate me, get it over with," she said behind her hands. Raelene stopped laughing.

"I don't hate you," she said in a small voice.

"Can't hate what you don't know," I said. Hadn't planned on talking.

The mother's hands left her face. She looked at me.

"Who are those kids?" Raelene said.

"It's my job. Got to make a living somehow."

"All done!" the kids called.

"Go read *Miss Moppet*," Raelene's mother hollered. The anger she felt at being surprised got stuck inside the word *Moppet*.

"I'll be there in a while," she called, trying to sound nicer.

She turned to Raelene with her blue eyes. She said, "I know what you're thinking. I know you're thinking it's damn funny of me to take care of other people's children when I can't take care of my own. But I have to. Only job I could get, Rae. My middle name's not exactly Skills and Education."

Raelene looked at me, then at her mother.

"Delia won't give me the book!" one child shouted.

The mother got up and started talking to the kids like a foul-tempered Donald Duck. Very talented. Raelene's mouth hung open at this. I wanted to reach over and close it.

"Be good for ten minutes, then we'll have cookies," said Donald Duck.

I looked at Raelene and widened my eyes. She rolled her eyes up in her head. But then those same eyes landed on her mother. And stayed there. Desperate. All the sudden I felt I shouldn't be there.

"Maybe I should go," I said to Raelene.

"No," she said. "No." Looked at me, just as desperate.

The mother came back. "I memorized a whole speech for you a long time ago, Rae, and the damn thing's gone now." She slapped the side of her head. "My mind's a sponge somebody wrung out too many times. I still remember the Gettysburg Address, but not my own speech to my daughter."

"I don't want a speech," Raelene said.

The mother was digging under the couch now. She

brought out a shoe box. "I'll show you some photos," said the mother. Here, let me sit down.

So I stood up and let the mother sit down. I sat on the chair across from them and looked out at the sky. I said to myself, Of all the places in this world, here I am.

"This one's your great-aunt Sara in her Jackie O. glasses. She was like a mother to me. She took care of me when I first came out here."

"She looks nice," Raelene said.

"Nice? Nice? That's not the word, sugar. She was the one who understood. She was a survivor. Everybody else was saying, 'Cheer up, honey, keep your chin up!' But not Sara. Sara knew how heavy a chin could get."

Raelene's mother turned the snapshot so I could see. It shook in her hand. I nodded my head.

"And here's my friend Dot. She was my roommate in the bin. Dot Miller. Not very attractive, but kind. We did the Thorazine shuffle together for years. Be glad you got your daddy's genes, Raelene, or you'd be Thorazine shufflin' yourself. See those fuzzy slippers? We called them our dancing shoes."

Raelene held the snapshot. She couldn't look up. She couldn't talk.

The kids started coming toward us, crawling on the floor pushing cars.

"This is me, believe it or not," she said, turning the picture toward me. She was on the beach in a plaid two-piece. Next to her a handsome man in sunglasses. A towel gripped in his hand.

"He was a piano player. Vury jazzy. When I got walloped he thought he could cheer me by playing some music. I'd lay on his couch and he'd play for hours. Vury jazzy stuff."

"Sounds great," Raelene said.

"But he didn't love me, he just loved my body. He admitted that in the end. They all do, you know. Nobody loves you when you're walloped."

"Walloped?" Raelene said.

"Way far deep down in the dark-ass walloped." She laughed, her eyes watered. "Depressed," she said. She pulled out another handful of pictures, her hands shaking. Then she put them back in the box. One of the kids was singing loud, right by her feet. She yawned a big, sudden yawn. Loud and rude, but she couldn't control it.

"I don't know what else I can tell you," she said. "Maybe come back tomorrow. It'll be a better day tomorrow. I'm so tired. It's nap time here."

The children had turned into dogs, crawling and barking. We stood up. She saw us to the door.

Raelene and I got into the car. I was at the wheel. I figured she could sit back and digest it. I started up the car, I pulled out to the road. Then we hear, "Hey, Raelene, stop, stop, stop, stop!"

The mother is at my window. Leaning in and saying, "Stay with me, Rae, stay and have coffee and sleep one night at my place. I'll get you back in the morning. I'm, I'm, I'm . . . I have to go back up there now, please . . . "

Raelene looked at her like she was undecided, but she weren't, really. "Go on, Raelene, go on," I said.

"Are you all right?" she said.

"Raelene, I'm a grown woman. Don't think I need you, I don't."

She looked hurt, I remember that. But it was true. I didn't need anybody.

She got out of the car, and away I drove. Too fast, probably. I didn't much care for the whole journey. I wished I'd never come. I found a telephone booth. I thought I'd call Ivy and tell her, "I'm headed home. The whole trip's been abnormal." I stood in that glass booth on the side of the road and the phone rang and rang.

The next night was the night Gus Gunados and I danced to some sorrowful old man band called The Starlights. The old fart who sang was a 112 and still using Great Day on the three and a half hairs he had on his head.

Gus was handsome for a sixty-year-old in bifocals. I suspected we were headed toward romance. I'd known him for weeks and I was lonely. I'd been lonely for years but now I was lonely in a strange place. It's better that way. It's worse being lonely in a place you know well. So alongside the loneliness was a kind of pleasure. And I liked Gus's way of telling stories. He had six kids scattered across the country. He talked to three of them every Sunday. And they were all doing crazy things. He'd tell me about them in that dark bar with Johnny Cash singing "I Still Miss Someone" or "San Quentin" and he'd get me laughing. For instance his oldest boy was a shepherd who didn't speak between the months of December and February. He didn't say a damn word. He told Gus it was his winter cleansing. He told Gus he needed "a world without words" in the winter. The only word he wanted in his head was *baaa* from the sheep. This boy changed his name from Johnny to Shepherd. Gus said, "Am I wrong, Gladys, or does this sound like the behavior of a lunatic?" It's not that funny, but to hear Gus talk about it, it was. Because he was so damned confused about every last kid he ever had. Gus was the sort to try to figure them out. His one daughter, Olympia, she had two husbands named Jack and the second one she married under water.

Your life might not pan out, but you can still tell your story. Gus knew that much. He never put me to sleep with all this. Fact he never bored me much at all.

Which is why I started missing James. Because the feeling of not being bored was what I had with James. Yet James never had to talk as much as Gus to give me that feeling. And I believe James understood the world more and was more generally offended way down deep.

Gus and me danced and drank. I'm talking whiskey or rum. That one night after dancing to the Starlights,

Gus and me decide we're going to the hot springs. We heard about it from some young girl named Stacy. Stacy was one of your Greyhound gals escaped from a group home in West Virginia. She had streetwalker blonde hair and hippie clothes and was always getting loaded. She had a boyfriend named Stephen who was handsome except for an obvious Adam's apple, but not wrapped too tight.

Stacy and Stephen did their slow dancing next to Gus and me. The elderly Starlights are destroying a good song, "The Great Pretender." Gus and me are dancing the old-fashioned way; he's leading and there's space between our bodies. Our feet know something about where to step. He's looking to the side or over my head. Meantime Stacy and Stephen are draped over each other like they're dead. Hardly moving. Eyes closed. I always found that modern style a little pitiful. As I moved around the floor with Gus, I kept my eyes on Stacy's face. She looked too young to be dead.

After the song Stacy says to me and Gus, "Stephen wants to take us to these, like, *hot springs*. It's like a cure. You just go there and sit down or something."

Tall, long-necked Stephen said, "It's like up in the mountains. It's like a dream world up there. And it's free."

Everything was always "like."

Gus said, "Whatever you want, Gladys, I'm like too old to think."

I said, "Let's like go." I said it because as I danced to

that bad music with Gus and looked at Stacy's young face with her eyes closed I started feeling a need to be distracted from the loneliness of it all.

So we traveled, the four of us, up to the mountain. One of the Cascades. I had to hand it to Stephen. He had a sense of direction. He found where we were going quick. So he parked his Dodge on the side of a pitch black road. I could see the mountain was covered with trees. You could smell the leaves. I said, "I don't see any hot springs." Gus said, "Gladys and me aren't big on hiking." Stacy laughed. Stephen said, "There's a path, just follow old Stephen."

So we all follow old Stephen single file. The path is wet dirt soaking through my sneakers. First I complained. "What the hell are you getting us into?" But then I didn't much care. Because it smelled so good in there, and the stars were so bright and low it was like a dream. And after a while we reached the springs.

Now if the path was a dream, the springs was a nightmare. I mean initially. The air was steamy and moonlit. The two pools in the ground, I mean the two hot springs, were filled up with naked people. In the one hot spring was three men and two women. They were all crammed in there. It didn't look too kosher if you want an understatement. We stood a ways back. A small fire burned to the left. I guess they'd had a cookout.

In the other spring was just one man. And he was reading a book. He was the one I looked at, not the others. I looked at him and felt almost right away like I wanted to be beside him. Not talking, not touching, but reading a book. I hadn't read a book in a long time. And the man looked so peaceful.

"We can go sit with that man," Stephen said. "That's a big spring."

"I'm not disturbing him," I said.

The man looked up at me then, then back to his book.

Stacy said, "Who wants to smoke a splib?"

A splib was what she called her marijuana cigarettes.

Well, Stacy and Stephen went to smoke while Gus and I stood side by side mumbling things like, "You going in?" "Don't know." "Didn't expect it to be so well lit." "Is there like a full moon?" "Why are we here?"

So they come back naked, Stacy and Stephen, and then the four who were crammed in together stand up and walk naked over to their little fire. They stoke the fire. They crouch by it. Cavemen. Stacy and Stephen go into the spring where the four people had been. I'm beginning to get a little disgusted. I'm not the queen of clean, but I never had the urge to sit in another person's bathwater either.

Gus, he just took off his clothes and glasses real quick, folded them neat. Then he went to sit with Stacy and Stephen. When he was in there he said, "Come on, Gladys, this is heaven."

Stacy said, "Come on, we don't care if you're fat."

That Stacy had a lot of class.

She was too young to know that I could be happy being a big woman. She was too young for knowing much of anything. If I wanted to go sit in the bathwater of strangers, I would've stripped and they would've seen a big, strong, healthy-enough body. That's how I look naked. Powerful. I know I do. Despite the excess.

"You three have a nice soak. I'll just look at the stars," I said.

But I kept looking back to the lone man with the book. He was young, maybe thirty. His hair was dark and thin. He wore glasses and his shoulders were strong looking, the kind of strength some men seem to get from a lifetime of tension.

Well, the man puts his book down all the sudden. Then he looks at me. "You should take a soak. It's good for the spirit," he said.

"What's the temperature?" I said. My heart was racing. Because I knew I was going to do an extreme thing.

"It's just warm, just warm enough. It's just like putting on a silk robe that's sat in the sun all day."

"A silk robe," I mumbled. "A silk robe."

And then I got out of my clothes and walked over to that spring and climbed in. I wasn't Mrs. Graceful. I sank down and put my head back on the earth and looked up at the stars. I could hear my heart. The stars looked like they were beating, like they had hearts too.

My three cohorts in the other spring joked, "Guess we're not good enough for her!"

The man across from me said, "Nice?"

"Real nice."

"You should come here every time you want to die," he said.

I lifted my head off the earth and looked at him. We looked at each other for five seconds or so. Finally I said, "Why would I want to die?"

"You might not. I just took a stab."

"And you?"

"And me?"

"Do you want to die? Do you come here when you want to?"

"Oh, most certainly. Johnny got his gun. Uh-huh. Johnny had his fun. But Johnny can't talk to anyone. If you get my drift."

I didn't. My friends in the other spring were now singing,

> *Carry me over,*
> *Carry me there*
> *To leave the hills of Caledonia*
> *Is more than the heart can bear. . . .*

"Your name's Johnny?"

"My name's Thomas. I'm sorry, I should've kept quiet."

For a while we sit there. A breeze in the high leaves above us.

Then our feet were touching. It felt good. I felt my foot move against his. He moved his foot against mine.

"I believe it's usually best to dwell in silence," he said. "To dwell in silence," he said, "is to dwell in possibility."

Fanciest thing anyone ever came out and said to me personally. I'll never forget it. He moved his leg, stretched it forward. Now his leg was lined against my leg.

"So you got a way with words," I said, too quiet. I don't think he heard. Maybe he heard my heart, maybe he heard my heart beating like a jazz drum.

Soon it's our legs are entwined. My cohorts are still singing the same song, doing harmony now. I wanted them to sing on and on. I wanted this *man*. I admit that.

And all the sudden I knew he'd been to Vietnam. I knew he'd been hurt. I knew he was one of the wounded souls who couldn't sleep.

"My son was over there," I said.

"Over where," he whispered.

"Over there."

"Is that right."

"He died over there."

Then we were quiet, both looking up at the stars, and he said, "Ursula?"

I said, "Ursula?"

"Yes, Ursula. Let me read you this nice sentence."

He picked up his book and read, *"The new house, white, like a dove, was inaugurated by a dance."*

And he'd pulled his legs back. We weren't touching anymore. And all I could do is say, "Read it again." And he read it again, four times.

Well, I've had an odd life with odd encounters but this was the strangest.

Not so much the man, but what he called up in me. The kind of hunger. The kind of loneliness.

He said it was time to go after a few minutes. And the feeling was mostly gone. Just scraps of it were left, and a kind of deep pit inside me where the scraps floated. Now I was just sorry I'd come here. I watched this man. He stood up, he climbed out. I looked up at him. He had a strong young man's body, but it looked so alone I was filled with the heaviest kind of sadness. And when I closed my eyes, I saw Wendell. I saw Vietnam jungle rice paddies. Dark green twisted confusion. Flames. Someone screaming. Wendell a boy on a bike. I opened them quick. The man dressed and said good-bye, and "I'm sure I'll see *you* here again sometime."

But in the Valiant on the way back to town I knew I'd never see that place again. Gus and the others sang all the way home, the same damn song. "Damn! We're good!" they said. And I stared out the window. Everyone was strangers to me. I missed Wendell. I couldn't talk. My throat was filled up with missing him.

I wrote Raelene a note. I told her if she needed anything, call.

On the bus back home I leaned my face on the window like a dreamy girl. Mostly because I was tired. And because I didn't want to talk to the blonde woman next to me. Or her children in the seat behind me. They all had colds. The one boy kept kicking my seat. I sunk into myself. I pretended I was deaf. I made my eyes look blank too. The blondie maybe thought I was retarded. I could hear her thinking, Just my damn luck to end up sittin' with a deaf retard.

On that ride home I remembered all kinds of things from long ago. My mother's vegetable garden. My mother. I remembered how she'd take me and Ivy to the ocean. She'd wear a bathing cap and earplugs. She swam all stiff, like she was made of tin. It always bothered me. I'd want to rip the cap off and dunk her head under, hold it for a while. So she would come up alive and kicking. I don't know why I was born with this kind of mean spirit but I was.

"Mom! He farted on purpose!" the child behind me screamed.

"Did not!"

"You did too ya big fartin' liar!"

The woman, the blondie mother, she just sat beside me and pretended she didn't know these kids. The kids got louder. I finally had to say, "Aren't those your kids?" Surprise, the deaf woman can talk. She stared at me. And then she whipped herself around and talked to those kids through gritted teeth. They shut up for a good five minutes. The bus rolled on.

And I remembered James. I remembered how James and me knew how to spend a winter day. Light a fire, open the curtains to the gray sky, get under the blankets. I kept remembering that one thing over and over again. I didn't go trailing into other things. I controlled my mind. And when the woman settled down those kids for the fifth time, I drifted off into half sleep; I dreamed about the same thing. The fire, the gray sky, the blankets. And James.

So it didn't surprise me when I got back and James was there. Thoughts are like spirits. You think a thought about someone and the thought will travel right into that someone's heart. Whether they know it or not.

Or so I started thinking.

It did surprise me to find out he was with Ivy. I have to admit that surprised me quite a bit. I didn't know what to make of it, it seemed so odd. I wasn't hurt, initially.

It had been eight years since I'd seen James. We thought we had a lot to talk about. So we tried to talk, right there in the house. Ivy just let us be. For a few days, we'd sit at the table and try to talk. I wanted to talk, but it wasn't working.

"So, what have you been doing these past years?" I'd say.

"Well, a lot of things. Working hard. Living."

"So tell me some of your jobs."

James looked about the same, a little older I guess. He was tired looking, but he was always tired looking. One of those men whose face tired out before his body.

He didn't tell me I looked good. And I knew I didn't. Four days on a Trailways at my age will leave its mark. Still, we felt our connection to each other. A few times at the table, talking, we felt it. One of those times it was what you call a fierce connection. It stung. I couldn't breathe.

I would've done anything James asked me to do. I had nothing to lose with him. I had wrecked mine and James's life together long ago. After we lost our girl. Plenty a woman lost a child and recovered right alongside the child's father. For me, it weren't possible. I remembered James saying, *Please, please, please, don't leave me.* Like he was a child too. But I'd already left him. I left everyone. I was in a land of my own. Soon as I knew she was gone, I went to that strange land. Had to. At the time I didn't see another way.

So what James wanted after all was to go to the

pond. The pond where we lost her. Where we slept while she drowned.

"I just want to see it," he said. "We can get there in three hours."

Meanwhile Ivy was out walking, walking, walking. She worked in the garden or out in the field raking up leaves with the kids, she came home to eat, but otherwise she was walking. She wouldn't talk much to me. She had her chin lifted high. She was holding on to dignity. That's Ivy. That's what she did her whole life.

"Well, whatever, James. I mean, if you want to see it, why not go see it?"

"I want you to go with me."

"That's fine then, I'll go."

All I had to do was close my eyes and I could see the pond in my mind anytime I wanted. But I went along to help James through it. It helped me to be in my own skin to feel like I was helping out James.

"It's so strange, being with you," he said in the car. It was autumn, but the air was strangely warmed up with Indian summer. The leaves were all fiery yellows and reds. And it was evening. I just smiled over at him. Wasn't like him to say something so obvious. Made me sad, somehow. He was not the old James.

"I thought about you plenty," he said.

"Well, me too," I said. "Me too."

But our words weren't sinking into the other's heart. You could feel that. You could feel the words just stuck in the air of the car. Homesick words. I thought to myself, *Where do the homesick words end up? Where do they go if they don't sink in?*

And I knew it was hopeless, but James kept trying.

"What's your read on Jimmy Carter?" he said.

"James, I don't pretend to know. What about you?"

"I've arrived at the age where I think anyone who manages to be president doesn't deserve to be."

"You were born at that age, James, weren't you?"

He laughed a little.

"I know I was," I said, though that was a lie.

Silence. I watched the trees rush by.

"Remember that old dog called Wilma?" he said. He looked over at me with his dark blue eyes, then turned back to the road.

"Wilma—one ear," I said. "She thought you were her mother."

He tried to laugh.

I was thinking, Why Wilma? Why bring up that stray dog we got in Wilmington, Delaware? Of all memories, why Wilma? I couldn't figure.

"And the cat, Mr. Horse?"

"Mr. Horse," I said. "I always liked that old cat. Course even that cat liked you better than me."

And then James began to laugh at the wheel. It wasn't his old laugh. Fact, it scared me because it didn't sound a thing like him. And his hands were holding too tight to the wheel. His knuckles were all white. And then just as quick he stopped laughing. And I could see he'd laughed himself into his tears.

They just sat in his eyes. I was glad. I wouldn't have known what to say if James had tears running down his face.

"The last time I saw Wendell, that time he visited me before getting shipped off, he talked about all the pets we ever had," James said. "I think about that day a lot. He kept saying he was grateful that we'd had all those pets, really grateful."

"I should give you some pictures," I said. "Of him. I have them all."

It wasn't seeing the pond itself. It wasn't even the swim we took. It was the dreams that came afterward that changed me most. Because in the dreams there was a door. A door on the bottom of that pond. Under the water I'd bang on the door, bang on the door, using all my strength. In the dream was hope. A hope that somehow the door could be opened. Somehow I'd step through the door at the bottom of the pond and there she would be. There she would be. In the white sundress Ivy made her. Patiently waiting.

But the swim, it's not forgettable. James and me stood at the edge of the pond. I didn't want him to talk. But he felt like he had to. He said, "I never said good-bye to her. I never knew how."

"That's why we're here," I said. I wanted to say, Just be quiet. But I wasn't about to.

The pond looked smaller to me. The whole area did. I had my arms crossed. I wanted to go. I believed I'd said my good-bye. Or that I was always saying it, somehow. Wasn't that the real truth? I believed I was in the wrong place at the wrong time. It was like the place was too small. The place in my head, in my heart, it was gigantic. It was oversized. Bigger than life. This place, this real place, it was so small.

But James looked like this good-bye would take a while.

"I'm real sorry," I told him, suddenly, looking out at the trees. "For all I did wrong. For all I never said. I'm just sorry."

He looked at me. I think he thought I could read his expression. But I couldn't read a thing. I couldn't trust a thing. He could've been looking at me with the eyes of a murderer, or a saint. I wouldn't have been able to tell. Finally James looked back at the water.

"I think I'm going swimming. I'm going in."

"It's too cold to swim."

He was taking off his shirt.

"You sure about this?" I said.

He looked older to me, his skin looser. Different from how he looked stored in my mind. Now he was taking off his pants. He had on the oddest boxer shorts, flannel, a wildlife scene on them, a bear and a fish or something.

"You coming in?" he asked me.

"I don't know."

I felt sad just looking at him. But I felt something else too, some old urge. I felt both things at the same time, along with other things. Confusion.

"You should come in. That's what I think, anyhow."

It began to feel like I was dreaming. Just like when I dreamed about this it felt like it was real. It seemed to me there was a siren blaring in the distance, but there weren't. It was just silence. Silence that sounded like a siren getting louder and closer.

I took off my shoes, not my dress. I waded into the water. In my dress. Now the siren was gone. It was just the sound of water disturbed now. Then James came in. And then we were swimming out into the middle of the pond. The dusk above us. And out there in the middle I said, "James, this was a bad idea." And I began to shake, like I was freezing cold. But the water wasn't that cold, he said. I treaded water. James dove under. He stayed under for a while and I looked at the purple sky and shook. James came back up.

"It's not deep," he said.

Then he was swimming toward the bank, and I was too. And he dressed and rushed to the car. I thought he was going to leave me behind.

Instead he ran back with two blankets. A red one that smelled like gasoline, and a white flannel one with yellow roses on it. He said, "Wrap yourself up." I used the white flannel one.

I took the red one and put it on the ground. We sat on it. It wasn't a bit comfortable. Nothing was. I wanted to weep. Because I could remember the ease that used to be between us. I could feel how James was stunned that none of it was left. Where was it? Where did the ease go? And how was it we could stand being in that pond? We sat there for about ten minutes. James had a small stick he was biting.

He said, "What did Ann *think* when she was drowning? What did she think of *us* for not coming to save her? I still think about this every night."

"Don't. Don't."

That's all I could say. I stood up.

"I'm sorry," he said. "I wanted to talk for so long. To *you*."

"I'm sorry," I said. But I wasn't as sorry as I was angry. Not so much that he said what he said. But that I let myself go into that pond. I don't even know why I was angry about that. But I wished I'd never gone in.

"James. I wish I didn't go in. Wish I'd stayed dry."

"Gladys, please. Please sit beside me. I miss you. I miss you."

I went back and sat beside him. He put his arm around me. I'll tell you what. His body did not feel familiar. The way he had his arm around me did not feel at all familiar. Still, there was something in him, something about him, it felt like my home.

I fought that feeling. I closed my eyes and said to myself, Take me away from here. But meanwhile my body just leaned right into his. And meanwhile we kissed each other. And he said, "We're not strangers, we're not strangers, we can't be strangers." Like saying it over and over would make it true.

And it was true. We held on to each other.

"Did it help?" I asked him. "Did it help to swim in the pond?"

We'd had a long, quiet drive back. We were walking toward the house now. The porch light was on. Ivy was in the kitchen. I could see her in the window. She was sitting at the table with a beer.

"Help? I don't know. I guess not. No, it wasn't what I had in mind," James said. He stopped me and held on to me for a second, his eyes on Ivy in the window. "Thank you for coming along," he said.

Later I gave him sixteen pictures. Eight of Wendell, six of A., and the others of the two of them together. Wendell holding A. I said, "It's high time you forgave yourself, James." I said this out on the back stoop one night when the moon was bright. The night Ivy was cooking a stew and listening to Billie Holiday. That stew was the last meal the three of us ate together. A few days later, the two of them were gone. I'd told

James and Ivy, "Don't worry about me. I need time alone."

And what I thought I felt watching them drive away together was a small amount of sorrow or pity for Ivy, because James loved me. I knew that. And Ivy loved James. I knew that too. I imagine she always had. Couldn't blame her.

I stepped in and took over Ivy's job canning vegetables with the kids. The kids didn't much care for me. I wasn't Ivy, asking questions like *Have any hobbies, honey?* But nothing about it was terrible. We canned, we put up the squash, then got the ground ready for the next summer. They mostly laughed and talked and weeded. And ignored me. Unless I stepped in to tell Connie Kaiser, the ringleader, to cut the mean crap when they teased the child with the wayward eye. That child ended up working quiet beside me, grateful I think.

I worked with my hands in the dirt, and it was saving me. The dirt was. How my hands felt digging. Gripping on the roots. The smells out there. The dark mornings. It made me feel stronger than I was. Because I had my hands on the earth. And the earth needed my hands, or so it seemed. And for those hours I didn't think much, or if I did the thoughts didn't feel as real. I'd think of Raelene. I'd think of Gus. Of James. Of Ivy. Of James. I'd think of worse things, like giving birth.

And then the thoughts would float away easy as a balloon, and I was back to the real dirt. Taking a deep breath, starting all over.

And the children all around me sang rock and roll songs sometimes.

But there was an undersong. I mean something *under* all the sounds of the day. A voice, almost. Poking me in my stomach. *You've had your loves. You've had your chances. You've lived your life. Now who are you? Who are you? Who do you love?*

Do you love? Do you? Did you?

"Let's keep up the good work here, kids," I'd say.

And the undersong would play again, softer, and I'd be both relieved and regretful that it didn't play louder.

Some nights I'd sit out on the stoop with a beer. And a blanket. My book beside me because I'd be tired of reading. I'd start wondering when I'd hear from Ivy or James. And a moment would come when I'd feel like I'd never hear a thing. Does it matter, I'd wonder. Does it matter at all if I ever see their faces again?

I supposed not. That's what I told myself. *I suppose not.* But that's when I knew deep inside I'd be hearing something soon. Most likely James would circle back this way.

I began in the middle of that month to have the strictest routines. I felt for the first time that house maintenance was important. I painted the whole house except for the basement, I cleaned with a vengeance. I also began to feel that getting exercise was important. I was like Ivy now, walking, walking. And I spent more hours in the garden than I needed.

I'd go down there in the evening sometimes. The child with the wayward eye, her name was Marie. Marie and her sidekick, Kate, they began to take a liking to me. Kate was twelve but acted more like ten. Didn't seem on the verge of anything like most of your twelves. And she had terrible horsey teeth. Marie with her eye, Kate with those teeth and when's-the-flood-ma'am pants, and me with my whole life inside me like a car wreck.

But in the evenings it got cool and the sky was pretty. Pretty in that violent purple way the sky gets in the evening when late autumn's coming at you like a train. And Kate and Marie would stop playing and sit down on the cool ground and talk to me. All about their teachers or parents who were mostly "boring," "crappy," or "so stupid you wouldn't believe it." Camp was over, school was started. These children were in sixth grade. They'd gone home to their rich parents for three weeks between camp and school.

Kate, she had herself a fake English accent. She weren't from England but she had an accent and she came out with things like, "You bloody well bet-tah!" and "Have you gone round the bend?" which meant "Have you lost your mind?" which she was always asking Marie. Along with the wayward eye, Marie was one of your children who lived in the land of outer space. I couldn't get too involved with her. Or not in a human way. I think I got involved with her the way you get involved with a dog. Because she started hanging around the back stoop at different times in the day. She'd just hang around, not saying a word. Just sort've sniffing around like a dog. Finally I'd spot her and open the door and say, "Marie, hello, want a treat?" And she'd smile her martian smile and walk into the house and sit down at the table, her bony hands crossed. And I'd give her a cookie or a cracker, some small treat. And I'd want to say, Don't you ever scrub your fingernails? But I kept my mouth shut.

Then she started bringing Kate. They'd eat and look around the house and look at me, just glad they weren't in the school building, glad they were here in this strange woman's house getting away with something. One day Kate might come in and say, "Marie loves Tony Romoni." And I'd say, "Why? What's the story with Tony Romoni?" And Marie would get beet red, and Kate would say, "He's conceited! He thinks he's God's gift to women! And he got thrown out of class because he raised his hand to say his balls hurt!" Marie wouldn't say a word, just stared at her hands, her face crimson. I was glad to have them around. A good distraction. Because I was beginning to be afraid that James and Ivy really wouldn't be calling. I'd be thinking *sonofabitch, Ivy and James. Of all people.* And then I'd freeze my mind so it wouldn't think about it.

I went back to the kitchen in early November. I was glad to return. Glad because I knew that kitchen so well. And the woman they'd hired that September weren't bad at all. She was a pretty thing built like a pencil and just wanted to be left alone. She liked her talk radio, her Wrigley's spearmint, and spotting birds out the window. "A convention of warblers," she might say, nodding her head. But that was about it. Mostly we worked listening to a bunch of talk radio strangers. It would've been pleasant if I was the type who got comfort from hearing how many people were crazier than me. But it was better than talking. I was in the mood for moving through the days, just moving right through, and waiting. Waiting.

You can only be hiding in a life of routine for so long. The heart of autumn will come. It'll come when you're all alone in your bed, in your cleanest, whitest sheets. It will come when you smell like Jergens soap and your hair's still wet.

I had showered, I was there in that old dark room with the mirror on the closet, and I brought my hands up to my face and smelled the Jergens soap I'd always used. All I can tell you is the smell was too old, too familiar. I felt I'd been alive forever and in the next minute like I'd only lived a second, like I was a small child.

And why'd I let him go off with Ivy? And why'd Ivy go

off with him? Why would she do that to me? And why hadn't I found a goddamn thing to say to him to find his heart again? And if I'd found a thing to say to him to find his heart again, what then?

And then I thought, *You didn't let him go off with Ivy. You are not the boss. You are not in charge. You did not have a say. Did your goddamn sister even ask you?*

And then I thought, *He might very well love Ivy. And you, you who had this idea in the back of your tired head that someday you and he would circle back. Well you are the fool. Fool. Fool. You are.*

You are the fool smelling your own hands in the night, not a soul you could call on the telephone, not any old relative, not some lost friend, not Raelene.

Maybe Raelene.

I hoisted myself out of that bed, shaking. I had the Oregon number. I let the phone ring twenty times, then hung up. Then I got something to eat, a thin sandwich, and ate it in the dark. And I knew as I sat there listening to myself chew that I had to hear a human voice. Any voice.

So out I went. Out went the big wet-haired lady into the cold night. And she walked like hell, walked into town on the black narrow road, ridiculous and afraid, because don't I know it's only the crazy people out at four in the morning, crazy and lonely.

One place was open, that was the spoon called Vinny's. I made it a point never to go in there. The rumor in the early 1970s was that Stan the counterman, Vinny's jailbird brother, made rat burgers. But that night I walked right into Vinny's and sat down in the first booth and a man behind the counter with a Walkman on his head said, "Hello," and his voice broke like it was still changing. He wore a T-shirt that said I'D RATHER BE SNORKELING on it.

And the only other person in there was an old man eating a plate of baked beans at the counter. His black cap sat on the counter. His feet were in sandals.

The man with the Walkman came over to my booth, his small gray eyes open now. "Rice pudding?" he said.

"Yes," I said, though it was only him saying it that made me want it. "How did you know?"

"I been in the business long enough to know a rice pudding night owl from a burger-and-fries night owl," he said. He was too young to talk that way. He was acting. Who could blame him? And he saved me from myself that night. He brought back a small dish of rice pudding and a tin of cinnamon, set it down and said, "So what brings you out tonight? Can't sleep?"

"Can't sleep at all."

"I myself haven't been a night sleeper since I was eleven," he said, "which is why I got this job. It's perfect. You meet all these interesting folks. And they all got a philosophy of life. I truly hope you don't have one. Or if you do I hope you keep it to yourself." He looked right at me but he smiled like he thought a hidden camera was on him. One of these people who watched so much television they think they're *on* television.

"Don't worry, Buster." I had the urge to call this man Buster. So I did.

"Really? You're just here to eat some pudding?"

"That's right, Buster."

"I think I'm in love," he said, and put his hand on his heart. I smiled at him like I thought he was cute.

"Will you marry me?" he said, and went down on his knee, down to the dirty floor. "I've been looking for someone with no philosophy for fifteen years now. Marry me."

I laughed a little laugh. The baked bean man turned on his stool to look back at us, then went directly back to his food.

"Sure, let's go get married," I said. "Let's go get married and adopt seventeen unwanted crippled children and live happily ever after, Buster."

He was taken aback. He didn't want someone joining in like this, he wanted to be the entertainer, the only joker.

He yawned. "So. More pudding?"

"I'll pay up."

I went to the counter with two dollar bills and told him good night.

"Stop in again, we'll talk about the wedding," he tried, just the sort of fellow not to know when the mood was all gone.

I walked outside. I started up the road. It was still

pitch dark. But I felt somewhat better. Comforted some-how. I inhaled the leaf smell. In the air I could catch a hint of real winter. Of snow coming soon. I crunched some leaves under my feet. And then after a minute of walking I hear someone saying, "Miss! Miss!" and I turn and it's the old man.

He stood there, his hat off his head, his hair all white. He stood up straight.

"Good night!" he said.

"Good night!" I called back.

We waved at each other.

When I got home, I slept. I hung on for a month before I got a phone call. It wasn't James.

"Gladys, it's Ivy. I'm on a pay phone. We're in Canada. I miss you. I just wanted to say I miss you."

"What the hell are you two doing in Canada?"

"James has some friend out here. Some woman."

"Is that right?"

"Are you mad at me, Gladys?"

"Mad at you? Why the hell would I be mad at you?"

The operator came on and told Ivy to feed the phone.

"I'm out of quarters."

"Put James on," I said.

But that was it, she was out of quarters, the line was dead.

And I waited and worked and drank too much through a sunless winter before I got the next call that mattered.

"Raelene had a boy!"

It was her friend, Hambone West. He'd been in the delivery room.

I wanted to say, *Hambone, come on out here, bring Raelene and the baby boy, come on out here and stay with me a while, I'd like that, so just come on out whenever you can, stay with me and save a little money.*

"We're headed to Philly," he was saying. "Anthony too. We're all going back to the East. I'm the godfather," Hambone said, in Marlon Brando's voice.

"Baby's name?" I said.

"Moses. You like it?"

"Uh-huh." *Moses? Someone tell me he didn't say Moses.*

"Well, Raelene'll call you sometime from Philly. Raelene would've called you now but she's passed out. But you were number two on her list of people to call."

"Who was number one?" I said, in spite of myself.

"Raelene's father. I had to call him first. He didn't have too much to say."

"Really."

"He's sending her some cash, though."

"Well, good luck," I said.

Somehow I knew I'd never hear from Raelene ever again. Why should I? She had her new life.

So, I said to myself. Time to stop waiting. Time to start over. Time to move on.

But I didn't know how to move on.

Rage had me stuck. Rage at my whole life. Rage at Ivy, James, but mostly myself. And then the rage turned into something else, a kind of despair, where nothing in the world was interesting to me. Of course the girls, Kate and Marie, they stopped coming by. Because when they tried to talk to me, I just looked at them. I didn't have any words. I couldn't have small talk. They got scared of me. The woman I worked with, Nadine Fisher, with her Wrigley's gum and love for birds, she was the only person I talked to for months on end. Because all I needed to say is "We need more batter for the hotcakes," or "Does the walk-in feel a little warm to you?" and things like that. In the spring Nadine wore binoculars like a necklace. Tried to share the views. "Oh," I'd say, "that is one nice bird."

"It's a nuthatch," said Nadine Fisher. She wanted to teach me.

"A nuthatch. So that's a nuthatch."

I wish I could've fallen for those birds. James could've. Maybe even Ivy could've. Not Gladys, I told myself. I was not a woman who could fall for birds. In my mind a voice would say that over and over again, like it was some kind of explanation.

I kept on going through those days because I just never believed in the alternative. Not that I don't respect others who do. Just isn't for me, never was.

One foot in front of the other. Go through the days, I'd tell myself. Go through the days.

James
Strangers

I WANTED GLADYS AND I TO GO INTO THE POND WHERE we'd lost our daughter. I wanted some kind of healing to take place. I confused that idea of immersion with healing, I suppose.

Gladys was angry that she had gone into the water, and later told me it had felt like a sacrilege to her. She wouldn't explain any further, but I think I understood. I hated being in that pond too, finding out it wasn't deep, as if Ann's death was all the more preventable in my memory now, which is absurd, but that was what I felt when I felt the shallowness of that water.

I remember us sitting on the ground, shivering next to each other, and me touching Gladys, and thinking that I finally knew that she and I would not make our way back to each other, ever. That whoever we had been, we were now something else, two people who did not fit together.

I sat there in silence. It surprised me when I was overcome with a sudden feeling of longing for Ivy, and shocked me when the very next moment I wanted Gladys, and pulled her to me, and told her we weren't strangers. It was like a chant, *we're not strangers, we're not strangers we're not strangers*. And it worked. For a few moments, it worked. But only for those moments, and these had dissipated before we'd returned to the car.

Gladys stood in the driveway and watched me and Ivy leave, not waving, not smiling, but looking somehow bemused. But I couldn't read that face with any degree of certainty anymore. I didn't really know her at all anymore. Or so I felt then.

I had told Ivy that we were going to Ontario, where I knew an old Quaker woman who had a farm. I told her we could go up there and live, and work the farm. This woman was named Muriel; I had met her down south when she was visiting her daughters—two chefs upstairs from me whose apartment was too hot, so Muriel had slept on my couch for a while. She had given me her address, told me she'd put me up anytime. She was a nice woman, a Quaker like my mother had been. She wore her white hair in a long braid down her thin back. I described all this to Ivy as we drove, and the more I talked, the wearier I felt. I felt I didn't have it in me to go there, to go to a new place, to start up a new life with a woman named Muriel who was virtually a stranger, even if she had slept on my couch for a few months. But I would conjure the will; I didn't know what else to do, and money was a problem. I had lived frugally and worked hard on a series of shrimp boats and managed to save some, but I needed to find work as soon as possible in order to feel right.

Ivy sat beside me in the car. "Gladys seemed happy for us," she said. "But almost like a person gets happy after hearing a good joke."

"I wouldn't spend too much time worrying about that."

I drove on, drove north, going faster than usual, as if with speed I could get through my resistance.

Ivy said, "Traveling's not something I ever thought I'd like so much, James. Now I got an idea of how you must've felt all those years driving into new places."

It gets old, I wanted to say, but I didn't. I didn't have it in me to ruin her enthusiasm. The woman deserved to be traveling with a man who could look out the window and be grateful for the beautiful blue dusk. So instead I said, "Look at the sky over there, Ivy."

She whistled appreciatively, then smiled over at me.

I drove on, and on.

*　　　*　　　*

When we found Muriel's farm it was late morning, and up there the heart of autumn had passed and most of the leaves had already fallen. Muriel was out by the side of her house. I parked and got out of the car and she stood up with her hand over her eyes, peering out at us. She didn't recognize me from a distance. Ivy was saying, "This place is sure nice," and looking all around. I was looking at Muriel, as if I could will her to feel more familiar.

"James?" she finally said, and her hand came down. "The fisherman with the good couch! Am I seeing right?"

I went and shook her hand, introduced Ivy, and told her we were there to help her out.

"I do have to tell you this is a big surprise," she said. "And a welcome one. Come in, come in."

We followed her into the old white house. It was set way back from the road, and looked solitary and peaceful. Up close it looked like it needed a lot of work, but it had the feel of contentedness, somehow, not neglect. The feel of a house that was happy to be neglected, proud to fall into a kind of natural disarray, which I knew from experience was just the kind of house that responded best to being fixed up. A house with life in it, a house that seemed accepting of whatever shape you wanted it to take, a house that breathed as long as it was respected. On the porch a few cats slept next to a pair of men's work boots that turned out to be Muriel's.

She insisted on making tea and feeding us sandwiches. She said she had plenty for us to do, that we should feel free to stay as long as we wanted, that we shouldn't look at her as a sad old lonely woman who needed our company, because she'd never been happier in all her life. But it would be nice to have us around, she added, and she certainly could stand some help. Her intelligent face was lined and lit up, radiant, as if she'd somehow absorbed all that brilliant color in the last of the autumn leaves.

Initially we worked outside: she had two cows, four goats, and a bunch of chickens. One coop had been torn up in a storm. The barn needed patching. The loft had been virtually destroyed by carpenter ants. All the work waiting to be done told me I was in the right place.

She had a small tractor that I rode around on under the gray sky, or the sometimes shocking blue sky that would fill me with hope. I would take it into my lungs, that northern blue Ontario air, and I would be able to stay focused for long hours on what I was doing, on where I was, and the hope would change to happiness. Ivy and I worked on patching up the barn together. It was when we were working hard enough that I felt especially good. I would drive those eight-penny galvanized finishing nails into the siding of the one wall and feel like nothing else mattered but how the nail went in. Ivy knew how to work quietly, which surprised me because I remembered Gladys talking about how she talked too much when they cooked. Also, Ivy loved to paint, and knew her tools, and she also loved to hammer and sand. In the evenings—the muscles in our backs so sore it was hard to swing our arms at first—we took walks with Muriel along an endless narrow road that was lined with tall pines. Sometimes we'd walk down to Superior, and stand looking out at what might have been the ocean. A few dogs would always follow us down there, which I liked. Muriel wore old dresses, big sweaters, and boots. From behind she could have been mistaken for a child were it not for the bright white of her hair. She had a spring in her step, and she'd kick stones. She loved the landscape passionately, and this was easy for me to understand, because a great clarity seemed to be the thing that held the place together. The clarity of rock, pine, water, road. When we were up there at Superior, the air felt scrubbed with cold light. The trees on that road dwarfed us. I appreciated the feeling that gave me because I had long ago arrived at the age where I felt my own smallness in the scheme of things as a comfort.

During the winter months we worked inside that house, painting, wiring, sanding, and fixing floorboards. Muriel loved it. She worked at various charities in the town most of the day, and had given us permission to do whatever we wanted when she was gone. "Go to town," was how she'd put it. We got Muriel's old Christmas decorations out of the attic and dressed that house up and the three of us had a white Christmas, sitting up half the night listening to her old radio, watching the fire and the lights on the tree, fifty old-time figurines skating and singing on the white cotton snow of the mantel. Ivy talked all about her childhood Christmases that night, but I knew she was glossing over the stories, and she didn't mention Gladys in any of them. I found myself feeling grateful for that ability of hers to weed out the unsettling. Muriel listened and told some stories of her own, mostly about what Christmas was like during the Depression, how she and her husband had managed to create joy out of thin air.

January was the hardest month we spent there because there wasn't enough work to pour ourselves into, and Muriel was always having neighbors over. Neighbors from a mile away would ride their tractors through the snow and sit in Muriel's dining room around her table in their wool socks drinking hot rum and cider and talking about people they knew who Ivy and I didn't know. Muriel always tried to invite us into these conversations, but mostly we sat in silence, listening, Ivy listening with her pure attention span and her natural ease, me listening with a growing restlessness, an unwanted knowledge that soon I'd probably be living somewhere else, because this wasn't my home. Hearing the generations of history these people had shared told me it would not become my home.

Then, in March, after a dose of false spring, I was up late and looking out our bedroom window when I discovered a tire on the lower roof, and in the tire was what looked like a bird, a goose. The goose seemed to be sleeping. It was a moonlit creature, very beautiful, with white patches on its face, a long black neck, and a gray coat. A Canada goose. I had always been captivated by the pure noise of their departures, and their designs in the skies.

I supposed the bird was nesting, and I was right. Immediately I felt happy about this, that I had a view of a nesting bird I had always liked. The next day Muriel told me the tire had been used for years as a nest, that she had witnessed the births of hundreds of goslings. "You should see them when they have to jump out of that nest. The poor little things land flat on the ground, then start walking behind the mother toward the lake. It's a long walk for those little goslings, but most of them make it. It just stuns me, the kind of hunger for life that nature packs into such tiny bodies."

I watched the mother on her nest every night, and sometimes during the day I'd come in from the fields where we were working on the soil, and I'd watch the big, beautiful goose covering the eggs with her own down, biting it from her own coat and adding it until she developed a painful-looking bare spot on her underside. Sometimes she'd leave the nest and come back dripping wet. I'd watch her stand over her eggs, dripping water on them, then adding more down. A few times she looked toward the window, seemed to see me. She made a honking sound that I took as a greeting, though I knew it was more likely a warning not to come closer. At night she sometimes looked toward the window so intently I believed she was trying to find me, so I finally turned on a small lamp. Ivy never woke up, and for reasons that weren't very clear to me at the time I never told her about the way I was keeping what amounted to be a kind of vigil.

But she came into the room one afternoon when I was at the window watching this goose fix more of her down over the eggs, and I looked away from the window quickly, and immediately felt resentful of Ivy's presence. I couldn't understand myself in these moments, but I knew enough not to be rude to her, knew it was my problem. So I said, "A nest of Canada geese on the roof." She walked over and stood beside me and watched the mother goose for a moment.

"I used to love watching them fly in the autumn. I'd just lay on my back and watch and listen to their honks. They sure are some loud honkers."

I was happy when Ivy left me there, alone, happy that the goose hadn't turned to look at her, though I was not obsessed with the goose, not strangely attached as it may sound. I just felt the need to have something of my own, something purely interesting that I could observe with my own eyes, and my own mind. Muriel told me it took about four weeks for the eggs to hatch, and I was happy to learn that, glad to hear that the drama of their birth would take some time.

When I stood at the window, I could see far out into the fields, where the snow still layered the ground. From the attic window, upstairs, you could see Superior. I knew that when the geese were born they'd have to learn to fly down to the lake. I was already thinking of how I could watch them learn to fly, how I could study them as they swam and dove for food.

For a while there wasn't much to see. I'd stand and make eye contact with the mother, and I wouldn't leave the window until she looked away. Sometimes she held my gaze, or so it seemed, for a long time, and I'd find myself staring beyond her out into the land, thinking back to New Orleans, probably as a way to avoid thinking back further, but as a man learns soon enough, memory never walks a straight line.

In New Orleans, I'd met a hard-working woman named Nicoletta Graves. She held down two part-time jobs, one as a graveyard shift security guard, and one as a waitress in the fine restaurant where I first saw her. I wasn't eating in that restaurant but delivering fish in the morning, which I did twice a week, and after I first caught sight of Nicoletta, on subsequent deliveries I lingered in that big kitchen, hoping she would come through the swinging door in her white uniform and meet my eyes. When she did, she smiled, and I took this as a cue to ask her how she was doing. Beg your pardon? she said, because I'd spoken too quietly. She stepped closer to me, looked up at my eyes. "How you doing?" I said again, holding steady. She said she was doing just fine, thank you, and smiled. It was not a smile that suggested she knew I was uncomfortable; I had never approached a woman this way before, mostly because I'd never had to. Her smile was easy, and her eyes unburdened.

A few weeks later, after several more of these easy smiles, I finally said to her, "What are you doing tonight?" and she said, "Tending to my kid and my nephew."

I said, "Alone, or with a man?" and stepping closer because again I was too quiet, she said, "Pardon?" "You want company?" I said, and she said, "Depends on the company." And I said, "Well, I'd like to see you again."

Again she smiled and said, "You would, would ya."

Later she told me she agreed to see me because I reminded her of her father. She was forty-two, and her father had been dead for nineteen years.

She was tending to the children alone, outside of the city in a house that looked small as a child's toy when I first drove up. It was pale pink, with a gray metal chair on the lopsided porch, and my first thought was that I'd be too tall to fit inside the place, and my second thought was that the place could be taken up into the sky by a strong wind.

I had taken three showers before driving out to her place to make certain I would not smell like fish, which tells you my intentions were to eventually seduce her. Two nights before as I laid down in bed it had dawned on me that I hadn't been with a woman in over two years. I can't say it was a physical hunger I felt so much as a fear that I was turning strange that sent me toward Nicoletta Graves without my usual hesitations.

Nicoletta answered the door in a dress, looking prettier than I'd expected, and said, "Come on in and have some wine, the kids are almost asleep." I walked in and we sat at her kitchen table in the smallest kitchen I had ever seen, small enough so that as we drank red wine I felt that we were *huddled*. I studied her as she stared out the window and said nothing, and I don't know how to say why we were both comfortable in that silence, but I remember I wanted it to last, because I could hear her breathing, and it had been a long time since I had heard anyone's breathing but my own.

She had some questions, however, which didn't surprise me. First she wanted to know why I'd picked her out. I told her I couldn't explain that, but that I imagined many men had picked her out before me. She said that was true, but she wasn't used to someone like me choosing her. At the time she wouldn't go on to explain what she meant by that. She also had the predictable curiosities: where was I from, had I been married, and if I had kids.

I have always been as wedded to truth as I believe a man can be, which is a trait that never served me well, because as most everyone knows this land of ours is built on lies; men keep jobs and wives because they're willing to lie, and all of us are supposed to agree that a little lying is what you need to keep the American peace. I never accepted that, mostly because I knew I felt unable to discern a white lie from a real lie. I felt if I started lying, I might fall into a state of confusion and never return. I'd had truthful parents, parents who never even told white lies when they were drunk, or at least they managed to give me that impression, so telling the truth was an inherited habit of mine, one I couldn't imagine breaking without effort before that night in Nicoletta's house.

I said I was from Kentucky, originally, but had lived all over. I said I had been married, and that I had never had children.

This last statement came out of my mouth as if the words had their own will. The lie floated like a black balloon in the air between us, and stayed there all night, and a few times I was tempted to throw a dart that way, but I didn't.

I can only say that I felt there was no room for the real stories of my life in that kitchen. I must have felt that if I let them escape from my heart, the room would disappear, the stories would take over, and I'd feel emptied out and incapable of seeing this woman. I'd be unable to see much of anything if I let what I had lived come into the room; even stating the facts would be too much. So I sat there with Nicoletta, and I made up a life for myself, a simple life that allowed that room and woman to exist for me, and the longer they existed, the more I knew I had needed them for a long time, needed someone like her to help dismantle my isolation.

"Always wanted some kids, but it just never happened. I was only married for a few years, then went to Korea. When I came home it was clear things were bad with my wife. That's all ancient history," I lied. Then rushed onto the truth. "Anyhow, so I've moved around a lot, worked construction, welding, worked as a fisherman like I am now, a painter, a substitute mailman. Lived in all kinds of places."

That was fine as far as she was concerned.

"I just wanted to hear ya talk a little more than you do at the restaurant," she said. "Just wanted to make sure you were normal."

We had almost finished the bottle of wine when Pie Pie Graves appeared in the doorway of the kitchen in a pair of white pajamas that looked new.

"I'm hungry," she said. She was a sturdy-looking three-year-old child. She looked at me, unsmiling but not suspicious. "Hi, Mister," she said. "Are you the plumber?"

Her mother laughed and said the plumber was coming in the morning. Pie Pie explained that their sink was clogged for a week and that it was disgusting. I told Nicoletta I could fix it, but she said no, she had too much experience with nonprofessional men saying they could fix things, she'd wait for the plumber.

Pie Pie ate some applesauce, sitting at the table in the dim light of that kitchen. She ate, and kept her eyes on me, and when I looked over, she'd look away.

"Back to bed now," said Nicoletta, and the child didn't argue. But a minute or so later she called out from her bed, "Hey Mister?"

"Sleep!" her mother said.

"Are you Italian?"

And then we were laughing together, her mother and I, and I called back that no, I wasn't Italian.

Nicoletta said, "The new woman in the day care is Italian, or so she says. She looks about as Italian as my pet frog."

"I'm Italian!" Pie Pie shouted.

"Go to sleep!" Nicoletta hissed back. "The day care lady, she's got all these tiny kids doing some ancestor project. I told Pie to tell everyone she's American all the way back, and we forgot the specifics. End of story, ya know what I'm saying? I got a black grandfather, and I don't trust people with that information unless I get a real good vibe. *Real* good. We got a lot of racists in our midst, James, in case you never noticed."

I told her I noticed. I told her I was a man who noticed a lot of things mostly because I couldn't help noticing. I told her I'd noticed way back during the Second World War, when it was all just taken for granted. I noticed how the military treated their own black soldiers like animals.

"You were in that war too?" she said. "You're older than I thought." She smiled, like the fact that I had stepped into my fifties added to my quality of harmlessness.

I did not seduce her that night; I kissed her, and tried to feel whether or not she wanted me, but I couldn't read her clearly; I felt no resistance, but no invitation, either. Because I liked her, and her house, and her girl, I decided I would wait.

Two nights later I took Nicoletta, Pie Pie, and Jack, Nicoletta's nephew, out for catfish dinners. We sat in a circular booth by a window looking out at the crowded street. Jack was a thin boy with good manners and clear, happy eyes, like a child on an old television show. He asked me if I liked being "a laborer," and said he was going to be a professional football player, they made a lot more money than "laborers," did I know that? Didn't I ever think of getting another job so I could drive a nicer car? "I never minded an old car," I told him. "But you never know, someday I might go into law, or medicine."

"Definitely," he said, "you definitely should. It's not

too late," he coached. "Never too late to go after your dreams."

"Well, thank you," I said, Nicoletta and I smiling at each other.

He was only staying with the Graves for a week, then he would go back to his mother, who had just had a new baby, Nicoletta told me. Pie Pie, hearing this, said to me, "You can sleep in Jack's bed some night when he leaves."

Again we laughed together, her mother and I, with an ease that continued to surprise me, but in the middle of that laugh something in me lurched forward toward the child in a way that was painful, and suddenly I wanted to look at her mother and say, I had a child, a girl, she was just about this age, and she died.

But I went on eating the catfish, my face hot. I was grateful when Jack started talking in detail about some linebacker on the New Orleans Saints.

During times like this I'd try not to think of Gladys, of what she was doing, of how she had gotten through. When she came into my mind, which wasn't too often anymore, it made my stomach feel knotted, and I'd had enough of that feeling. Of course when a man works specifically to block things out of his mind, they'll get bigger, stronger. So as the little boy Jack talked on, and I looked at Nicoletta, the hollow of her throat, the fine dark eyes, the rippled hair, the face of Gladys was almost superimposed there, so that I had to rub my eyes.

That night I stayed at Nicoletta's. In her bed by the window where she'd hung what could have been blackout curtains from the Second World War, it was clear to me that Nicoletta had something to tell me, and I her, and it would probably take us a long time to finish the conversation.

For over two years it was good to be with her. It was not a home, but it was company on a daily basis. I was forced to have some human interaction each day. I'm a man who can drift into solitude too easily, and I never particularly enjoyed it or knew what to do with it, other than work too hard and read books until my eyes stung and the real world blurred.

I still had my belongings in my own place, and once every so often Nicoletta and I would take Pie and spend the night in that bare apartment, Pie packing up dolls and clothes in an old-time red hatbox she used as a suitcase, acting excited like going to my place was a vacation, though all we did was play the board game *Sorry* and listen to the music from the downstairs apartment, which was live blues, and which we all loved.

Pie became attached to me, but I became more attached to her. More than I knew. I enjoyed talking with her as much as anyone. I told myself I loved her mother, but now when I think of those years I can see clearly that what connected me to that house was mostly the child. I knew as it was happening that she was somehow slipping into the space Ann had left behind, that I was turning back into a man who knew how to be a father. This should have felt like a betrayal, but it mostly felt good. I was tired of hating myself for Ann's death. I thought I'd been punished enough.

I would sit out on the steps in the humid evening while Pie Pie played with her cars and dolls in the dirt under the clothesline. She was a girl who loved dirt, who made dirt seem clean somehow. She would sit out there and talk her endless talk about all kinds of things I knew weren't true, things she got from TV and her own imagination. I knew this age well, knew how to go along and ask the right questions. These times on the steps were when I felt most at peace during those years, because the great distance between myself and that little girl, which was the same familiar distance I felt between myself and the world, was filled up with love, so that there were moments when the gap dissolved, when I'd rise from the steps and gather her up into my arms without thinking.

At night when Nicoletta slept beside me, it was not Ann I thought of, but Wendell. This surprised me, because I thought I was done with remembering him other than the times he'd flash in and out of my mind for no reason like a blinding light.

But there beside Nicoletta I wasn't remembering him as he'd been, but thinking of him as he would've been had he lived. He would've still been a young man in his prime. He would've been in love with some woman, some beautiful woman he would not yet know how to satisfy, but she would wait, she would understand that he was a man whose body could learn.

They would've had a child or two, and he would've made a good father. (I felt certain I had always known that.) He would bring his children over to see me, and I'd hold them in my lap and press my lips to the top of their heads, and each time it would surprise me again how warm the top of children's heads can be.

I would have a man to talk to, if Wendell had lived, a man I loved to talk to, a man I loved.

It was a new way of missing him, and I was both weary that I'd discovered it, and surprised that it had taken me so long.

I suppose it led to this dream.

I was living in a strange city overseas, everyone was speaking a different language, but no language I remember hearing when I was over there during the war. A tremendous feeling of homesickness overwhelmed the dream so that I felt like a boy, but clearly I was a man. I met Wendell in the street, and felt such tremendous relief I wanted to wake up, wanted to test the dream and make sure it was real. I tried to wake and couldn't, so it was real. "Let's go fishing," I said. "My son," I added. "Sure," he said, and we walked along in what felt to me like a stream of pure joy until suddenly he stopped. He turned and looked in my eyes, and in his own eyes there was a message for me. At first I couldn't read it. He began getting smaller now, shrinking, his eyes steady and looking at me. Now he stood beside me, clutching my leg. It began to rain. Then a woman came and placed him in my arms, and he was an infant, looking up into my face. His eyes had the same message, and now it was clear to me that if I couldn't read the message in his eyes, the city would be bombed. I looked into his infant face, his blue eyes. *You left me, so I died. I went to war without your love. I stumbled without your love.* And then he was dissolving, pieces of his body merging with the air, and my own hands trying to grip him, trying to stop him from leaving, until finally there was nothing but a siren, and everyone running in the streets, the sky dark.

When I woke I was drenched in sweat. I opened the black curtains to a moon and looked out the window. Nicoletta sensed something. She sat up and turned to me in the darkness and said, "You all right?"

I sat up on the side of the bed and looked out the window. I said, "A dream." I felt like any second now I'd weep, which I did not want to do.

"What dream?" She sounded irritated that she had

to be awake. I had already noticed that the slightest show of weakness on my part made her angry.

I couldn't say anything for a while, so I sat and held my head in my hands.

"What was the dream, James?" she said.

"It was . . ."

"Tell me about it."

"You go back to sleep," I said, because the irritation in her voice was more pronounced.

"No. Tell me the dream."

I said, "I had a son. I lied and told you I never had children, but I lost a son in Vietnam."

I felt her hand on my back. She began to rub my neck; she was sitting behind me, naked.

"I'm sorry," she whispered. "I'm real sorry."

But she didn't even want to know my son's name. She didn't have a single question for me, and I sat wanting to be questioned, wishing she would interrogate me. But she just rubbed my shoulders and ran her hands through my hair, and finally it seemed the dream had left my body, and we slept under the warm breezes that came in through the window, our hands entwined.

A few nights later in bed I asked her why she never had any questions for me. Why she didn't want to know about who I'd been before she knew me.

"We don't have that kind of love, James. We're not

young enough to do all that again, are we? You haven't asked me too many questions, either."

She was right. It was true it wasn't that kind of love, but it was also true that I wished that it was. I was not young, but I was young enough to hope for that possibility. I wanted to tell her, at the very least, about the dream I'd had while sleeping beside her, because in some way I felt she had brought the dream on. A part of me knew I was thinking of Wendell because I was with a woman, and it was good, and Wendell hadn't ever had a real chance with women. He had been a boy with girls, never a man with women. Never had he experienced what for me seemed like the center of life. With Nicoletta, I'd come to realize the truth of that.

I wanted to tell her about what Wendell's eyes had said in the dream. I wanted to say to her, "I thought leaving him when he was fourteen years old was not that important. I thought by then he was on his own. He hardly seemed interested in me by then. What do you think?"

So I tried to tell her this, late one night when we shared a bottle of wine in the kitchen as we had the first time I'd been to the house.

"When you were fourteen, were you a child?" I asked her.

She laughed. "When I was fourteen, I was a mother. Or could've been. I was pregnant, let's put it that way. And I was no child, James. I was a savvy little P.S. 454

bitch with my fake rhinestone ankle bracelet and pints of rot gut hidden in my bedroom." She laughed again.

"Fake rhinestone ankle bracelet," I said, in an attempt to enter her spirit of levity, but she heard it as the lie it was.

"James," she said. "Just let it go. You have a life, right? A life to live. Today. Here. Don't you? If you think for one second your son would've lived if you'd never left him, you got a mighty inflated opinion of yourself."

I looked at her. I was struck by the wisdom of her words. It made me want to go out and take a walk.

Pie's father, Nicoletta's ex-husband of ten years, was a comedian. He was onstage at a couple of clubs in the city where tourists liked to go, and he traveled often, to cities in the East and Midwest. The first two years I spent there I saw him five or six times; his career was just starting to take off, and when he came by the house he had the excited air of a man on the brink of success. He dressed in what I recognized as expensive, under-stated clothes. When he spoke to me, it was with polite restraint, and in his dark eyes I saw a kind of confusion I recognized, and maybe it was just the confusion of a man displaced.

But when I watched him talk with Pie, or play with her in the yard, I felt sorry that she felt she had to per-form in order to keep his eye. She had a whole personality she would put on just for him, a Shirley Temple kind of act where she giggled and tossed her head and spoke as if she were much younger. She had lived with him for the first two and a half years of her life, and clearly he was inscribed in her heart for good, and she would break her back trying to tell him that. I could see that he had a man's typical impatience for children, a man's typical ambitions.

As for Nicoletta, when he came around she grew tight-lipped. But when his back was turned, she studied him, and when he left she'd say things like, "That sonofabitch didn't even rinse his glass out. Am I still his maid?"

With that kind of passionate anger still inside of her, it shouldn't have surprised me when he began to come around more and more, shouldn't have surprised me when Nicoletta explained to me one morning in a coffee shop that she and him were going to give it another try.

"I have to say I'm surprised," I said.

"Well, so am I."

"Are you sure about this?"

"Yes."

I looked out the window. I couldn't feel much of anything, or make myself think.

"I still want you as a friend," she said.

But we weren't friends. We'd never been friends. We were lovers. To her credit, she reached out and put her hand on my arm and said she knew that probably wasn't possible.

But it was the thought of Pie Pie that made me unable to turn from the window to look at Nicoletta when she asked me to.

"You got a lotta stuff at the house," she finally said.

"I'll get it today."

"You can still see Pie, of course. You're like an uncle to her."

"You mean like a father," I said. "I've been like a father to her, not an uncle." I turned to look at her.

Nicoletta lowered her eyes, then looked up.

"You can see her once a week or something," she said. "Like we're divorced."

"That's right," I said. "Like we're divorced. Let's get going."

"I'm sorry," she said and began to cry. "I miss you already. I wish I could have you both."

I put my arm around her as we walked out of the diner; anyone watching would've thought I was the one who was saying good-bye.

Pie and I went and saw two movies together, and three times we went out for ice cream, and I took her to the dock where I worked just to point it out, just to give her more of myself. But driving out to that dock, I was hit with a forceful memory of Wendell. A memory of him when he was seven or eight, wanting to go watch me work down at the shipyard when I was a welder in

Delaware. I told him I'd take him someday. I drove, trying to remember if I had taken him, or if I only imagined that I had. I drove half listening to Pie, but her voice somehow became part of my memory of Wendell. I decided that I never had taken him down there. I remembered thinking it would be dangerous, and not interesting enough for him. Or was it just inconvenient for me? Who had I been to him, really?

In the car with Pie, I had a few moments that were almost like panic, because I wasn't sure about any memory I could pull up that concerned Wendell. I couldn't make myself see his face clearly, much less hear his voice. Pie talked on. I groped after one clear memory of Wendell, and in that groping broke into a sweat. And finally, when I gave up, which was like being punched, I saw Wendell as clearly as if he had suddenly appeared in the road. Wendell as a baby, not a boy.

I decided to pull into an ice cream stand and get Pie a cone. I gave her money and she went up and ordered a cone by herself, and I sat in the car, and let myself remember another life, a life when I was still a boy, a boy alone with an infant. I had been overseas, never on the front line, but I'd seen enough suffering so that I had an understanding about life that Wendell's mother did not. When she left me alone with our son, I felt almost relieved that I would no longer have to make conversation with her. I concentrated on Wendell. The other men I knew at the time were working and buying nice houses and raising families with wives who went to hair salons. Soon they were buying television sets. People I'd grown up with saw me in the market exhausted from sleeplessness and the shock of a life I'd never chosen, Wendell in my arms with his bright eyes and bald head and stained undershirts.

"You all right?" they'd ask me, but it was with suspicion in their eyes, not concern. They had never figured I'd turn out completely normal, I suppose. There were times during that first year with Wendell that all I wanted was to be someone else.

I had never known until that day in the car why it was that the loss of Wendell was in some way harder for me than the loss of Ann, even though I held myself accountable for Ann's death, even though I had not forgiven myself. It's morbid to compare the two, but I always did, in some faraway region of my heart. Maybe because he was a son, I reasoned, or because I had known him longer. But those explanations never convinced me. The reason I think his loss was harder was because he was mine, my baby. I knew what a mother knows then, not a father. It had been Wendell and me alone for the first three years of his life. He was my teacher, the child who taught me how to father. Ann was Gladys's baby. I loved Ann more deeply that I could say, but Gladys and Ann, they were the real pair. Inseparable. Which was why I allowed myself to go to sleep at the pond that day. I knew Gladys never would, because I had seen Gladys stay completely focused on Ann for three years. Another man might have blamed Gladys for this reason, but I never did. That may have been because she so badly blamed herself.

Wendell was thirteen when Ann was born; he and I spent those long days together, just the two of us, throwing the baseball, or walking in the woods. He had my love of nature, my love of peace and quiet. In the car that day was the first time I remembered that about him, his love of quiet, how he would request, "turn it down, please," when anything got too loud, how he had to leave the gymnasium at school during loud basketball games just to step outside and hear the quiet for a minute, as if he feared it would vanish, and noise would take over the world.

Pie got into the car with her cone that day, and offered me a lick. She seemed less familiar to me now, alongside the memories of Wendell. She was in first grade now. She appreciated our time together, but when I took her home, she was glad to see her father. She jumped into his arms. "Why can't you live here too?" she asked me many times. "There's room." The adults laughed good-naturedly.

I left the explaining to Nicoletta. And I left Pie a long

letter when I decided to leave New Orleans, a few months later, when I understood that she would, of course, be perfectly fine without me. I could too easily imagine her mother's voice saying *If you think she'll fall apart without you, you have a mighty inflated opinion of yourself.*

As I drove north I felt like I was driving myself out of a long dream, a long sleep. I was driving toward an idea of home, home to a camp in New York State where Gladys would be cooking a big meal or reading a book on the back stoop.

I loved a little girl almost like I loved Ann, and it tore me up again, Gladys.

And unlike Nicoletta, Gladys wouldn't say, *Just let it go.*

Would she?

But Gladys wasn't there when I pulled into town.

When she showed up, when we went to the pond, I should've told her then what I knew. I should've told her that I wasn't thinking as much about Ann as I was about Wendell. I was seeing how he'd looked that day, sixteen, dripping wet, his girlfriend by his side. I was seeing him running and diving into the water. I was hearing his voice, still in the process of changing. I was seeing his wet boy face coming out of the water, his eyes closed, then opening and asking me if I was going to come in and swim.

Maybe if I'd looked at Gladys and told her what I

was really thinking that day, she would've returned the favor. How could there be any moment of truth between us when I had withheld so much? And how could anything good come about in the absence of truth? I knew, thinking of this at that window in Muriel's house, that I needed to see Gladys again.

I watched that Canada goose day after day, then watched the goslings hatch one gray morning. They were a handsome yellow color, and bright-eyed. I watched them for nearly an hour that morning. Ivy came in and watched with me.

She hadn't noticed the distance opening up between us; at times I thought she was capable of deliberately ignoring it, that she insisted on not leaving the island of contentedness she had created for us. I had already left—if I was ever there. I felt her standing beside me, but I was far away, and whenever I looked at her, a knowledge that I'd used her would overwhelm me, so that I found it hard to say anything.

She had been my refuge. She had allowed me to figure some things out. She had made for me a warm place where I could stop and think back. Now I wanted to go back and see Gladys, not because I was interested in any kind of life with her, but because I wanted, somehow, to tell her what had happened at the pond. I wanted to explain my withholding. I wanted to tell her how I'd come to feel about Wendell, and to ask her what those years had been like for him, those years after I left, those last years of his life.

I watched the goslings line up and get ready to jump off the roof, then walked outside and followed them as they followed their mother down the pine-lined road toward the lake. I followed as if I were just another hungry goose, and before I knew it, Ivy and Muriel had joined me.

The day was blue, the sky seemed closer to the earth than usual, the sun was so brilliantly present I felt when I walked I was kicking pieces of light.

We watched the goslings enter the water. "Whee-ooo," they said. "Whee-ooo."

Ivy said she had never seen anything so sweet in all her life, and when I looked over at her face, her eyes were teary, and she wouldn't look my way. When Muriel walked down along the stony beach, Ivy said, still looking at the geese, "Don't think I don't notice we're not like we used to be, James. Don't think I'm blind, deaf, and dumb just because I know how to stay cheerful."

"I'm sorry," I said. "If I hurt you, I'm sorry."

"You hurt me," she said. "But I expected it all along. Part of why I came here with you was to push us into the future so we could lose each other. Because I knew it had to happen. I think it's probably time you took me back home."

She looked over at me finally, and smiled, and I wanted to change my mind about her, almost did change my mind, almost said, No, Ivy, I'll come back to you, I'll come back to that world we had for a while.

But I didn't have the ability to return, and I knew it. We stood and waited for Muriel, then the three of us headed back down the road.

By the time we packed up our car the goslings still couldn't fly. Both Ivy and I felt an urgency about leaving.

"I wasn't lonely before you got here," Muriel said. "But you can best believe I will be when you leave."

"I'll come back and visit you," Ivy said.

"You'll both be back," Muriel said. "You won't be able to stay away." She smiled, and we got into the car. Ivy rolled down her window, and the two of them had their last conversation.

"You remember what I told you," Muriel said to her.

"I will."

"You remember that every day," Muriel added.

I didn't ask what Muriel meant. I didn't have the right. I drove off, with Ivy waving out the window until Muriel was out of sight.

Ivy was quiet for hours. The land rushed by us, and a kind of bravery returned to me, a kind of optimism that I can't help but feel when I'm on the road in a car, as if all the motion, which has always seemed to me like an illustration of how time flies, all that knowledge of the shortness of our time on earth just weeds out every-thing complicated in a man, weeds a man's soul until what's left is something simple and good. Because time was short, I drove with hope for everyone I knew, even as I knew the source of that hope would disappear when I stopped the car, when the world and time slowed down, became what it was.

Ivy was asleep, and didn't wake up until I stopped for gas.

She looked at me, got out of the car, went inside to the rest stop, and returned with popcorn, which she sat between us on the front seat. We were careful to avoid each other's hands now.

When I asked Ivy why she was so quiet, she said she had nothing to say. That was the moment when I recog-nized the loss of her, a necessary loss but not an easy one for me, either.

It was late at night when we got to Gladys's, but a light was on. We sat in the car for a moment, and I wanted to say something to her as we looked at that light in the window.

"Ivy," I said, "thank you."

She didn't say anything at first. She waited a while, then got out of the car, then just as quickly got back into the car.

"That's a terrible thing to say," she said.

"I'm sorry, I didn't mean it that way."

"Don't thank me for loving you, James. A person can't help who they love, and you should know that by now. A person is absolutely *helpless* when it comes to who they love."

She got out of the car again, gently closed the door, and walked toward the house.

Ivy

Good Night, Children

I SAW THE END OF ME AND JAMES COMING AT ME ALL ALONG, just coming right down the road like truth in a truck, rattling closer and closer until it stopped at my feet, and then everything under those cold blue skies got real quiet up there. Even though the early birds of spring were whooping it up in the tops of pine trees and waking me at four in the morning, it always seemed quiet. There must be a certain quiet that comes into a person's world right before someone they love is about to say good-bye.

I knew days before James said anything that our love was over, because I could feel how he wasn't really in his hands anymore when he touched me. It was like he somehow found a way to keep himself out of his hands, so that they were like the reluctant hands of a stranger, and yet even as I knew that, they were also the same hands I loved, with their hard, lined knuckles, their short, clean nails, their thick-skinned palms. I liked being touched anyway, even if his spirit was elsewhere, so even though I knew it was over, I couldn't bring myself to say a word. When he kissed me one cold night in his flannel-lined coat down by the lake I thought, *This is the last kiss, drink it in*, and every time he touched me that week, whether it was accidental in the kitchen when his arm brushed mine to reach for butter, or on purpose in the bedroom when he ran his hand through my hair I'd think, *This is the last touch*. I'd try to memorize the way it all felt, because I was afraid he'd be the final lover in my life, maybe because I wanted him to be.

Then he went and got all involved with a pregnant Canada goose that was out there on the roof at Muriel's. It came to me one day that I couldn't compete with that goose, and if a woman can't compete with a goose, well, I'd call that a problem too big to fix.

It was a sad ride back home, sad, dark, and quiet, and when he dropped me off I asked him not to come in, and he agreed to see Gladys some other time and I was grateful because it would've been more than a little awkward with me, James, and Gladys sitting in that kitchen. When I got out of his car I took my shoes off and stood on the grass and felt the cool earth on my bare toes while he backed away. I'd been wanting to take my shoes off the whole time I was in that car, but somehow it seemed like a personal thing to do, another thing I wouldn't do anymore with James, so I kept them on. My feet felt good that night in the cold dark grass, and since they were the only part of me that felt good, I tried my best to concentrate on them while he left.

When he beeped a small good-bye it was like the sound of the horn was a hot coal in my throat, but I looked up at the moon and said to myself, "You will be fine." And I walked across the cool grass and smelled the spring and then out of nowhere, I found myself whistling the song "That's the Night That the Lights Went Out in Georgia," a song I hadn't even thought of in over five years, and when I raked my mind I couldn't come up with one reason why such a tune came to me in that moment, but I kept on whistling. I didn't want to face Gladys, because I felt like a failure and I knew I was right where she'd expected me to land. Another part of me wanted to face her and get everything out in the open.

I walked into the house, feeling the oddness of being there but still whistling and the kitchen was empty and orderly, with the clock ticking and the old foreign dolls that Louis had sent me lined up on the shelf. I went and picked each of the dolls up, one at a time, then put them back. "Hello, Gladys?" I said to the empty living room. I flicked on the light. The couch and chairs were exactly where they always had been, but for a second they looked littler to me, and the one blue chair that I always thought of as Gladys's chair looked worn out and faded like a five-dollar item in a garage sale, and I wondered why I never noticed before. Beside the chair was a biography of Harry Truman and on top of that book a white rock. The rest of the room looked pretty much as usual only on the table near the window was this little statue of a boy with a bluebird on his shoulder, something I knew had to be a gift because Gladys weren't a knick-knacker and never would be. I'm by nature a knick-knacker, but Gladys never did permit me displaying my items. Years back we went through a time where I'd try every so often to set out some cute little china statues of dogs I collected, and she'd try to live with them for a few days, then she'd end up saying, "Ivy, about those dogs?" and that was my signal, I knew they were driving her crazy, so I'd box them up and try again a few months later, but she never changed.

I went and picked up the statue of the bluebird boy and looked out the window, like maybe Gladys would be marching toward the house out there in the dark, but all I saw was the moonlit air, and the black trees in the distance on the far hill, and then my heart started pounding because I hadn't checked the bedroom yet and somehow I started thinking Gladys might be sick. I hadn't even talked to her for months. I actually even thought she might be dead to tell you the truth, and I can't explain why I got that feeling, but it made my hands and face go cold and my heart pound and as I walked to the bedroom door I didn't breathe. First I knocked. Then I opened the door and the first thing I see in that dark was the wind puffing out the white curtains, new white curtains I noticed, I could tell they were whiter and nicer than the old ones even in the dark. The rest of the room was completely the same as far as I could tell, and when I flicked on the light and saw how much things hadn't changed I felt both relieved and disappointed. And I looked at my old twin bed and something twisted in my heart. Because I'd be going back to being a person in a twin bed, after so many nights in a double. And then I looked at Gladys's bed and imagined her sleeping here all these nights alone, and I wondered about what state she'd be in.

I put some things in the closet, undressed, showered, and got into bed. It was the loneliest, strangest sort of feeling, to be in a single bed again, just myself, waiting for my sister and not knowing what she would say when she saw me. I waited and thought of Gladys but also my mind was still on James. James was in my mind, stuck there no matter how many other things I thought.

I laid under the sheets with my eyes closed and soon enough my head started to feel like it was stretching out behind me like a road, and James was driving and driving and driving, and my head was getting longer and longer and longer, and I felt there was no end to what shape your head could take when a man was driving in it. I tried to imagine him stopping the car so the road could end and I could drift to sleep, but it didn't work, he just kept on going with the windows down and the spring night blowing in his hair. So I sat up in bed and looked through the curtains into the starry sky and shook my head until I finally got that road out of my mind, and laid back down with a normal-shaped head. Still I could smell his body, and see his hands on the wheel, but gradually it all faded and for a minute or so all I saw was the room I was in, the curtains, the moonlight, the nightstand between the two beds, the sheets, and the mirror on the back of the bathroom door like silver.

Then I had about an hour of just lying there in that bed, with my thoughts drifting way back into my childhood, way back to my mother, who would walk down the hall and come into our first-floor room at night when she thought we were asleep. I remembered how she'd stand and just watch us for a few minutes, her two little girls sleeping, and I'd be awake and wondering what she was thinking as she watched her sleepers, and I always had the feeling she was praying for us, just praying that we'd be happy in our lives, happier than her, that we'd find love and happiness as we grew and turned into women. And when I was about eight she'd still do this and I'd feel her own unhappiness, or sadness, but I never really thought about it much, never really asked myself why she seemed sad. It was just the way she was, a sweet but sad type of woman, with big dark eyes, married to a man who hardly ever spoke a word to her, and now here I was, a grown-up woman nearing fifty all the sudden missing her more than I ever had since she died years ago. Because I thought if she was alive I would call her on the phone and tell her I was heartbroken and she wouldn't say, "Serves ya right for runnin' around with your sister's man." She would say, "Oh, Ivy."

She would listen, and she would say, "I'm sorry." And she wouldn't know what else to say, and she was always a woman who just said nothing unless she knew exactly what to say, and she hardly ever did. So I'd just fill in the silence on that telephone and tell her not to worry, I'd be all right, and then we'd hang up. But since she was dead of course I couldn't make that call, so I just lay with my eyes closed and started feeling like she was in the room, like I was a child again pretending to be asleep and she was in the room watching me and thinking, Let her be happy. Let her turn out a happy woman. Let her have a good life, Lord.

I had the oddest sense that my whole life was stretched out in front of me for me to live.

That was when I heard the kitchen door squeak open, slam shut, and the old, familiar, solid footsteps of Gladys head toward the bedroom, while my heart pounded in my ears.

"Gladys?" I called out, to warn her.

I heard her footsteps stop.

"It's Ivy." I sat up in my bed.

She wasn't moving, and she didn't say hello. Not for a minute or so. I didn't say anything either. We just felt each other in the house, and I tried to slow down my pounding heart. She seemed to be rifling through some papers or a book out there, and I heard her clear her throat.

Finally she came back to the bedroom and stood in the doorway and looked at me.

"So. When did you get here?"

"Just a while ago."

"Where's James?"

"He dropped me off."

"He dropped you off?"

"Yes."

She went and sat on her bed, took off her Cuban-heeled black shoes. She wore a blue dress with three-quarter-length sleeves that I'd never seen before. It weren't her style, it was one of those baggy dresses with a real low waist and some kind of black embroidery around the hem which I can't say was fancy or pretty. It actually scared me for a second because I thought it meant she lost all her good taste, and if she lost her good taste, what else did she lose?

"This old girl had a blind date tonight," Gladys said. "With a man who installed us a new industrial dishwasher."

"Was it a nice time?" My heart was still pounding. Her voice sounded flattened out to me.

"I don't know. Is listening to someone talk about industrial dishwashers for three hours a nice time?"

"I'd guess not."

"The fella took me to his apartment," Gladys said. "Showed me his collection of empty cough syrup bottles."

"Empty cough syrup bottles?"

"He's got over eight hundred."

"Does he fill them up with colored water?"

"No."

"Little stones?"

"No."

"Does he decorate the outsides or something like that?"

"No, Ivy. Stop hoping it's normal. It's not normal to have over eight hundred empty cough syrup bottles. Why the hell would you think that was normal for one second?"

"Sorry."

Of course I didn't think it was normal, I was just trying to fill up the air in that room with something other than the strangeness I was feeling.

"So did you have a good time in Canada?" she said, but I could hear something in her voice that made me feel cold. "Did you have a real good time?"

"I'm sorry" just spilled right out of my mouth.

"Are you? What are you sorry for?"

"I'm sorry if I hurt you."

She shook her head, then gave me a kind of laugh, or chuckle, one of those unreadable chuckles she gave me all her life, then said she was tired and went into the bathroom. When she came out she was in a nightgown and her hair was brushed and she didn't say a word. She got into bed and turned away from me.

"Gladys?"

"Ivy, I'm tired."

"I was going to say I'm real glad to see you."

"Okay."

I lay awake half that night, and wished I could whisper over to Gladys, I was thinkin' of Mama, and how she'd come in and watch us sleep, and it made me miss her. But soon even when I tried to think of my mother, I couldn't. I couldn't see anything but a pair of her old blue sneakers she would set by the door in the kitchen. And remembering my actions with James seemed to pin me down on the bed so I couldn't really move at all.

I lay there trying to figure out why I'd been with James when deep inside me the whole time I knew that Gladys loved him and always would. Or did I know that? Maybe it only seems that way now, looking back. Maybe at the time I didn't know if Gladys really cared all that much. The problem is, I don't really know. So I couldn't sleep.

*   *   *

The next morning Gladys had these sad-looking red sneakers on her feet, the kind you buy from those big bins at the supermarket and then never wear, hopefully. She wore a pair of white shorts and a shirt with a flower print. She had dyed her hair darker and her face was made up like I'd never seen it before, with mascara and smoky eye shadow and dark pink lips, and she had her old cat-eyed glasses on that I hadn't seen in years. She looked all right, she had nice legs and everything, but actually she also looked a few bricks short. I don't know why she was in those 1950s glasses, and I don't know why her hair was so dark, but she thought she looked good.

"The worse you feel, the better you need to look," she said when she caught me staring at the breakfast table. Then she winked and laughed.

"So you better go talk to Brent Quinn, Ivy. You might not have a job anymore. You were gone longer than Brent thought you'd be. Hell, you better go talk to him now."

I didn't know why she said that, because we both knew Brent was absolutely not the firing sort, not just because he was nice and liked the two of us, not even because he had one of these big hearts that just forgives every human foible, but because he was lazy and wouldn't want to go through the trouble of firing someone, he'd just rather shuffle us around, put me back in the garden or something.

I went to see Brent that night. His cabin was filled with the purplish light of a spring evening, and jars of wildflowers all over the place. He was in his pajamas as he often was, only he had work boots on instead of bare feet or slippers. He said, "Hello there, mystery woman." He poured me beer in a big mug that was all frosted up from being in his freezer. We sat at his table and he didn't turn any lights on because his whole house ran on solar energy and golf cart batteries. So his white hair looked like it glowed in the dark.

As it turned out, he wanted me back in the kitchen with Gladys and Nadine because he said there would be more campers this year, but I got the feeling Brent really just wanted me back in the kitchen so Gladys and I would work side by side because he liked the idea of that, he told me a long time ago that he had a brother he hardly ever spoke to because they'd had a terrible falling out years ago, and every time he saw me and Gladys together he envied us and admired us. Well, I felt like saying to him that night in his cabin, "Brent, you can stop your admiring now." Because I could feel how things with me and Gladys weren't the same, and maybe never could be.

So there I was, back in the kitchen with the new dishwasher that didn't make much noise like the old one, and Nadine the bird woman who started wearing all

kinds of gypsy jewelry and smiled too wide whenever I
looked at her, and Gladys in her cat-eyed glasses, who
bit down on her lower lip and hardly said a word. We
weren't exactly three happy clams on the half shell. But
we were busy, it was orientation week for the new summer counselors, and we were supposed to cook our best
meals for these kids so they'd look forward to coming
back up for three and a half months. Things like blueberry pancakes with whip cream, pizza on prebaked
shells, melted cheese on their baked potatoes at night.
I'd cook and whistle and try not to think, but I could feel
something, even with the oven blasting out its heat,
something I didn't have words for, and maybe all it was
was Gladys. I could feel Gladys. And she didn't much
feel like the old Gladys to me.

"You should come with Gladys and me bird-watchin'
sometime," Nadine said.

"Gladys and you go bird-watchin'?" I said. I looked
at Gladys, trying to picture her with binoculars and
rolled-up pants.

"What the hell is so surprising about that?" Gladys
snapped out at me all the sudden. It was the strangest
thing, and I just stared at her for a few seconds.

"Nothing," I said. "I just . . . "

"You think I wouldn't be the sort to like birds."

"No, I don't think that."

Gladys looked at me and I couldn't read her expression.

"Ivy," Nadine said, "why don't you come with us this

evening? We'll be looking for the red-winged blackbirds this evening. They're just stunning, aren't they Gladys?"

"Stunning little buggers," Gladys said, nodding.

So that evening I walked through the woods with Gladys over to see Nadine, and I was feeling happier because Gladys was acting more normal, more like herself, and telling me a story about Nadine's crazy sister.

"Her name's Carmella but they just call her Mel. Isn't that cute? So Carmella's got these damn twins. She hauls them up from Camden, New Jersey, to see Nadine for Easter time. Well, here's what happened. Mel is just driving along. Driving along in her banged-up Futura. One of the twins looks up ahead and sees a little rabbit. A little brown rabbit by the side of the road. This little twin is named Leanne, by the way. Leanne and Stan are the twins' names. 'Look at the cute rabbit,' Leanne says. So her mother says, 'Honey, I think that's the Easter bunny!' She drives another few seconds. 'Why, it *is* the Easter bunny!' So the twins get excited and start bouncing up and down. 'The Easter bunny! Mommy can we stop! Can we stop and see the Easter bunny?' Well, the rabbit darts right out into the road. Poor Mel just slams on those brakes. But it was too late. She kills the damn thing. So now she's got little Leanne and Stan crying with red faces and tears. They're saying, 'Mommy killed the Easter bunny, Mommy killed the Easter bunny.' They cried and chanted for miles. Mel said they must've said it two hundred times. She said she was ready to stop the car and kill them too."

I laughed at that story, laughed until my eyes teared, mostly because I was grateful for my sister's company as we walked through the woods, grateful to hear the tone of her old voice, and grateful to hear her laugh.

"Carmella tried to tell me the story like she thought it was a sad story," Gladys said. "Like her kids would be scarred. But I started laughing. So she started laughing too. She said I had what she'd call a sick sense of humor."

"I don't think so."

"I don't either. You could just tell it was the kind of thing that always happened to Carmella. You could tell by looking at her. She might as well have been voted 'most likely to kill the Easter bunny in front of her children' back in high school."

I laughed, and then I smiled over at Gladys. I thought maybe it would be a nice moment and she'd smile back, but she just got an odd look on her face and the green in her eyes got darker. They got about as dark as the pine trees in Canada, I thought to myself.

Nadine and Gladys and I took turns with binoculars down by the river, spotting red-winged blackbirds. I had a nice enough time, but every time my sister spoke she looked at Nadine, and not at me, so I began to feel terrible. We all walked back up to the old blue house about eight at night.

Nadine wanted us all to sit on her back porch and listen to the wind in the chimes and drink some beer, but I just thanked her for the bird-watching and said I'd go on home, and I did, I went on home.

Between breakfast and lunch the next day after Nadine went home I followed Gladys out of the kitchen, all the way back to our house. About ten feet from the door leading into the kitchen I finally said, "Gladys? Did you know I was following you?"

"Yes," she said, and walked inside. And I followed her into the kitchen. It was half in shadow, half lit up by the morning sun. I said, "Gladys, I'm worried about you. I'm just nervous you're not doing so well. I can't tell where you are, how you're doing."

"Fine. I'm fine."

"What I mean is, I can't tell if you hate me or if you're just sad."

"Well, I can't tell either," she said, running the water at the sink.

"Don't hate me, Gladys," I said. "James doesn't even love me. We're over." I waited, holding my breath after I said this, and she waited before she said anything. She kept her back to me, kept on running the water over her hands.

"I don't hate you, Ivy. I'm too tired to hate people."

"What is it, Gladys?"

"Ivy, you wouldn't understand. You're a different person."

"How do you know I wouldn't understand?"

"Ivy, I don't have the words. All you need to do is let me be."

"No, I can't. I can't because I feel guilty as Adam's house cat. I think I did a wrong thing, Gladys, and I don't know why but I need to make it up to you."

"This isn't about you, Ivy. I can tell you that."

"Well, Gladys, why don't you do yourself a favor and talk to me!" I was getting upset, my voice was rising, and tears were in my eyes now. "Just talk to me instead of keeping me shut out of your whole life! You don't even turn around to look at me."

I have to say a part of me was in a state of shock that all this was coming out of my mouth.

Gladys sat down at the table.

"I feel confused," she said. And the second after she said that she said, "And now I feel angry as hell because I said 'I feel confused.' That sounds like the biggest goddamned understatement I ever came out with, goddamnit."

She got up from the table.

"You gotta start somewhere," I said to her, and winced because I was figuring she'd turn around and scream at me, but she didn't.

She walked away from me, through the living room and into the bedroom. She closed her bedroom door.

Any other time I would've just walked out of that house and let my sister alone, but something just pushed me toward the bedroom door and had me knocking before I knew it, and had me opening the door and saying, "What's wrong? If you want James back don't worry because he's going to visit you. He told me. He wants to see you. He'll be back, Gladys. I bet he still loves you."

It didn't feel too good saying that. It felt terrible, and I felt a burst of warmth come into my face, and I figured it was the truth I'd blurted out.

She was sitting on her bed with her back to me, looking out the window and taking a deep breath while I said what I said.

"I'm not a little girl on a television soap opera, Ivy. Don't talk to me if all you know how to come out with is horseshit."

"I'm not saying horseshit, I'm just trying to find out what your problem is. You just waste your life like this! You just waste your whole precious life!"

Then, real quiet, Gladys says, "Bingo."

I don't say anything. So she says, "I wasted my life. That might be what's ailing me." She turned around to me, and for a second her face looked like someone else's face, some stranger's face you see in the street and think, What happened to that poor soul?

"Maybe you wasted your life too," she said to me, and then she smiled.

And in my head a voice was saying, "Certainly did. We all do. You could look at it that way, couldn't you."

But to Gladys I said, "I didn't waste my life. And neither did you."

"You wasted your life pretending you were happy," she said.

"I am happy."

"Horseshit, Ivy."

"I am happy!"

"Ivy, what in the goddamn world do you got to be happy about?"

And a voice in my head was saying, *Not much, not much.* But another voice was saying *No. Don't be like her. Be yourself! Be Ivy. You are Ivy.*

"I got a lot to be happy about! I got people I love, I got a good job, I got a good home, and I got my health. I got a nice son who visits a few times a year. I'm not starving out in Africa and I'm not dying of leukemia. I count my blessings, Gladys! All you do is look at the bad side of things!"

"So when's your nice son coming to visit?" she said. She stared at me like she was putting holes in my head.

"I don't know, sometime in July he usually comes."

"You don't know what the hell it is to lose a nice son, do you, Ivy?"

"No, I don't."

"Do you know what the hell it is to feel your life go down the drain when you lose a nice daughter, Ivy?"

"No, I don't. But if I did lose one, if I did lose one, I wouldn't waste the rest of my life over it licking my wound."

My face turned bright red. I could feel it. I was saying something without thinking about it, but as I said it, I realized I'd thought it all along, and I was glad I finally said it.

"Get out."

"I can't."

"I said get the hell out of this room."

"I can't. I can't move." It was true, I couldn't. I felt like my sneakers were glued to the floor.

A long silence fell. I just stared at her back and tried to pick one of my feet up off the floor, but I couldn't. Something shifted in the room when Gladys sighed.

I said, "You can't just go on and on and never get over it."

"I can't?"

"Well, maybe you can. Maybe you can. If that's your choice."

Then I left the room.

Next thing I knew things got worse. Gladys with her face dark red and her green eyes on fire came out of her room yelling at me, "Just because you ran off and had a love affair with my husband doesn't mean you got the goddamn answers to my life!"

"He's your ex-husband!"

"What the hell difference does that make? You think

you got all the answers now. You think you can march back in here and tell me I wasted my life! Maybe I got reasons for how I live. Maybe I think about that. Maybe I'd rather live by my losses, Ivy. You want me to whistle through this goddamn shithouse of a life? Would that suit you?"

"He was your ex-husband and he came here for you and you weren't even here! You left me first! You got on that bus with an oddball little girl and went way the hell across the country and couldn't have cared less that you left me behind. You didn't even miss me and didn't care if I missed you, and when I told you James was here you didn't even say you'd like to talk to him! You acted like you didn't give a damn about the man, and I did. I do. I care about him! I got ways of showing I care! And I loved Wendell and Ann too! Maybe not like you did, but I loved them both!"

Gladys just kept looking out the window.

I didn't say anything, I just stood there, feeling how everything between us was different now. A terrible feeling came into my stomach, and I missed us, I missed the old Gladys and Ivy, where Gladys was strong and somehow kept to herself and Ivy tried to cheer her up and never crossed the line. I wanted to take back everything I said to her and just start acting like the old Ivy, but I really wasn't the old Ivy anymore. I was shaking.

"Ivy, can you stand here and tell me you really thought I didn't care about James anymore?"

I couldn't.

"I want you to know something, Ivy. This is not about James. We're talking like it's all about James. What it's really about is something bigger. It's about my life, Ivy. My whole life. And yours. And as far as I'm concerned, you went off with James because it was your chance to get back at me for being our father's favorite."

"What?"

First thing I'm thinking is, Gladys, you finally lost your last marbles. Then I'm thinking, Does she have a little point?

"You felt left out your whole life because he loved me. And didn't give a cow's last shit about you."

"Don't tell me that. I didn't feel left out."

"Oh yes you did. That's why you had to turn on the cheer. A welcome wagon lady. You had to whistle and smile so you wouldn't know how left out you felt. I know how you felt. Like you're not worth a cow's last shit."

"Maybe that's how you felt," I said, talking real quiet now, because it was like she punched me hard with something and I didn't yet know how I felt. "Maybe you felt like that because he made you into his little wife. That's not exactly the right thing to do, Gladys. If you had a nine-year-old girl would you buy her fifteen aprons and make her cook you dinner every night?"

She didn't say anything for a long time, and I knew why. I knew she was sitting there thinking, *If I had a nine-year-old girl, if I had a nine-year-old girl.* But I didn't respect that feeling of hers just then. I didn't feel like just saying nothing anymore and I didn't feel like walking away, and I didn't feel like going way back into the past where our father made some oddball decisions, because that time was over and I don't care if I was loved or unloved in that time, it was gone, and it always would be gone, and I said as much to Gladys. And then I said she ought to try to see things different, she ought to try to appreciate what she does have instead of mourning her whole life away. I even told her in the old days people lost dozens of children and they just picked their feet up and went on, including our great-grandmother, whose picture used to hang in our bedroom in a big frame and scare us at night until Gladys begged our father to put her in the basement.

"All those people might have lost their children, Ivy, but they didn't kill their children. They didn't turn their backs and let their children drown."

"You made a mistake!" I said, and all the sudden I started crying when I said that. "Can't you understand you made a human mistake?"

Gladys looked down at her hands in her lap and wouldn't look at me, and I kept crying and wishing she would cry too, wishing she would come over to my arms, but she didn't move.

She said, "If someone else let her drown, I'd never forgive them. Why should I forgive myself?"

I sat there for a while. I looked at her. She had her

head bent down and her eyes closed. I said, "Because that's all you got, Gladys."

And then she didn't say a word, and we had to gather ourselves together to go back to work. It was a relief to be in the kitchen with a big supper to prepare, to go through the motions of shelling beans and stirring sauces and mashing potatoes and chopping carrots and onions. After that, we got out the rolling pins for pies. "You two sure are quiet today," Nadine said. And we were quiet like that for days before the ice broke.

The children from the winter school were going home now, and the summer campers and counselors would arrive soon. The last night the winter school kids ate in the dining room their teachers told them to sing "For they are jolly good ladies" to the familiar tune of "For he's a jolly good fella." We were in the kitchen still refilling the bowls of food, and we didn't even think much about the kids' singing. They sang a lot of songs. But then we started hearing our names, "For Gladys's a jolly good lady! Which nobody can deny!" "For Ivy's a jolly good lady! Which nobody can deny!" "For Nadine's a jolly good lady! Which nobody can deny!"

Well, we felt like we should open the wooden shutter that closed our view to the dining room so we could thank the children for their song, so we did, we rolled up the shutter.

One of the teachers started them off clapping, and we stood there looking at them. They looked like nice little kids, and a few even put their heart into the song, and two little girls were waving at Gladys. Then Gladys took a bow. So I took a bow and Nadine took one too. Then Gladys took about ten more little tiny bows, and I watched her and started laughing, and she started laughing too, and the kids kept clapping and then they sang another round of their song, and Gladys spread her arms out wide and took a more dramatic bow and said "thank you thank you thank you" the way Ed Sullivan used to, and Nadine and I just bowed right along with her.

Afterward we pulled the shutter back down and Gladys shook her head and said, "It's hard being a star, ain't it girls? Now let's be jolly good ladies and clean these damn pots so we can go the hell home."

We stepped out the back door of the kitchen into the evening of bright stars and moon in a dusky pink sky, and I thought we'd just walk down the hill and up the hill back to our house as usual, but Gladys was real quiet with a small smile on her lips and then right out of the clear blue she started singing. She started off in a real quiet voice. "For I'm a jolly good lady, for I'm a jolly good lady, for I'm a jolly good lady! Which nobody can deny!" She started singing it louder, then real loud, and she swung her arms, and I thought she was either going crazy or getting better, it was hard to tell. She just sang and sang and marched with her swinging arms and from the distance we heard Brent Quinn yell "Encore!" when she stopped. So she sang another round, and then one of the teachers yelled from her shack in the woods, "Again!" and she sang it again, and then decided she would march all over the flat field behind the dining hall, so I kept walking with her, sort've running almost because she was going fast, and when I said, "Where are we going?" for an answer she just sang louder, "Which nobody can deny!" Soon a bunch of kids were racing toward us and following us like Gladys was the pied piper, and they were laughing at her or with her, I wasn't sure, but they kept following and she kept marching and singing, and walking down the path through the dusky woods. A little girl with a wayward eye walked right beside her, looking up at her the whole time like Gladys was her hero. In the woods the kids started singing along with her. "For she's a jolly good lady," some of them sang, while others sang, "For I'm a jolly good girl," and some boys sang, "For I'm a jolly good fella," and some wiseacre kid named Tony Ramoni sang, "For I'm a jolly good asshole!" which inspired a few cronies to join in, and all the different voices and words were bumping around in the dark and sounding so good I wanted it to keep going and never stop even though a part of me was afraid Gladys was about to walk off the deep end.

But she didn't, she just walked around that way for a while, back out of the woods and into the flat field and down the hill, then suddenly stopped so all the kids slammed on their brakes behind her and she turned around and started walking, this time real quiet, so we could hear the kids' teachers ringing bells and blowing whistles. I just followed Gladys, and so did the kids, and they were whispering, "What's she doin'? Where we goin'? How come she's so quiet?" But they kept on her trail up the hill, and followed her right to our house, just ignoring the bells and whistles, and for a second I thought Gladys would invite them all in for a party, but she just stood on the stoop like the queen of England and looked out at her followers and said, "Good night, children." And then she went inside.

They ran off laughing and singing and I went inside and found Gladys in the living room in her blue chair opening her Harry Truman book like nothing had happened.

"Well," I said, standing near the couch. "That was something else!"

"Oh yes," she said, not looking up from her book. "It sure was."

"That was what I call a lot of fun."

She still didn't look up from her book.

"Those kids, they loved it."

She just kept on reading, and I said good night, and she said good night, and I went into my room and laid on the bed and smiled.

*   *   *

She was pretty much back to normal the next day and didn't want to talk about her pied piper night, so I dropped the subject. Some kids hung out of bus windows yelling to her as we walked to the dining room, and she gave a brief wave and kept walking and I understood she was embarrassed about it all. She was glad those kids were going home and a new batch was coming, and glad to be in the kitchen with Nadine, working.

One night she was up at Brent Quinn's drinking some beer with him, which weren't usual, and I was alone in the living room trying to get interested in the Harry Truman book when I heard a car pull up. I was still in the stage where every time I heard a phone ring or a car pull up I thought *James?* and so I went to the screen door and stood looking out into the darkness, and I could sense it was him even before my eyes adjusted to the night. He walked his long-legged easy walk toward the door and I stepped back and let him in and he said, "Ivy, hello," and bent down and kissed my cheek. He was clean shaven, in jeans and a blue work shirt, and his eyes looked bluer and he seemed taller and I wanted to stop looking at him so I opened the refrigerator and said, "Are you hungry?" He said, "I just ate a while ago." I said, "Well, how've you been these weeks?" He said, "I picked up some work a few town's over. They're putting up a new motel."

I told him to have a seat at the table, and I sat down across from him and was disappointed to feel myself heartbroken again, and I had an urge to stoop to a very low level, I had an urge to go over to him and pull on his sleeve and say, James, just come back to me for one night, just tonight let's go off somewhere, and that's all I'll ever ask you in this world. Instead I kept my bearings and talked to him about his construction work on a new motel, and when he said, "My body's getting too old for this kind of work," I felt a twinge of pleasure or relief at that, but it didn't last long.

"I thought I should wait a while before coming around, Ivy," he said. The clock ticked. That kitchen could be so quiet. I wanted Gladys to come home and I wanted her never to come home.

"Well, I appreciate that," I said, real quiet. "Gladys will be glad to see you."

"Well, I came to talk to her but I also came to talk to you."

I raised my eyes to his face and waited for what he'd say.

"I know you said not to thank you. I understand why you said it too. But you helped me a lot, Ivy. You helped me more than you'll ever know."

"Why? Why did I help you? How?" I noticed my tone was harder than I wanted it to be.

"That's hard to put into words. But when I was with you, I had room to think. I had room to figure things out. You gave me a kind of shelter. Nobody else gave me what you gave me, Ivy, and I wanted to tell you that. I wanted to tell you I'd always remember it."

"Is that right?" I said. "Well, so will I."

Again my tone wasn't what I wanted it to be. I just sat and looked at him, and he looked away.

"Ivy, I know I used you."

"Used me? Is that what it's called?"

"I'm sorry. I wanted to say I'm sorry. I wanted you to see that I never meant to hurt you. I'm just sorry."

I could see he was feeling bad, and my heart softened up a bit. I said, "Thanks, James, for saying that."

And then between us a little bit of ease set in, and I started telling him about working with Gladys and Nadine, and how Gladys liked birds now. He told me about a man he worked with who used to be a millionaire and lost all his money in the stock market. I got him a glass of water and put out a bowl of chips on the table. I told him Gladys was up at Brent's cabin and might not be home for a while, and if he wanted I'd go on up there and bring her back to the house. He said, "Why don't we both go on up?" Maybe he was curious to see who Brent was, maybe he was thinking Brent was Gladys's lover. I just let him go on thinking whatever he was thinking, and we took ourselves a walk in the dark and I didn't much care for that walk, that space between our bodies that felt like it was marked by a fence that would shock me if I tried to touch it.

At Brent's we stood and looked through the window and saw they were having a little party that consisted of Brent, Gladys, an old man I didn't know who was probably a townie, a pretty young woman named Sylvia Micheski who taught pottery in the summer, and a real old black woman named Minna Kates, who'd been hired as a storyteller for years, and who was sound asleep now sitting up straight in one of Brent's old armchairs with a smile on her lips.

"Well, let's go knock on the door around the side," I said, and James said, "Why don't you, and I'll stand back here."

So I guess James stood at the window and watched me step into the party and watched everyone say, "Ivy!" "Hey Ivy!" and watched Gladys say, "Little lambsy Ivy!" She was drunk, I could see, but looked nice in a simple green dress and bare feet because she'd taken off her sneakers, and she was wearing her wire frames instead of the old glasses. I sat next to her on the couch and said, "Gladys, James is here. He's outside right now."

And she said, "What?" And I said it again. She stood up and excused herself, said she'd be right back.

About five minutes later she pops back in and thanks Brent for a nice evening, and then she's gone. And I'm there at the party. And I started to drink. I drank and drank and drank that night. I drank like I never drank before. And in the morning, when I woke up in Brent Quinn's bed, I didn't know what had happened.

Brent wasn't beside me. Maybe he'd just given me his bed. It was a pretty room, so pretty I had to take a moment just to look around. He had paintings hanging, including a pretty one of a woman in a bathtub with a dog on a mat beside her, and another one of a laughing old man in a café, and another one of the ocean, and all of them were in old frames, and the shutters were half open so the light streamed in, and on his bed was a handmade quilt of every color, and on the sills were jars of flowers and little statues, and I'm just looking around thinking, This is certainly one way to live, when Brent appears in the doorway holding a tall glass of fresh squeezed orange juice.

"I bet you feel about as good as I do," he said, smiling. Now, I didn't know how to take that remark, as you can imagine, so I just sat up and said, "I bet." And I couldn't look him in the eye, but I took the juice and told him he had a real pretty bedroom. He said Sylvia Micheski was making pancakes out in the kitchen, why didn't I come on out and join everyone. I made myself look at him, and he looked back at me, the sunlight in his eyes making them hard to read. What happened last night? I wanted to say, but couldn't, so I smiled, and I said, "Well, it sure is nice to wake up here," and next thing I knew I was at his long oak table in the kitchen feeling a little sick and watching pretty Sylvia flip jacks, rocking back and forth on her small, sandaled feet. Old Minna Kates and William, the man from town who seemed to be her good friend, were over on the couch, talking quietly with mugs of coffee. When Brent came back into the kitchen, he stood beside me with his hand on my back, while he and Sylvia talked about blue-berries.

I walked back home to get ready for work. It was Sunday. I'd be making stew. Gladys had off. Gladys and James weren't in the house and I didn't have the energy to won-der about where they might've got to. I got dressed and walked down to the kitchen with my head splitting open from one of the worst hangovers I ever had, and Nadine was there waiting for me, cutting up the vegetables. We stood side by side and cut vegetables for almost two hours. I told her I just wanted to be quiet.

After work I was still hungover. After all I wasn't a spring chick, and somehow that was a sweet feeling, that feeling of knowing all I could do was sit in a tub, soak my bones, get into a nightgown, and slide my body in between the sheets, which I'd just recently changed, so they were crisp and cool and I cried from the happi-ness of how they felt, and the happiness of having no other choice but to sleep, and then I slept.

Raelene
Blessings

WHEN MY SON WAS JUST OVER TWO YEARS OLD, BACK IN 1979, this nice lady named Bernadette Myerly from south Philadelphia was watching him every afternoon while I worked at a boardinghouse for pregnant teenage girls. The house was called the Second Mile, and it was run by these Catholic nuns who were devoted to helping girls who, as the one nun liked to say, "got in the family way before they got in the family." Me working there was odd, since I wasn't much older and wiser than those teenagers, and I'd done the same thing. But I'd had two years of being a mother, and that changed me. I was raising my boy alone, doing okay I suppose. Moses' father went back west just after Moses had his first birthday. He wasn't ready to settle down. He made that real clear by cheating on me twice. So it was like, hey,

nice knowin' ya, Anthony. I wasn't in love with him anymore anyhow. I was too much in love with my baby.
They don't tell you that's how it'll be if you have a baby.
A grown man with stale breath and bristles, even a man
as pretty as Anthony, looks mighty undesirable next to
the magic of your baby, at least for a while. Anyway,
Hambone had come back with us, and the truth is, he
was more of a father than Anthony'd ever be.

Two of those teenage girls weren't easy to like, I mean
they were loudmouths and pissed off at the world. One of
them, Charlene, who'd been beat up for years by her own
father, ripped a chunk of my hair right out of my head
when I told her she couldn't smoke in the kitchen. I
couldn't fight back or I'd be fired. What did I do to control
myself? I looked at that wild girl with her angry red face
and with all my concentration I thought how she was
once an infant in somebody's arms. It was the only way I
could feel a shred of compassion for that human being.

My son had broken my heart like all babies do when
they first come into this crapped-on world, and for more
than three years after his birth, I couldn't stop myself
from looking at people and seeing them as they must
have been as innocent, cute little babies. This became
such a habit with me that it was like the whole human
race started to cooperate; I would look at their faces and
they'd give me this secret look of their old innocence.
Okay, maybe I was warped. But it got me through some
shitty situations.

I held that job for almost a year for a big four dollars an hour, and I think I kept coming back day after day in order to learn some kind of secret from the two of the nuns I worked with. I could've made more as a waitress, but I was learning something from those sturdy nuns who loved (I'm not talking tolerated, I'm talking loved) that Charlene girl who could spit in your face as a way of ending conversations.

At that age I wanted to believe that love was something you could have for a person if you just had enough willpower. Nobody was outside the possibility of love is what I wanted to believe. I guess deep down I wasn't sure whether I was inside or outside the possibility myself. I was back in Philly, I was taking my kid over to my father's and trying to pretend he was a normal grandfather and not an addict living on a couch. He was trying to pretend too, going to King of Prussia mall one day and buying little cars and stuffed bears and a shirt that said I LOVE GRANDPA, and a year's supply of animal crackers. He didn't have a girlfriend anymore, as far as I could tell. He'd been in and out of NA. "NA is not for people who need to quit, it's for people who want to quit," he told me. "And I don't want to." I had to quick pull out my trick of seeing the baby inside the man, because believe me, the man made me sick.

I was living in a house on Sansom Street with a bunch of kids—students, mostly. Rooms were fifty bucks a month, and the kitchen was never kept real clean, and the bathroom sink had fallen out of the wall and now sat in the hallway. The carpet was burnt orange shag, the sort all the slumlords bought in the early 1980s. Some of my roommates played in a wanna-be Lou Reed band and spent their time drinking and practicing at night. I would try to join them, but it didn't work. You can't just forget you're a mother. I couldn't relax the same way I used to. I'd have moments when I wished my baby would just go back to wherever he'd come from, and then I'd feel so guilty for thinking that, I'd have to leave the room and go upstairs where he was asleep in a wooden crib next to my bed. I'd crouch down and look through the spokes and whisper him promises. Sometimes I'd pass out on the floor, and when he woke up in the morning, he'd look down at me through the bars and smile.

I left work early one day because Bernadette Myerly's husband called on the phone and said Moses was a little under the weather, and he really wanted me to come get him. As it turned out, Mr. Myerly was sugarcoating the truth so that I wouldn't drive like a maniac and get in a wreck.

Moses had slipped through the railing and fallen off the black flat-top roof of the Myerlys' house. Bernadette had turned her back for three minutes in the TV room because she'd gotten a phone call from her mother. Moses wandered out of the TV room and walked up the narrow stairs that led out to the black tar roof, where chairs were set up for the Myerlys and their friends to enjoy the city lights in the evenings. Bernadette heard footsteps, hung the phone up, and rushed upstairs, but it was a second too late. Moses crawled under the railing, and fell two stories down to the sidewalk, and lay there unconscious.

They had him rushed to the hospital. I got to the Myerlys' and Mr. Myerly told me the real story, then drove me over to the hospital, where I had to wait for over two hours before I saw him, before he was assigned a room. And when I saw him, he was a ghostly white, still unconscious, dressed in a tiny blue gown, with a plastic bracelet on his wrist just like when he'd been born, and nobody could predict when he would wake, and though they weren't yet using the word *coma*, it was stuck in my mind and stomach, believe me, and it grew louder and bigger like an echo until I felt like I lived inside it. I called Hambone from the hospital, and he came as soon as he could. He was not a good support because he was so afraid. I wanted to cry whenever I looked at Hambone, who stood biting his nails and rocking from side to side, because I'd never seen him that way before, and it scared me.

He went and fetched some peanut butter crackers and Cokes for us to share. "What else can I do?" he begged. He wanted to be busy, couldn't stand sitting there by the bed where they had Moses on an IV.

I looked at him and said, "Call my friend Gladys."

"You want me to call Gladys?"

"Yes, Gladys. Tell her to come. Just tell her I need her to come because it's an emergency."

I wanted her there, that's all I knew. I guess I imagined she was someone who would understand how terrified I was. Gladys was still in my heart almost the way she was when I was a child writing her letters. I have that sort of heart, once you're in, you're in. I didn't want to call my father; he wouldn't have known what to say, what to do. Even if he was straight, he would've needed my comfort. Gladys, on the other hand, was Gladys. When she came into my mind in that hospital room, my heart pounded. I thought, She'll understand. Gladdy is the one who will understand me now. I was so relieved it was like I thought her understanding could give me the strength to wake my son.

But I didn't really think she would come.

She arrived the day after Hambone called her. She'd asked no questions. And she brought James, who I had never met. He was a handsome man in my humble opinion, tall with windburned cheeks and lines around his serious-looking eyes, his hair not entirely gray; his hands were strong with long fingers, and rough from work. He stood blinking in the doorway while she walked into the hospital room. I was sitting in a chair with my head in my hands and didn't see them at first.

"Raelene?" she said, and stopped walking toward me when I looked up and saw her. She was like the sun itself. I got out of my chair and went over to her and I wanted to throw myself on her, but stopped for a second, sensing she wasn't real comfortable. But then, she must have sensed *me*, or the terrified feelings inside of me. She must have sensed it, and recognized it. And she stepped up and pulled me toward her and held me for a moment. It was a hard, stiff hug, and when she let me go I looked in her eyes and saw she had backed off from the intensity of that hug, and she was somehow trying to escape from the room. I wanted to cry. She turned toward the doorway.

"James, this is Raelene," she said.

James came over and shook my hand. He looked at Moses in the bed, then looked back at me. He said, "Can we get you something to eat or drink?" and I said no, and then I was overcome with a sense that my fear had not been settled at all by their coming to the hospital, but only seemed deeper, now that I'd had that moment with Gladys, that minute of human contact that seemed hard to hold on to. A big gap opened up between us, while they stood and talked awkwardly about the traffic on the way, and talked about the weather, and how Philadelphia was more crowded than they imagined. They'd gone to the house and found a sleepy Hambone, who had told them how to get there.

It was like I began to sink into a hole. And in that hole I thought of Charlene, the girl I worked with in the home for unwed mothers, the kinds of breaks she had never been given, and how my own life, hard as it had been in ways, already had a ton of luckiness too, considering how I had been given a good brain, a decent personality, good friends, a healthy baby, and it struck me hard for the first time that of course I could lose my boy, of course whatever God there was could easily let him slip out of this world, since after all, these things happened every day to people, and that was just the nature of life. I didn't deserve any special treatment. Why had I ever thought I did?

And when I looked at Gladys, I imagined for the first time that I knew what the inside of her heart felt like. I wanted to look over and say, "Gladys, now I understand you," but in the same moment I wanted to push that understanding away, with all my strength, so I did.

Because her child had died. Her child was lost to her forever. I felt sick with a terrible confusion; a part of me regretted calling her now, like her life was contagious. It was like now that Gladys was in the room, my little boy would drown inside of himself, never to open his eyes again.

I sat down in my chair and looked at Moses, and suddenly felt just like I was paralyzed. I couldn't take my eyes off him, or even shift in the chair. I felt the most terrible, unjust kind of emotion toward Gladys now, a resentment that she was in the room, she who had lost her girl who was just a year older than my boy, she who had slept while that little girl drowned. *How can you live with yourself now? If my boy dies, I'll die with him. I'll just die with him.*

Gladys was standing beside my chair now. She put her hand on my head. James had left the room.

"I was surprised when Hambone called. Surprised to hear from him. But I'm glad to be here," she said. She cleared her throat.

"Thanks for coming," I said, but I felt that if she left her hand there for one more second, I'd have to reach up and push it away.

She did not move her hand, and I just didn't have the nerve to push it away, so it sat on my head, contagious, burning, so heavy I felt my head would split open.

Finally she lifted her hand. "Moses will wake up," she said. "He will?" Every emotion but hope disappeared inside of me, and I sat looking up at her. It was like I was hanging on her words as if she were some kind of prophet.

"Moses will wake up," she said again.

"What makes you think so? Why do you say that?"

"I have a strong feeling about it," she said. "Very strong."

And when I looked up at her, her face seemed unbelievably strong, and the strangest thing was, it was circled with some kind of light. Maybe it was real light, from another plane of existence, or maybe it was just what I needed to see at that time. It doesn't matter in the long run.

The nurses made me go home and sleep. Four of them together had to work on convincing me to leave. They assured me I would be called the second he woke, and it was this kind of assurance that made me leave because hearing the words "the second he wakes" rather than "if he wakes" shot me full of wild joy. *The second he wakes*, I kept whispering to myself. *The second he wakes I will hold him and hold him and hold him.* Gladys and James and I left in James's car, and went back to my house. *Pick him up and kiss him and never let him go.* They walked around my long, narrow room looking at the pictures of Moses on the wall, and Gladys kept going back to the one of Moses in the flat field with the huge windy pine tree behind him, a black and white I took myself when he and I went camping for his first birthday when we still lived out west. Moses had just learned to stand. It was spring, and the world behind him looked huge and filled with all this positive energy. And Moses seemed a part of it. Gladys smiled at the picture, and showed James. He took it in his hands and stared at it a long time, so long I almost asked him why he found it so interesting, but something told me not to intrude.

The next morning it rained, and we left for the hospital before dawn, the three of us in the rainy dark of James's car, me huddled right between the two of them in the front seat, the morning news on the radio. I could feel the exhaustion and stiffness of their bodies; they were in their fifties, and James had slept on a pull-out couch in a tiny room off of the kitchen, Gladys on the sofa in the main room in flannel pajamas. I'd offered to help pay for a hotel, but they said they weren't picky. I was always so lucky with friends.

Gladys had fixed us each a cup of coffee, and I had to hold James's mug for him while he drove, along with my own mug, and when he took the curves I looked down at the coffee in the two cups, one yellow and one blue, and I thought, *Okay, God, if nothing spills out of these mugs, that means he's waking up today*, and nothing spilled until the very last moment when I was getting out of the car in the parking garage, and I told myself that didn't count.

At the hospital that rainy day, something interesting happened between Gladys and James. I think about it whenever I think of Gladys, which is often.

James sat on one side of Moses' bed, and Gladys sat on the other side. I sat in the chair at the foot of the bed, reading a magazine, just waiting and praying. I stole looks at Gladys and James for a while, hardly knowing I was doing so until finally it registered that the two of them were talking quietly to each other, and that those quiet words were crucial, so crucial the room's atmosphere changed. Yet when I overheard some of the words they confused me because they were so simple. "Potato chips" and "rain all day" and "dogs" were some of the words I could pick up, and I almost laughed because the contrast of what they were saying and how they were saying it was so extreme. Finally I was staring at them, and I trusted what I felt more than what I saw, for what I saw was simple enough.

They looked at each other with naked faces. You know how a face can be naked. Like whoever lives in the face is right there, pressed up against the face's window. They held each other's gaze for a long moment. Then James reached his hand out across the bed to Gladys, and her hand met his. She squeezed his hand hard. They held hands like that, and James winced, as if the moment was just too much for him to bear.

Then Gladys stood up from her chair, and walked out of the room, and James followed, his head held high, as if he were still bracing himself against all the emotion. I waited for a second, then got up from my chair, and went to the door, and watched the two of them walk down the hall together, a space between them just big enough for a young child, and for a split second she was there. Their girl. And for another second, Wendell was there too, and he turned to look at me with the same soldier's face I'd known as a child who had his photograph, a girl who had imagined she loved him. And when both of them disappeared, I could still sense their spirits, hovering around James and Gladys, and then the two of them turned the corner. Maybe it was just me and what I was feeling. But it seemed real.

Two hours and twenty-five minutes later, Moses opened his eyes and said, "Mama."

In my mind, Gladys had something to do with this. I don't pretend to understand it. But it felt like Gladys had something to do with my son waking. I believe that feeling. So I'll always miss Gladys. I'll always wish she lived down the street.

That night we celebrated in the hospital with Moses, who had lost much of his ability to speak, but they told me this damage was temporary, and his eyes were nearly as happy as they had been before his fall. We filled the room with balloons, and fed him green beans and chocolate cake, and I brought his tape recorder in along with his favorite music (Bob Marley) and his Pooh books, and after an hour or so we were told he had to sleep, he had to be quiet and heal, and that everyone should go home but me, though they advised that I also leave.

I couldn't leave. I couldn't yet trust that he'd stay awake, that he wouldn't slip back into the dark. But Gladys and James said they were going back to New York, and each of them gave me a kiss good-bye, and kissed Moses. They left quickly, it seemed, and when they were gone I felt afraid and the room felt hollow for a moment, but just as quickly it was filled up again just as if the sun was shining, because my boy was awake, and pointing to a Big Bird balloon on the ceiling, trying to say one of the words he had mastered months before. "Look! Look!"

In less than a week, Moses was home with me. The Myerlys, who had sent flowers and offered to pay the hospital bill, had called me, asking if I was planning to sue them. I told them of course not and a week later received a check for two hundred dollars in the mail, which at the time seemed like a huge sum. It came with a note telling me to do something nice for Moses, and that they missed him. See what I mean about luck? I collected unemployment for two months, and then the nuns decided I could come back and work night shift, and bring Moses along with me. He played with his cars and coloring books in the kitchen at the long wooden table, and lightened the mood in that room for the girls who were on dish duty. Later, he would sleep on the gray cushioned bench in the front hall beneath the bad painting of Saint Theresa, who'd been given a goatee by one of the girls. They'd cover him up with this red homemade quilt.

"Check him out!" the girls said. "Sleepin' like an

angel." They'd pat his head, kiss his cheek, stare down at him with expressions of longing. None of them were keeping their babies, as far as they knew.

I would call Gladys that year, late at night, on the pay phone in the halfway house when everyone else was sleeping. I had thanked her a thousand times for coming to the hospital, but each time she said, "I think it's me who should thank you." And when I asked her why, she said, "Doesn't matter why, just accept my thanks."

I knew why, anyhow, of course. I knew she and James had gotten to the other side of their grief.

She didn't tell me much about James, but I know he stayed around New York State for a while. It's difficult to say what was happening between the two of them. Because Gladys would tell me things like, "Later on I'm sneaking out to meet James in the woods," and then she'd laugh. "Really?" I'd say. "Just to take a walk," she'd say. "Just a walk with a friend."

And one night Ivy came home and told Gladys, "I'm in love." She had fallen in love with a sixty-eight-year-old man named Brent Quinn, and the two of them planned to live happily ever after in Brent's cabin. Since I had worked at that camp when I was a girl, I knew who Brent Quinn was, and had even seen his cabin once. I had even looked at him as a girl and thought, If I ever loved an old man, it would be a man like him. He had an odd, comfortable habit of wearing old striped pajamas and worn work boots, and his face had aged real nicely. The one time I saw his cabin, on a late spring night when he had an open house for the counselors, it was filled with bright, beautiful colors—quilts and flowers and paintings. His walls lined with books. He had great food on the table, though I didn't recognize what any of it was. Stuff from other parts of the world. And he had several jugs of wine. He loved life, I guess you could say. He seemed to know what matters.

I couldn't go to their wedding, but when I talked to Gladys, and asked her how badly she'd miss Ivy, she didn't have much to say. Gladys never wanted to say much about her loneliness. Instead, she told me what she thought Ivy would miss: "It'll be our music, trust me. That foreign music Brent Quinn listens to is gonna drive her crazy. All that singing about how happy someone is, or how sad, and you can't understand a damn word about why. All you get is the feeling. And I don't think Ivy's the type to be satisfied with that. Ivy's the type to want the story behind the feeling. Ivy likes George Jones. Johnny Cash. She's got taste."

The next year on the telephone when I asked Gladys about James, Gladys said he had gone south to New Orleans where he worked on a boat, but that the two of them kept in touch, but not all that often.

"He's my friend, Raelene," was what she said. "My old friend."

*   *   *

That year, when Gladys was fifty-four, she enrolled herself in the community college. She took all kinds of night courses—English, history, economics, math, physics. "I think I'll be a professional student," she told me in a letter. "Or maybe I'll get a real degree and start teaching the little winter school kids. Imagine that. Gladys at the chalkboard."

As it turned out, she was a teacher the last time I saw her.

Me, I was a mail carrier. I was making decent money—twelve bucks an hour. And I liked the job. I liked being out in the elements. I took some days off and decided to visit Gladys.

I hadn't called ahead to tell her I was going to visit. I guess that's an odd habit of mine. I don't like to call ahead. I like to pop in. "You're afraid if you call ahead they'll say don't come," a friend once said, but I don't think that's it. I think I'm afraid of visiting, so I don't call ahead, part of me hoping they won't be home when I get there. But whatever it is, this isn't a good habit to have these days. People's lives are too full of structure and privacy to allow for droppers-by. But with Gladys I didn't fear she'd mind. I had not seen her since that day in the hospital. Over eleven years ago! It didn't seem that long. I hadn't been able to make it up to her graduation from Mercury Teachers College. She sent me a picture of herself in blue cap and gown, unsmiling, one eyebrow cocked up, classic Gladys. Her friend Doreen who she'd written me about, standing beside her grinning.

A neighbor girl stayed with Moses, someone named Nancy who was twenty and always brought her cassette player and turned him on to funky music. So I took myself up to see Gladys like I'd wanted to do for years.

On the bus I sat next to this kid who looked about seventeen or eighteen with a Walkman on his head. He was slumped down, all pissed off in his seat, and his face was set in anger. I recognized the look. I probably never wore it on my own face in high school, I was too busy trying to pretend I was good, but I recognized it all the same.

When I had first sat down, the boy had looked at me with hatred I took personally at first, until I realized I looked old to him. I was a grown woman now. To a seventeen-year-old who hated the world, I was old. I was of the world. Settled. An adult. Part of the group who betrayed him, in whatever way. Why was it shocking that this kid would see me like that? Why did I feel like defending myself? *Hey, kid, I'm just a letter carrier, a mail deliverer rain or shine, just a person trying to get by, I'm not an enemy.* A few miles into the trip, when that boy shifted in his seat and touched my arm, I felt an electric charge from his body, something I hadn't felt from anyone's body in a long time. After this happened I spent an hour or so shifting my own body in order to brush against him. I know that's warped. He shifted toward me too. It was a kind of conversation I'll never forget. I hadn't had a serious romance in three years, and this boy's touch told me I'd been starved.

We sat that way until it was time for him to get off the bus. Neither of us even said good-bye, though before he stood he grabbed my arm until it hurt, then turned and gave me a small smile before he stepped off the bus, a smile that pretty much shocked me, because I saw what a baby he was. I watched him walk down the street of a small, dead-looking town in upstate New York, the street lined with spindly bare trees, the gas station like something from 1950 with old Coke signs in the window. Someone in a dark coat stood under an awning before a small newsstand, holding a cup of coffee. Watching the boy walk away I felt like I was losing him, like he'd been a part of my life for years, like he was leaving for no good reason. I pressed my forehead into the window as hard as it would go. But the smaller he got, the more he moved into that place, the more the feeling went away, and it was gone when I realized I was old enough to be his mother.

It came to me that we're not really one age at all. We're all the ages we've ever been.

As I rode the cab to Gladys's house, I might've been the girl I was the first time I surprised her. My racing heart was slamming inside my chest. Like I said, I'm afraid of visits, so the closer I get, the more nervous, the more excited, the more uncertain I am about who it is I'm going to see, and who I am. My palms sweat, my stomach swirls, I talk to myself like an old woman.

I knocked on Gladys's door, and Gladys's friend Doreen Manchester answered. Gladys had written to me about her—how she was a good friend, the divorced mother of four grown sons, how she was constantly asking people to call her "Door" and how nobody, for some reason, ever did. She was tall and sort've bony with burnt orange hair and tight lips that seemed permanently amused, as if any second now a huge laugh might escape her. The sight of her at Gladys's door surprised me.

"I'm Door at the door and you're?" she said, eyebrows raised.

"Raelene Francis from Philadelphia."

She waited, thinking for a second.

"Raelene, Raelene. Well come on in. Don't I know all about you. Gladys is out back, she'll be in soon enough. She's getting some wood. I'll fix you cider with a cinnamon stick in the meantime unless you got somethin' against it."

We sat at the old Formica kitchen table, the same one that had been there years ago, white with silver boomerangs. The kitchen had been painted bright yellow, and a beautiful painting had been hung of a pretty woman in a rowboat. On another wall was a framed diploma. Doreen began telling me about the antics of her sons, as if she'd always known me. "One of them likes a girl named Hildegaard. You know, like the saint? Can you imagine naming a baby Hildegaard. The last name's Smith, so I guess they thought they'd give her a real stunner of a first name. Well, this Hildegaard's no saint. Last Sunday she spends the night at our house— that's right, I allow them to live in sin. I tell myself there's worse things than sex, but sometimes I'm not sure, you know what I'm saying? So this girl, who by the way won't let anyone call her Hildy, no sir, it's always Hildegaard, anyhow she wakes up in the morning and comes down to my kitchen hanging out of her night-gown like Fritz the Cat's wife and says, 'Mrs. Manches-ter, Brendan wants to know if you have any frosted Pop-Tarts. . . .'"

The kitchen was filled with the warmth of this new friend, and I imagined Gladys and Doreen Manchester had spent a lot of days together, and I knew even before I saw Gladys that she was doing better than I could've imagined. I relaxed.

Gladys walked in and said my name, dropped a few logs on the floor, and said, "I'll be damned." Her face was thinner, her eyes greener, her hair completely white, a beautiful color on her. She was dressed in a big fisher-man's sweater and red wool pants. Her skin glowed from the cold air. I thought she looked perfect.

"So what brings you up here?" she said.

"You," I said. "What else?"

She smiled. "Long way to travel to see the likes of me."

"Oh, Gladys," Doreen said. "She'd come round the world to see you, isn't it obvious?"

"Poor thing," said Gladys. She picked up the logs and went to the living room to stoke the fire. We followed her.

Gladys stoked the fire and said she hoped I planned on staying at least until Monday, so I could see her teach fourth grade. Then she turned around and studied me, smiling.

"You don't look half bad," she said. "You got a new boyfriend?"

"No."

"What's the problem? I'd think they'd be lining up at the door."

I had Monday and Tuesday off, so I decided to stay, after calling Moses. Doreen was there for most of that weekend too, and Ivy and Brent came by for Sunday dinner. Brent looked fragile to me that winter day, but also happy. He'd developed Parkinson's disease and looked like he was constantly shaking his head no. Meanwhile his bright eyes were always saying yes. Ivy, who wore sapphire earrings and her silver hair in a braid now, brought most of the dinner over.

"Here's to our faraway guest," Ivy said, toasting me at the table.

We ate her excellent vegetable stew and rolls. Beyond the kitchen window the snow fell whiter than the thin curtains. The sky behind the falling snow was dark, dark gray. The sort of air that makes everyone inside feel huddled together.

"This is real good, Ivy," Gladys said.

"Good for what ails ya." Ivy winked.

Gladys and Ivy, I noticed, studied each other whenever either of them spoke. They might have looked alike, but Ivy studied Gladys with an interesting expression. A kind of confusion and awe. Meanwhile Gladys studied Ivy from a sort of amused distance. But it was a softer look than it had been years before. It seemed to me she had a kind of tenderness in her face.

"So today Brent and I were out driving, and we see this big fat man selling flowers in the parking lot of the Duke of Bubbles. The duke was standing there in his lace-up boots talking to the man."

"Who's the Duke of Bubbles?" I said.

"Oh, some car wash fanatic, thinks he's a duke, so anyhow, this fat man's selling his flowers and we pull over to see what they are, well, they're all roses. All different colors. So I lean out of the car and say, 'Hey, Duke, what's your friend charging for those roses?' so the duke asks the fat man, who says, 'You can have a hundred for three dollars!'"

"My God!" Doreen said. "I would've died!"

"Well," Ivy said, "don't get too excited. These roses

had one foot on the banana peel. They'll only last one more day, but it's worth it. To have a hundred roses in your house for a day. Right Brent?"

"Oh, yes, it's lovely," said Brent, all the while shaking his head no. Later that day he joked about it, saying it was a new dance he was trying to make popular called "The Perpetually Disagreeable." I had to laugh at that.

I ate my soup and watched Gladys listening to Ivy. It was clear to me that she was thinking about the fact of Ivy's existence as Ivy talked, and not the story Ivy told. Later, when Gladys talked about one of her students whose mother called and yelled at her, Ivy hung on Gladys's every word, as if she believed that if she could listen hard enough she might finally understand the mystery of her sister. Watching them, I started to wish I had a sister of my own. It wasn't a small wish, it was a deep wish, it was a desire that made me lonely at that table. I kept watching. I was thinking that for all the great space between Gladys and Ivy, for all the stuff they were never able to protect each other from, a real close-ness existed between them, one that nobody else at that table could touch. I think that with a sister, that kind of closeness could be made up of confusion, misunder-standing, and a kind of distance.

After that meal, we had pie by the fire. Gladys smiling at me across the room.

*   *   *

"So before ya leave, you should come to my classroom."

"Of course."

Gladys had been teaching for five years. This was her first year with fourth graders. I sat in the back seat and imagined being one of her fourth graders. What would she look like to me? I don't know if I would've liked her. I would've feared her. I would've tried to impress her. She was not a natural for the job because she grew too easily bored with the children's answers, which tended to be rambly or too short.

I felt her impatience when a pale boy with strange pointed sideburns that looked oiled into place answered her question about a character in a book they had all read called *Harvey the Doggone Ratfink*. The boy said something about how Harvey really was a nice person inside but he didn't know how to show it because he was too concerned with the lizard and maybe if he got to the cotton candy stand in time that girl with the bare feet could explain to him could explain to him could explain to him—the boy got stuck on this phrase, and I wanted to go help him out, and wished Gladys would help him out, but she just watched him and patiently waited, and finally he said "could explain to him about the lizard" and Gladys just nodded at him, said "Okay," and called on someone else.

She wasn't exactly filling up the room with her warmth. Yet the children responded to her. They all wanted to answer her questions. Maybe she was a great teacher. She had her classroom decorated with the kids' own art and a fish tank. One bulletin board had red felt letters that said LIFE'S SHORT: DON'T BE AN IDIOT.

After class it was time for lunch.

"So, Raelene, what's new? You been here for two days, and I don't even know what's new with you."

I told her about Moses, how he's off with his friends a lot now, how he gets decent grades.

And then I tried to tell Gladys that I'm almost glad that he fell off the roof that day, how after his fall and recovery, I became a different sort of mother, more grateful, more alert. I wasn't trying to brag. I was trying to bring us back to a time when I needed her, a time that brought us together. Gladys lowered her eyes, nodded her head. It was like she didn't want to remember those days. Like she had moved too far away from that time of healing in the hospital. Too far away from James, and that old life, that old Gladys. I was sorry I tried to talk this way, and for a minute felt foolish and alone.

What I really wanted was to have her remember me in the past, to talk about it some, but I could feel her resisting that. So I didn't say anything else.

"You have a good life," she told me after a while, then squinted at me, as if thinking hard. "But don't be a loner."

"I'm not," I said.

"It's important not to be a loner," she said. "You need companionship."

"I know."

A silence fell between us. I felt really disappointed, and didn't know why.

"You have a pretty good life too, you know," I said, trying to keep the talk going.

"For an old dame who never loved the ways of the world," she said. "I'm ready to retire, though, Raelene girl."

I was glad she called me that. It pulled me closer to her for a moment.

"I figure if I'm one of the lucky ones, I got about ten, twenty years left of this life."

"Or more," I said.

"Whatever. It'll fly," she said.

I said good-bye to Gladys then, who had to go back and teach. "You come back soon," she said. "You should come see me too," I said, though I knew she wouldn't. I knew the happiness she had now depended on this rooted life of hers, this living every minute in the present. She gave me a quick hug and patted my back, then turned and walked away, dressed like an old-fashioned teacher, in a wool navy blue dress and heeled shoes to match. I wondered when the next time I'd see her would be. I didn't think it would be soon.

I was sad watching her walk away. Something between us was gone now. It was just *need* that was gone, I told myself. I didn't need her anymore. Or maybe it was just that Gladys didn't need me. What was left was memory, I decided, there on the bus, riding back home. And she didn't particularly want to remember. Maybe I'll never see her again. Life goes that way sometimes.

But in the next moment I couldn't imagine that. Couldn't imagine that I'd never see Gladys again. Of course I would. I would visit when Moses was older. Maybe I'd visit her for a long time. Maybe I'd start to go up there for Thanksgiving sometimes, bring Moses along.

That night when I got home it was snowing. I opened the front door and found Nancy curled up under a blanket on the couch, The Wailers on the stereo.

"Hi! Where's Moses?"

Nancy, the baby-sitter, sat up and brushed her hair down, and blinked at me, like I'd caught her with a lover.

"He and Ruthie are out walking in the snow. We all watched *The Birds* tonight, and it freaked us out."

"So was everything all right?"

"Yep, like I said on the phone, he's a doll, and he's got good taste in music. More than I can say for my past two boyfriends. They were into this retro seventies stuff like Kansas."

"That's too bad."

Nancy had the house looking great. I paid her, I went

and took a shower and got into a nightgown, and combed out my hair. But I couldn't shake that sense of loss I'd felt the whole way home.

Why did I feel as if I'd lost something important? I'd had a good visit with Gladys. I hadn't lost anything, really. I'd been lucky enough to see that she had grown into her own brand of happiness, or acceptance, or whatever it was she had grown into.

And I had my brand too. That was true. I had a great son who had his health and his happiness. I had a good job. I had two or three friends. A full-enough life.

When I came out of my room, Moses and Ruth had just stepped into the front hallway. Both were bundled up in hooded coats. "Hi!" they sang. For a few seconds I just stared at them, taking them in.

I went to hug Moses, and he let me.

"How was it," he said.

"Excellent, and Nancy said you were great too."

They both had bright, dark eyes, and the kind of beauty I've noticed comes to kids' faces when expectations of the future are so high they can't be contained. I thought of myself sitting next to that boy on the bus whose touch had sent a shockwave of desire through my body, and I could hardly believe it had happened. If Moses and Ruth knew about such a thing, they'd laugh or feel disgusted, or probably both, for good reason. I stood in front of them in my bathrobe, feeling middle-aged for the first time in my life. I was envious of them.

I should've been relieved that I'd already survived all that, but I wasn't. I was envious and my heart was breaking.

Ruth was weirdly quiet, dreamy almost. "We saw *The Birds*," she told me. "It totally freaked us out." She didn't look freaked out. She looked in love. *Girl, you're a baby, get that look off your face.* "Well, we just came in to see if you were home, now we wanna go for another walk," Moses said. "If that's all right with you," he added, cocking his head. I was glad that he was forcing it a little bit, the way he did when he was being sarcastic; I was always glad for those few times when I didn't feel too much love for him.

"Be my guest," I said. "Bring me a snowball."

Really, I wanted them to stay. Or invite me. I wanted my son back.

They turned and walked out the door. I turned out the light in the living room, and thought I'd go to bed, but stopped at the window when I saw them on the sidewalk passing by. They moved together like they were one person, slowly and surely in the darkness, not holding hands, but together all the same. The snow had already turned the street white. I watched them and their dark footprints that followed in a trail behind them until they turned the corner. I stayed right at the window, watching the night, empty of people.

Did my mother and father ever love me the way I loved my son? I supposed they had, at certain times. I knew they had. I could remember the look of my mother's face when I came home from third grade one day, hurt by the words of another child. I could remember my father's eyes, dark with worry when I came in one night too late. I could remember his face when he first held Moses, how he looked at me with tears in his eyes and said he was so proud of me and he'd never find words to explain. I could remember my mother fixing me dinner the time I stayed with her out west, how hard she worked to make something special. I could still see that food arranged on the plate like a painting.

And thinking about Gladys and my mother and Moses altogether like that, I decided I would call her. My mother, I mean. I hadn't seen her since my visit years ago, which really hadn't been such a good visit, but I had called her three or four times a year, on various occasions, and she had sent me packages of clothes.

"Raelene?" She sounded glad to hear from me.

"Just thought I'd call and say hello. How are things?"

"Well, things are okay, considering I'm on a no-fat diet," she said. "I feel okay these days."

"That's good."

"And how are you? You're not in the area, are you?"

"No, no, still in Philly." I looked out the window into the night. A woman in a long white scarf was out walking her dog.

"So is everything all right? Nothing wrong?"

"Everything's fine, I just wanted to say hello."

"I liked that last picture of Moses," she said. "He's awfully handsome."

She'd stopped asking, Will I ever meet him?

"He's turning out real well. Right now he's walking in the snow with his true love."

She sighed, painfully, then said, "Oh, the poor things. I feel so sorry for the young. All they have to go through."

I said, "They're happy."

She sighed again, and said she knew all about happiness.

A silence came between us now. She rescued us from that silence. "Okay, well thank you for calling, honey."

"Sure," I said. "Sure, Mom."

It was not a good call, but I hadn't expected one, so it was all right. When I hung up I realized that what I really wanted was to talk about Gladys to someone. Maybe I'd wait for Moses. Maybe when he and Ruth returned I could talk with them about my visit. But I imagined them on the couch together with their cheeks red from the cold, me across from them on a chair, their faces trying to stay interested.

I turned the light off so I could see the snow falling, and the moon shining behind clouds. I could see the bricks of the narrow, empty street being whitened. I thought of Gladys, and even my mother staring out the window of their houses, where maybe it was snowing too. And it was all right. Everything was.

For a moment I saw the snow like it was breathing color, like it was freshly painted and set down before me as a gift to wake me up. It all seemed strange and alive, and so clear, and I wanted contact with it. I didn't want to just stand at the window and watch.

So I bundled up. I went out into that snow, into the wind, the flakes flying and shining in the streetlight. I walked through the silence for a long time. I had the feeling I was right where I wanted to be, seeing everything I wanted to see.

The wind blew, the snow fell.

Gladys

YOU LOOK BACK ON LIFE, AND YOU WANT TO ASK WHAT changed you. You want to point your finger. You want to say it was because you met this man, or you didn't meet that man, or maybe your mother died young, or she didn't. Or maybe it was something smaller, like you took in a stray dog. For me, I could have pointed to James, or Wendell, or to Ann, or maybe that day Ivy pried me open a bit, or Raelene, or when Raelene's little boy got sick, but in the end, I don't think it makes too much difference. Because in the end, you can't point. You can say this happened, and that happened. You try to say it, and you do say it, but you know the truth is you wake up one day and you've arrived somewhere else. You don't know how you got there. But maybe it's a blessing that you did.

When James sent me an airplane ticket to fly right into the New Orleans International Airport last year, I hadn't seen him in a long time. Eight years. We hadn't even talked or sent letters for about two years, so of course he hadn't heard that Brent Quinn had died, and Ivy was back working more than part-time in the kitchen at camp. She wasn't devastated by the loss. He'd been a good friend for a number of years, but even when they were married that was about all he was. In my opinion. Still, she missed him. She would stand with her arms crossed over her chest like she never did before. And you'd be talking to her and her mind would wander off, and she'd have to ask you to repeat yourself. And her hair finally turned completely gray.

Brent was replaced by a nice young fella from New York City who took the children's well-being too seriously, and Ivy complained about it.

I was still teaching school when I got James's card. I knew it would be my last year. I liked the job a lot. But it was too hard on me near the end. So many children with problems. I worked and worked for years trying to help them. In my own way. The way I knew. I took the loneliest ones home and fed them good food. Bought them books to escape into. Singled them out to be classroom helpers. Then, I started to get bone weary. A feeling of hopelessness would creep in. I knew it was time to step down.

Anyhow, James wanted me to come to New Orleans

for his seventy-first birthday. He didn't mention his birthday, but I knew.

It was October when that airplane ticket came in the mail. He had written a note. "You should come visit for a few days. James." To see that sincere and loopless handwriting again touched me. I didn't hesitate in my heart. My head hemmed and hawed a bit, but I knew I'd go. Not that I had any notion I was going to hitch up with James, because I wasn't. That was one place I knew I'd never arrive. But you respect the history you have with a person, and the losses too, and maybe, when you're older, it's that history you have to honor. Even more than the love you have left.

Doreen Manchester drove me to the airport. Doreen in the Sideshow, as she liked to call her 1974 Buick Electra 225. Doreen said whenever she drives the Sideshow she's scared a cop will pull her over. In certain up-and-coming parts, they pull you over these days if your car's not from the 1990s. They figure you committed the crime of being poor.

She paid the money to park and came into the airport. We were almost two hours early. I never had been in an airport. I didn't tell Doreen. She would've enjoyed that fact too much. She'd been in plenty of times and acted like my personal tour guide as it was. But I was glad she distracted me from the place. Personally I found it a terrible zoo. I don't like so many rushy rushy types around me. And I don't like the boy who bumped right into me. "Excuse me!" I said. "Kiss my ass!" he said. What the hell was that all about, I wanted to know. "The world's just falling apart," Doreen said. "That's all."

When I said good-bye to Doreen she got tears in her eyes. This is one woman who likes dramatics.

I said, "Manchester, I'm only going down there for four days!"

She said, "I know! I just hate good-byes! All good-byes! They remind me of other good-byes! They remind me of death! I hate good-byes and I always will."

"Well, good-bye," I said, walking away, and she laughed. She can always laugh.

So I fly to New Orleans. I wasn't too glad to be up in that plane. I'm not a natural flyer. I'm not the sort who kicks back and looks down at the majesty of Earth. I mainly sat with dripping palms and thought how in the goddamn hell do they keep this goddamn plane up in the air? Yes, I had a whiskey sour. No, I didn't chitchat with the gentleman to my left. They didn't have stewardesses on that plane. In fact they had boys. Stewards, I guess they call them. Two nice stewards with curly hair. Flying was normal to them. It's amazing what gets to be normal.

So James is there waiting for me at Gate 11. He's dressed nice in a green long-sleeve cotton shirt. He looks older. Still good, with ruddy cheeks, but older. His hair was silver and white, and his face thinned out. He didn't see me. Why is it sad when you see someone and they don't know you're seeing them? Because they can't protect themselves. They can't dress themselves up in their personality. They look naked and alone, and you're sorry you're seeing them that way.

A man you know all your life standing alone and looking for you in an airport makes your heart pound. I thought I might have a heart attack before I reached him.

He stood tall and thin with his chin lowered in that old way of his. His eyes moving to find me. Then he finds me. His face lights up. He walks over and takes my bag. He still basically had his same walk. Not jittery like some old men. I notice he notices my dress. I bought it new. Doreen dragged me to Divine's Lounge Wear in town, a store that for the past twenty years everyone thought would go out of business. The merchandise never rotates. Everything's in plastic bags. And Mrs. Peggy Divine's a three-hundred-year-old hunchback with asthma. You want to tell her, "Go ahead and die, Peggy."

The last dress I got there was for Wendell's funeral. I just wanted to get out of there, away from the mothball smell. "Fine," I said, "I'll take this dress." Off-white with miniature maroon roses. Fancy. I got out my black heels from another lifetime. I wore the whole outfit to that airport. And earrings. Doreen said, "Well don't you look like you're worth your weight in wildcats." "What the hell that's supposed to mean," I said. She laughed.

So James noticed the outfit. Looked me right up and down. I was glad he did. And he took my suitcase and said, "You travel light." And I said, "Always." He smiled down at me. And then we walked side by side through that airport. Anyone looking would see an old pair. And I felt old. Everyone I know, they say they look in the mirror and can't believe the old dame looking back at them is *them*. Well, for me it was an opposite story. The old woman I see now, she looks like me. Almost exactly. That young thing, she was the stranger.

James drove us to his house. It was a shotgun little house in a long row of other shotguns. That's what they call them down there in New Orleans. The rooms are lined up all in a row, so if someone wants to they can shoot a gun right through the house. Don't ask me.

James kept his house perfect. It was painted white with dark gray shutters. Trim green bushes out front. In the back, a garden in the moonlight. It was a James kind of garden, not too neat, and not too overgrown. Inside the rooms were painted white and the doors to the rooms were blue. It was night, and the light was dim, but I knew the place was clean. It had a watery smell to it. And another smell, which was like clean flannel shirts.

"Not a bad place," James said, "but I don't like the layout of a shotgun much. I don't like a house on one floor. It's too easy to keep it in good shape. Not enough to fix."

"I don't think it's so bad," I said. I didn't. It appealed to me. The clarity. But I didn't have to live there.

Next thing I knew he had two cold Budweisers and two glasses. We sat side by side on his couch. We set the beers on the table in front of us. Then he stood up and turned on a strange little antique mermaid lamp, came back and sat down and stretched his long legs out.

Then I surprised him. I took my glass and said, "Here's to your seventy-first birthday, old man."

He smiled, looking straight ahead. He didn't look surprised that I remembered. He looked over at me for a second with his distant eyes. In one second the distance in his eyes was gone, then back again, then gone, then back. He was that way even back in the beginning. I laughed because he was so much himself.

"Happy Birthday to you, happy birthday to you," I sang. He smiled.

But a kind of heaviness was creeping into the room. Call it the heaviness of our lives. A kind of uneasiness I didn't count on. And since I wasn't used to traveling, I wasn't settled in myself. Last time I'd traveled was with Raelene and Hambone. Hadn't heard from Raelene in a long time except for Christmas cards. Have to say I missed her down there in New Orleans. I missed her because I felt like a traveler, and she was the one who got me traveling all those years ago. The second day I was there, I got a postcard and sent it to her. I said I was having a good time in New Or'luns, as James calls it. I said, "Wish you were here" and meant it.

James had a lot planned for us. He wanted me to see

his whole life, all the places he went and all the friends he had. I was unsure why he wanted this. But he did. One night I met two men he'd worked with for years on a shrimp boat. The men lived in an old-timer boarding-house. JFK was framed on the wall in the hallway. The men were brothers named Yuri and Big. We went out and had what they call beignets. A kind of donut. And good black coffee. Yuri and Big were both recovered alcoholics, so we sat in a bright restaurant open twenty-four hours and drank coffee until we shook. Yuri would talk and Big would sit way back in his chair, and twist his mouth to the side of his face. I could see he was one of those people divided. One part of them doesn't want to listen to much of anything, but the other part's dying to hear it all. So he had to twist his mouth that way. Because Yuri was telling me his life story. He said he was in New Orleans because he was a jailbird at heart, and the original population of the city was jailbirds. Did I know that? No, I said. Oh yes, jailbirds, debtors, smugglers, and wayward Parisian ladies. That's the history of this place. "So I knew it was for me, because I came from a town in Texas that was filled up with God fearers. And they tried to beat the fear into me with splintery wood till I ran away when I was fifteen years of age. I was already on the bottle then. . . ." I noticed James looking at his friend with affection. I could tell these friends weren't really friends. They were people he listened to. They were two men James could sit and listen to.

"So, Gladys, it was lovely meetin' your acquaintance. Tell your boy here he oughta come see us more often," Yuri said. "Yeah," said Big. As it turned out, James hadn't seen them in a year or so.

The next day I met his next-door neighbors, Donny and Betty Fortunato, and we went out to eat Creole food together that night. They were nice enough people. Donny was a wiry man who talked fast and choppy. Betty had a smoker's voice and small blue eyes with drawn-on eyebrows. Both had dyed black hair and were about sixty-five. I got them onto the subject of grandchildren because I didn't want to have to be the talker. I wanted to sit back side by side with James, like I did with Yuri. Well, turns out the Fortunatos' oldest grandson's a juvenile delinquent named Ronny. Betty went on and on about him in her old smoker's voice. You'd think a story about a juvenile delinquent would be interesting table talk. Well, think again. Betty was one of these people who tell you all the details that don't matter. Like "So I went down to the store because I wanted to take Ronny some candy when I visited him. Let's see, that was about noon. No, that was more like one o'clock. Or was it noon? And so anyhow, I bought candy and I also bought baked beans and chicken. No, pork. I bought pork, that's right, it was Thursday and Thursday it's almost always pork." You got the feeling Betty Fortunato was talking to herself, just trying to keep her ducks in line. After that dinner James and me were relieved to be just me and him.

We walked around in the warm New Orleans November night. I could smell the Mississippi. I could feel the marshiness of the air. Between us was an old sense of ease.

"I just wanted you to see my life down here, Gladys. It's a good life. I feel at home here. I do. I feel this is a kind of home for me."

Now, I know this man well. Well enough to hear any falseness in his words. And I heard some. I looked over at him and knew he really didn't feel this was his home at all. But he kept talking that way.

"The weather's nice and warm. I don't know about you, Gladys, but I understand why older people go south now."

I didn't say anything to that. I didn't tell him how I bundle up and chop my own wood in the snow. How my arms and back ache for days afterward, which I like. I didn't tell him I loved snow more than when I was young. That I owned a man's navy blue parka that came down to my feet. That cost a hundred bucks. I put on my man's parka and Wellingtons and walk in the woods.

Maybe when I was seventy-one I'd understand.

"And it's not like other cities in the country, Gladys. Other cities are all alike now. Homogenized. Not this place. This place has character you can't even describe when you're right in front of it."

"Yes, it certainly does."

We kept on walking. We were in a different neighborhood now. The shotguns were gone and now the houses were big pink things with iron balconies. Music was coming out of half the windows. I'd say mostly jazz. James went on and talked about all the good music in the city. And then he's onto some sandwich you can get called a mufaletto. Then all the sudden something falls quietly out of his mouth.

"So Gladys, I was wondering what you'd think about moving down here. Down to New Or'luns."

I should've seen the question coming, but it shocked me to the point where I stopped walking. And my heart sped up. Not because the question excited me.

"James, you took me off guard there."

"I know, I know. Let me explain."

"No, don't."

"Let me."

We kept walking. He mentioned something about getting a drink in a corner café. Okay, fine. We walked a few blocks perfectly quiet. Then we get to the café. It's out on the sidewalk. We sit down at a table too small for us, and too many people are crowded around us. James was used to that. Not me. But there we sat.

"I think you'd enjoy this town, Gladys," James said. "Unless you've changed completely, I think you'd like it a lot."

"I do like the town, James."

"And I figure we could be a good friend for each other. As we get old. Allies."

A young woman next to me burst out laughing, then said, "No, no, I never said that!"

"I can't have this talk with all these strangers sitting on my lap," I said.

So we got up and walked on.

"It's that I don't know anyone like I know you," James said. I looked over at him. I looked at the side of his face as we walked. For a minute I felt his age, and the weight of his loneliness.

"If you're still you, that is," he added.

I didn't say anything to that.

We walked until we were back to his house. We went inside and laid down on his bed. We had all our clothes on. We just laid on our backs.

"You're different, Gladys."

"I am. I'm doing better."

"I know."

"I'm not doing so bad, either."

I reached for his hand. Now we were holding hands. My hand didn't remember his. It was brand-new. I thought that was strange. But I lay there thinking how I was glad to be there. For now I was glad to be there in the dark with him beside me.

After a while he asks me, "Do you believe there's any kind of life after death, Gladys?"

I didn't expect a talk like this. I didn't particularly want to go in that direction. But there he was, with an urgent voice, and holding my hand.

"I used to," I said. "You know that." And I lay there for a while remembering how I used to during the hardest years. "Not heaven. But I used to feel Ann out there in eternity. It was like she had hands and was pulling on my heart from eternity. I'd feel she was all alone out there. That's part of what killed me."

It was the first time I said Ann's name without hesitating at all. I did it on purpose, to prove something to myself, and to James. But it didn't necessarily feel good. Not bad, but not good, either. It was what it was.

He waited a few moments. Then he said, "And now you don't believe there's anything beyond this world?"

"I don't have conclusions. I think there might be something. Some kind of place for your spirit. But I don't know. Maybe the spirit's just as homeless in the afterworld as it is in this one."

I didn't even know what I meant by that. I prefer not to talk about this kind of thing because I start coming out with things I don't necessarily believe.

"I think there's a place," James said. "I don't know what it is, but I think it's there. Seems I've known it all along. Or so it seems. At least I've known we're spirits in bodies all along."

"I could see that too, but seeing it never helped me much. My spirit and body were too tied together, I guess."

"I don't think so."

We lay there in perfect silence. I had an urge to put

my head on his chest. I didn't do it, though. It didn't seem right, somehow. It was just an urge.

"I think of Ann a lot," he said.

"And Wendell?"

"Of course. And you?"

"Of course."

"What I try not to do is imagine what life would be if they'd lived," he said.

"That's a good thing to try not to do, James. It's a good thing to try to live your life as it is."

"It is a good thing."

"I'm not saying it's not the hardest thing to do."

"I know you're not saying that."

"I'm not saying that some days you get hit with a feeling like it was just yesterday when you could hold your child."

"I know."

"And other days when you're in a park and you see some family together with grown kids and babies and kids in between."

We just lay there and listened to a siren outside, and a few people having a conversation on the sidewalk. My heart felt pierced. It was a sudden thing. I didn't quite know why I felt it. Sometimes you all the sudden feel your heart pierced and you can't say exactly why.

Then James said, "How's Ivy?"

"Ivy's fine. She lost her husband. It was hard on her. But she's fine."

"Is she working, still?"

"Still working. She has a lot of back pain, James, but you wouldn't know it. This summer she burned her hand in the kitchen. It was after Brent died. She went and touched the dishes after they got out of the dishwasher. You know we got a hundred-and-ninety-degree dishwasher in there. Well, Ivy knows that as well as she knows her name. But she went ahead and grabbed a dish soon as it got out. It was a bad burn. Otherwise, she's herself."

He waited and thought about that for a bit.

"So they had some good years together, she and her husband?" he said.

"They were happy."

"Did she love him?"

"Oh, I think so."

I didn't see the point of saying no, she didn't really, she loved you, James. You were her real love. I wasn't even sure that was true.

"Well, someday I'll visit up there again. Maybe some Thanksgiving."

"We'd love to have you. I can say that for sure."

We were quiet.

"So I take it you're not moving down here."

"I can't, James."

He squeezed my hand and said he probably understood that even before he asked the question.

Soon enough, we fell asleep like that, and when I

woke up in the middle of the night, he was turned away from me, far on the other side of the bed.

Flying home was different from flying there. I was filled up with the visit. With all I'd seen, yes, but mostly, with James. So my palms weren't wet, not a bit. I sat in that plane looking down at Earth like I was born that way. It was a clear sky we flew through, so I had quite a view. I saw the tiny little houses, cars, and roads, the way it's all divided. How there's all these little lines drawn between yards and farms. So everyone down there with some luck and circumstance gets to stake out a little life on a little piece of rented ground.

Pretty soon I feel like I died and went to heaven. Heaven's in the sky, right? So I'm up there in heaven looking down and seeing James sitting in his shotgun house. Sitting in the wake of our visit. Sitting and wondering if he'd ever see me again.

He could die tomorrow. I remembered his face in the airport, smiling. The strength of his hug. How he didn't say the word *good-bye*, but just nodded. How he didn't say the normal things like, "Have a good flight," or "Talk to you soon."

And then I thought about the middle of the night. How when I woke up and looked at him over on the other side of the bed, I considered getting up and taking his shoes off. But I didn't do it. I turned away and went back to sleep. And let him sleep in his shoes.

It seems like a small thing, not taking off his shoes. Maybe it was being up in the plane that made it feel so big, so important. I had a feeling of regret that I could hardly stand. Why hadn't I done it? Why hadn't I gotten up and taken off his shoes when I had the chance? James from his deep sleep would've said, "Thank you, Gladys."

I knew up there in the plane that's how it would've gone. He would've thanked me from his sleep.

I pressed my hands over my eyes so I could stop the regret, stop the confusing tears.

And I stopped them. I took a breath. I took another breath, and looked out at the clouds. Couldn't see a scrap of Earth anymore. Bit my lip.

Doreen and Ivy picked me up from the airport. I'd only been gone four days. But it felt like longer, and when I looked at Ivy's face, it was like I saw her for the first time in years. She looked old to me in that airport. Maybe it was those lights. They make a person look green and tired. Or maybe it's just the truth. She's old. Ivy stood there at the gate, smiling. But something different was in that smile. She was trying too hard to hold that smile on her face. She hugged me hello, patting me on the back. She was wearing perfume she wore for special occasions.

That surprised me. Touched me.

Doreen was there with new red color in her hair and a bright silk scarf around her neck. She talked a blue streak as we walked out of the airport. I like Doreen. I will always like her. But she's too often on a blue streak. And this time I couldn't hear her. I heard the words coming out of her mouth, I can even remember some of them, but I couldn't understand the meaning. "Larry bought a motorcycle even though I told him a hundred times I'd disown him if he did and now he's taking those Keeley gals for rides down at that bridge where Tickle Abrams ran off the road last year. . . ."

I walked, I heard her, but it was like the English language was foreign. Maybe because what I was really listening to is Ivy. Which is a strange thing to say, because Ivy was quiet. Not saying a word. Just walking on one side of me in a blue sweater and green pants. I kept stealing a look at the side of her face.

She stared straight ahead. I hadn't really looked at her in a long time. Especially not from the side. Especially not walking in an airport.

We stepped out into the sunshine of day. Doreen's onto another tale. This time Ivy's laughing at it. It's a tale about a date Doreen had with an old man who plays tennis. He took her out to the courts. Doreen slammed back every serve. Only she slammed them over the fence. She didn't know she was so strong.

I was still mainly listening to Ivy.

Listening to her laugh.

Listening to her old cook's hands, the way they pushed back her hair that didn't have a trace of blonde in it anymore. Pure silver. Listening to her sigh when she sat down in the car.

Doreen drove us home, still talking. She never asked me how the trip went. She's not the most curious friend. She cares that I'm okay. She tries to entertain. The people she likes, she wants them to be happy. She doesn't care how they get there.

I thought I could feel Ivy's curiosity. Before I left to go down to see James, I'd considered how Ivy would feel. She didn't let on that she felt much of anything. She wished me a good trip. She didn't want to talk about it, really. But now, in the car, driving back home, I thought I could feel her curiosity.

The ride was a long one. Because I wanted to be alone with my sister. I wanted us to be in our own house. So she could say, "So Gladys, tell me, is James doing all right?" And I could tell her. I could tell her in a generous sort of way. The way I'd want to be told. I rode in the car, looking forward to it. To being generous as possible.

Doreen dropped us off. That was a relief. We walked inside, I set my bags down in the bedroom. Ivy was in the kitchen.

"You want some coffee?" she called in. I said I would. So she made some coffee while I took a shower.

I came out, dressed for November. We sat at the table and drank coffee. And I didn't wait for her to say, "How was your visit?" I just started talking, telling her everything. The color of his house, the way his face had thinned, his neighbors, the food we ate, even the way it felt.

Ivy didn't look at me when I talked. She wasn't smiling. Her eyes were lowered, her eyebrows were raised up. She listened to every word.

I talked on a bit more. And then I was quiet. Ivy said, "Well, it sounds like he's doing pretty well down there, and it sounds like you had yourself a nice visit, Gladys." She sighed, then smiled.

She smiled at me for a long second and I thought it was like she was suddenly on a plane, looking down.

"So how were your four days, Ivy?"

"My four days were just fine. A friend of Brent's was in town for one night, remember Bernard? He came over and we played cards. It was a nice evening. Other than that, I worked."

"How's your back?"

"Still there last time I checked."

"Why don't we go out for a walk?"

She looked at me funny. It wasn't something we'd done in a long time. In fact, last time we went for a walk together we were girls. Little girls in Delaware who laughed a lot. It's true. That's the last time we went for a walk.

But she went and got her old red coat. And we walked out the door, single file. It was four in the afternoon, November, not many leaves on the trees. But they were all over the ground. Mostly bright yellow, from the birches. It was beautiful the way the sun lit the leaves. We walked a long while, toward the road. Maybe we were headed into town. Don't think either of us knew.

Some skinny teenaged kid ran up to us down near the road. All out of breath.

"You ladies seen a black lab?" he panted. He was a painful-looking kid, with his acne and Adam's apple.

"No we haven't, but we'll be sure to keep our eye open for one," Ivy said.

"I'd appreciate it," he said. "If you find him, my numbers on the tag." He ran off.

We walked around in the woods after that, looking for the dog. Neither me or Ivy said much. But I was still listening to her.

I was listening and thinking how you're given a life, and certain people walk into it. Some make a small, but deep impression, like a kid from your second-grade class who shows up in your dream every three years. Others walk in and break your heart. Change you into who you are. You remember them every day.

Very few people, maybe one, maybe none, stay with you for the long run. It's a kind of miracle if someone's with you for the long run. A kind of miracle, I'd say.

Ivy hummed to herself, and tapped a tree trunk. She

picked up a leaf and put it to her face. Smiled. She looked over at me and said, "I could never decide what my favorite season was, spring or autumn. Yours used to be summer. What about now?"

"Autumn," I said.

"I knew it," she said.

We kept on walking, half looking for that dog until it was almost dark.

We found the lab when we were out of the woods, headed home. He followed us right inside. We called that poor kid. He said he'd be right over. The dog went and curled up on the couch. The house was quiet, so we put on some music. Then the two of us started making some soup, and when the kid came for his dog, we invited him to stay and eat with us. He said it was the best soup he ever ate, and we were the best ladies around for miles.

Ivy
Epilogue

WHEN EVERYONE YOU LOVED IN YOUR LIFE IS GONE, YOU have days when the wind comes into your house like a person. You get so alone the wind sits down at your table and tries to have itself a cup of coffee, but it can't, there's no time, it has to move on, it's the wind.

Don't think Oh, Ivy's off her rocker now and believes in ghosts. I'm not saying the wind is a ghost, only that the feeling of the wind, the whole notion of the wind, is different when all the people you ever loved are gone. It's not fresh air blowing through your hair and airing out your sheets and kitchen. No, sir. It's company. The wind is company that has to go.

*   *   *

Not very good company even when it's there, and neither are the trees, though I always thought I loved trees, and maybe I did. After Brent died I remember they consoled me. I'd walk in the woods and hear Brent's voice naming the trees and wildflowers.

Now the trees seem too filled up with meaning I don't have any words for, and the sky's the same way. All this meaning pressing in on my heart, making it pound like a drum. Maybe I don't want so much meaning all at once, but it turns out there's a lot I don't get to choose.

I go for walks with a cane now, and not because I need the cane for balance. The cane's just something I like to put before me, to reach into the spot I'm about to enter, like doing that could protect me from surprises.

So Gladys. Since you've been dead for only sixth months, I sometimes step into our old house feeling hopeful, as if your death was a bad dream and now we can go back to normal. Twice I even called your name aloud, then had to sit my bones down at the table.

I clean the house, I take walks, I shop for food, I say hello to a number of people, I sometimes put some music on. But mostly what I do is wait.

*   *   *

I called James right after you died, of course, and he wept without the slightest hesitation. And he couldn't speak to me, so he cleared his throat and said he'd call back later, which he did, and then we spoke kindly in hushed voices about the weather down there and the weather up here. "I miss the snow," James said, in his old man voice, husky and tired out. After that was a long pause. He said, "Well, I best be getting some sleep now." And I said, "And I should do the same."

I arranged a service for you in the Unitarian church, in the same bright room as the one we had for Wendell. Louis came alone. He's still not married, and I still see him once or twice a year, and he's still Louis, a warm and predictable son, but he couldn't stay for long. Back to sea.

James didn't make it up.

Raelene didn't make it either—she has a brand-new husband with an autistic son. Still, when I told her the news she was heartbroken, called me every day for a week. Just last month she sent me a card saying she hoped I was doing all right.

*   *   *

When they lowered you into the ground, everything in my body pulled up, up, up. I never felt so strong in my life. I thought for a second it would work, that I would pull you back into the world.

It doesn't have to be cold and rainy like it is today for me to sit at the table and drink tea and know in my heart I finally understand you.

I know now, Gladys.

I know why you couldn't just pick up the pieces and move on.

A certain kind of loss takes away your one heart and gives you another heart, a heart you hardly recognize.

That you had to die for me to understand you, Gladys.

Your voice, your face.

*   *   *

You could've got yourself a cane to match mine, and down the lane we'd have gone together.

I remember one night when Ann was three she whispered to me, "Sometimes I think we should all just skip in a circle." Her eyes were shy but shining, it was like she'd found a solution to a big problem.

What I'd like to think is you and Ann are somewhere now, united. I look up at the stars and think, Is it possible?
     Wendell's there too.

I can't be sure of anything. Nothing. It's surprising.

I believe in the chills I get when I look at the stars alone at night.

The chills I get.